"Pick Hendry was murdered, his head half blown off with a shotgun. He'd been workin' there in the Bonanza canyon and he'd struck gold. He was like a father to me! He was on his way to register his claim when you come up on him. You killed him and took his location papers and filed them, and now you're workin' his claim!"

Johnny's voice was thick, and he could not wait any longer. He lashed out with his fist.

"First I'm goin' to give you the beatin' of your life, fella. Then, when I'm done, I'm goin' to give you a gun. If you've got nerve enough to try and use it, I'll belly-shoot you. I'll stand by five days and nights and watch you die, you back-shootin' ranahan!"

KING COLT

LUKE SHORT

A DELL BOOK

Published by
DELL PUBLISHING CO., INC.
1 Dag Hammarskjold Plaza
New York, N.Y. 10017

ISBN: 0-440-14686-0

Reprinted by arrangement with the Author.
Printed in the United States of America
Previous Dell Editions #647, 962, 4686
New Dell Edition
First printing—June 1978

Chapter One: BUSHWHACK

OLD PICKET-STAKE HENDRY's features usually softened about this time of day. He had seen ten thousand sunsets filter through the thin desert air to wash the Calicoes and their shrouding thunderheads in all the colors that heaven's palette held, and it was always new to him. It was as close as he ever came to religion.

As the last gold shaft crept up the tip of old Monarch and leaped off into the blue, Picket-Stake's gaze returned to earth, and to business. He regarded the dead man sprawled before him.

"It might work," he repeated aloud, taking up his train of thought where he left it twenty minutes before. "He's got my sandy hair and my length o' leg. With my clothes on and a little mussin' up, it might work."

To Picket-Stake, the dead man represented only a small triumph. Two days before, Picket-Stake knew for sure he was being followed. It hadn't worried him, for he had been followed many times in his thirty years of prospecting the Calicoes. He knew the follower would wait until Picket-Stake led him out of the maze of canyon country to water before he gulched him; for Picket-Stake, rightly or wrongly, was deemed a rich man of the Cosmos country. His worldly goods consisted of two burros, a change of clothes, and a burroload of prospecting-tools, but only he knew that. To the rest of the country it seemed unreasonable that this gaunt, desert-blackened lath of a man should have prospected the Calicoes for thirty years and still have no gold. So they made him rich—in story. Didn't he always have money? Hadn't he taken in that waif and raised him to manhood, this same Johnny Hendry who was deputy sheriff of Cosmos county? Had either of them ever lacked for anything?

Pick could have told them that any man, if he's half smart, could make wages by placer mining at any of a hundred places on this side of the Calicoes. But what Pick couldn't have told them up to a week ago, was that a man could make a fortune, a solid, fabulous, undreamed-of fortune. He hadn't known it himself, for the mother lode of this field had always been a part of his dream. Now it was reality.

"I'm rich," he had kept saying calmly to himself these last two days. "So danged rich I'll never live to spend a hundredth of it—no, not even a five-hundredth."

In a tiny box canyon, just at the head of some copper stain, far up into the savage, waterless, and labyrinthine canyons of a vast and nameless valley of the Calicoes, his monuments were up. All that remained was to register the claim at Cosmos and watch the rush start—a futile, heart-breaking rush that would end where the rainbow ends. For Pick had it sewed up. He had waited until he was sure.

Then, two days back, two men had picked up his trail. Pick had too much to lose to try and shake them, for in the tattered vest he wore were the claim locations. Pick had been raised in a tough and deadly school, and he acted accordingly. It meant losing a half day to go around by way of the Kiowa rim, but he went.

There, perched a thousand feet above the foothill, the trail followed the rim around a series of pinnacle rocks. Close to sunset, Pick had hazed his burros on ahead, had cast one glance at his back trail, then had faded into the rock.

The only weapon he carried was a double-barreled der-ringer fitted for shotgun shells. So he waited, bellied down close to the trail. In an hour, the man came. He was a thin, rawboned man, afoot, packing two six-guns and a big canteen. Picket-Stake let him get within ten feet of him, then he called, "Hey!"

The man in the same second, in the same jump of surprise, was streaking for his guns, and Picket-Stake had let him have it—both barrels.

He figured the shots would blast the man over the rim, but they hadn't, and now Pick was glad.

Like all desert men, Pick was a philosopher, and as he lit his cob pipe to take his mind off his thirst, he reflected on the whims of fortune. "Funny how luck runs. That coulda been me. And the only soul woulda missed me woulda been Johnny."

But would Johnny, even? Asking himself that question, Pick laid bare the only real bitterness of his life. Twenty-five years ago, down in the Ute country, when the Indians were making reluctant way for the whites, Pick had found Johnny. He was prospecting in the Six Pillar country, and had stumbled onto a burning shack one afternoon. A glance at the dead woman and her husband inside the burning house told Pick the Utes had done their job well. He was about to leave when the dim wail of a baby came to his ears. A search revealed the baby hidden in a chest under the rough bunk. It had been the last protective gesture of a cornered and frantic mother.

Pick had taken the baby, had sweated blood corralling and milking wild range cows to pull it through until he could reach a settlement. And Johnny had been raised in the desert mountains of Calico.

He had grown to a big, amiable young manhood—too amiable, Picket-Stake knew. Johnny didn't care much about anything, and never worried a moment in his life.

"And that's bad," Picket-Stake mused, feeling his own seamed face. Not all those creases had got there from physical strain. Plenty of them came that time he nursed Johnny through double pneumonia over in the Panamints. "Worry shouldn't kill a man, but it's the fire he needs to temper him."

Picket was thinking especially of this last job of Johnny's —his deputy-sheriffship. Cosmos was a tough county, Cosmos town was tougher. Cattlemen were harried by rustlers, murders were committed and forgotten to make way for more murders. The law, under a slack, easygoing sheriff, was a mockery.

And Johnny, grinning through it all, said to Picket-Stake, when prodded, "Pick, you was in the West before I was in rompers. Like seeks like. Let the gunman kill off the gunman. If a man can't take care of his own, let him lose it. You never went to the law in your life. No *man* does. As long as women and kids is safe, let the best man win."

"Force is only for them that know when *not* to use it,"
Pick would say angrily.

"That's me," Johnny would reply, his eyes laughing.
"That's what I been tryin' to tell you. Crowd a peaceful
man and you got a killin' slated."

And Pick, never too eloquent, had no answer.

Yes, this dead man would fit the bill. Change clothes
with him, plant false location papers on him, put a poke
of dust in the tattered jeans. The shotgun derringer had
taken care of the man's face. He could dump the body
close to a trail.

He got up, lay on his belly, looked over the rim to the
country in shadow below. There, directly down, lay the
thread of a trail. It was used by the Bar 33 cattle as the
only entrance to a water hole abutting the rim some miles
to the south. Cows were calving now, and he knew some
Bar 33 rider would make the rounds of the water holes
on a last cleanup before the herds were moved into the
mountains for summer range. Buzzards would attract a
rider.

Pick reflected he had thirty days in which to file his
claim. Four of them were gone. In twenty-six days, he
would know Johnny as he had never known him before.

"And if he ain't what I hope he is, then my fortune can
go bum. I'll be ready to die," he admitted to himself.

By failing light, he wrote out his fictitious location
papers. Then he hurried through the distasteful job of
dressing the dead man in his own clothes. Finished, he
dragged the dead man over to the rim and put a poke
of dust in the pocket, along with several of Pick's own
recognizable belongings. Then, his mouth grim, he shoved
the corpse off the rim. An hour later he had caught up
with Jenny and Bertha, his two burros. He changed back
into his own clothes, burned the ones he had exchanged
with the gulcher, planted two pokes of dust on the burros,
then set out again.

At midnight, he picked up the old familiar pack
freighter's trail. He gave Jenny and Bertha the last of his

water, then cut them across the rump.

They vanished into the darkness, and he knew some traveler would pick them up in a day or two, or they would be found at one of the outlying ranches where there was water. At worst, they would wander into town from habit.

He listened to the night, to the dying patter of the burros. He fondled the six-guns he had taken from the ambusher. On them depended his food.

Off to the east lay the sparse water holes of the Calicoes, where game was to be found.

"Good luck, Johnny," Pick muttered. "An unbroke horse ain't no use to anybody, least of all hisself."

Chapter Two: LAW—ON ORDER

THE KIOWA HEAD SALOON at Cosmos did a booming business in the morning, a fact by which a shrewd observer might have sized up the whole town. For Cosmos, overcrowded with miners, punchers, saddle bums, and hardcases, did not work. It gambled and drank in the morning.

Of the four men seated at a rear table in the Kiowa Head, Johnny Hendry was easily the tallest. The game was stud, ten-cent limit, and the weary houseman was paying no more attention to the game than he could help. The other two players were chaffing him good-naturedly.

A man shouldered through the batwing doors, let his gaze rove first the bar, then the gaming-tables. Spotting Johnny, he walked over to him. He was a puncher, undersized, unshaven; and, like everyone else, he packed a gun at his hip. He was a little drunk, too. "Kin I see you a minute, Hendry?" he asked bluntly at the table.

Johnny looked up, frowning, for he had almost filled in a straight. He waited for the fifth card, saw he didn't even have a pair, and rose, swearing softly. "Well?"

"Outside."

He followed the man out. His walk was lithe, effortless, and there was a freshness, a tolerant good humor about his pleasantly lean face that placed him apart from the rest of the men in the room. On his left shirt pocket hung the badge of the deputy's office. He wore no guns. His range clothes were frayed though clean; his Stetson was dull black, flat-brimmed, hiding blacker hair.

Outside, the puncher turned and faced Johnny. "Well, I've got him nailed."

"Who?"

"Turk Hebron. Last night I hid out near that Dutch Canyon corral and seen him take eight head of my horses—seen him, mind you."

"What do you want me to do?" Johnny asked coldly.

"Do? Why, man, what do you always do to horse thieves?"

"Who saw him besides you, Cass?"

"No one. Ain't I enough?"

Johnny shook his head slowly. "Not by about two witnesses, Cass. You've been achin' to hang the deadwood on Turk, but it won't stick."

Cass Briggs flushed a little under his beard stubble. "What's a man got to do to prove his stuff is stole?"

Johnny grinned tolerantly. "If you'd seen Turk Hebron steal your stuff, Cass, you'd have shot him. Even if he wasn't runnin' 'em off, you'd've shot him." He shook his head. "If it'll make you feel any better, we'll ride out and talk to Turk."

"But I seen him do it!" Cass said.

"Then why didn't you shoot him? Everyone else cuts down on a horse thief."

"And get accused of beefin' him?"

"Then choose him on the street. He carries a gun, too. But I'm warnin' you. Make it even and in front of witnesses. Then try and get out of it."

Cass swore under his breath, but Johnny only smiled. "I'm not backin' up your play, Cass. Steer clear of us. If you got a grudge to settle, we don't want any part of it. After it's worked off, then we step in."

"Maybe you'll be wishin' I was backin' your play around election time next week," Cass sneered.

Johnny shrugged indifferently. "I'm appointed, not elected. If you got any threats, make 'em to Blue. He's sheriff."

But Cass was as persistent as he was vindictive. "You

say I ain't honest. Didn't I bring them two burros of Pick's in yesterday when they come to my place for water? Couldn't I have kept 'em—them and that poke half full of dust I found in a packsack?"

"Yes," Johnny drawled softly, "you could. You could've kept all of it instead of just half like you did. But if you had of you wouldn't've made me feel like I had to take sides with you today in that damned chinch-bug feud of yours with Turk Hebron. And also, you never know when Pick is apt to walk in and claim that poke." He gestured over his shoulder with his thumb. "Drag it."

But Cass stood his ground, alcohol inflaming his anger. "Trouble with you, Johnny, is you ain't man enough to hold down a deputy's job. Any other county, you'd've been fired months ago!"

Johnny's face flushed a little. "Listen, Cass," he said gently. "You're drunk. You're smaller'n me. But if you don't clear out of here, and right now, you'll wish you had."

Cass looked down at Johnny's hip. There was no gun there. He let his hand fall to the butt of his own gun and smiled evilly. "By gum, I got a notion to make you dance on the streets. You make us dance every time we ask for help."

"Try it," Johnny invited gently.

Cass's fingers closed about the butt of his gun, and he started to yank it from its holster. Swiftly, his palm held edgewise, Johnny struck down at Cass's wrist. Cass yelled with pain and dropped his gun; it clattered on the walk.

Slowly Johnny reached out, ripped Cass's Stetson from his head, then grabbed a fistful of Cass's thick hair. With his right hand he yanked Cass's head toward him and with his left he lashed out; his fist crashed into Cass's face.

Cass simply slacked down to the boardwalk and lay there, cold to the world. Johnny regarded him with impersonal distaste, then turned and looked over the street. He was mad, disgusted with himself at hitting Cass, and more disgusted at the fact that he had tipped his hand to Cass. He hadn't meant to reveal his guess that Cass had held back part of Pick's dust, but Cass had goaded him until it slipped out.

The poker game had lost its savor now, and Johnny turned up the street toward the sheriff's office. This thing about Pick was worrying him. The old boy, bless him, was as unpredictable as he was salty, but what if Bertha and Jenny's appearance did mean something? Pick was getting old and he took no care of himself. Traveling into the night after a hard day's work, it would be easy for Pick to stumble; and on some of these trails in the Calicoes, a stumble would mean death.

Then, too, Pick was carrying plenty of dust, and that was unusual. It wasn't reasonable for Pick to put his dust on his burros. Didn't that argue that he had so much of it that it was easier to pack it on burros? And if he had a lot of it, he would be well worth robbing.

Johnny had made plenty of guesses. Maybe some saddle bum working over the Calicoes had killed Pick on the chance he carried a road stake.

And the worst part of it was, Johnny didn't know where to look for him. Ever since Johnny had been grown up and shown a desire to roam, Pick had kept his affairs to himself. He and Johnny bunked together in the abandoned offices of the Lost Lady mine above town, but Johnny knew nothing of Pick's comings or goings.

His dark eyes narrowed a little, Johnny swung off the boardwalk into the Cosmos House. In every perplexing situation, he went to Nora, but after asking her advice, rarely took it. She had been working in the dining-room of the Cosmos House for three years now, a sort of stepdaughter to Ma Jenkins since her father died four years back. Six times Johnny had asked her to marry him, and she had refused each time.

Nora was clearing up after the last late breakfasters. She was dressed in a dark riding-suit whose somberness seemed to light up her ashen hair as the night does the stars. She wasn't tall, but straight as a ramrod. She had a full, friendly mouth, a straight nose inclined to tilt, and dark, depthless blue eyes that reminded Johnny of a pool at midnight.

"Mornin', m'lady," he said with a grin, and, yanking a chair away from the long table, slouched into it.

"Mornin', m'lord," Nora said, with a mock curtsy. She saw Johnny sizing up her neat riding-rig, and she flushed a little.

"Ridin'?"

"Going ridin'," she said.

Johnny shook his head. "It's wild country, hidin' bad buckaroos." His grin faded. "Seriously, the Esmerella paid off last night. There's still lots of red paint left in them miners—enough to make a lone girl ridin' just a mite careful."

"But I'll not be alone," Nora announced.

"Oh," Johnny said, flushing a little. "Who is it?"

Nora watched him shrewdly as she answered, "Tip Rogers up at the Esmerella. He's off for the day."

"Oh," Johnny said again. Then he grinned. "He's been off all his life." He shrugged. "Well, bad cess to him."

Nora sighed just a little and made a face at him. Immediately Johnny had forgotten his rival, it seemed.

"Nora, I'm worried about Pick."

"Worried? You?" Nora jibed gently. "Not Johnny Hendry, the man without a wrinkle."

"Cut it," Johnny growled, looking up at her. "Am I gettin' spooky, or what? It ain't like Pick to leave dust in a packsack."

"Not in this county," Nora said dryly.

Johnny looked up at her, puzzled. "You're sorta' proddy this mornin', missy."

Nora sat down on the table beside him, and shook her head. "No more than usual on that question, Johnny. You know that. If you run a shooting-gallery, then you pay for the clay pipes. Train a dog to eat at the table, and that's where he eats. Of course Pick could have been slugged and robbed. What do you expect?"

"A little sympathy," Johnny said.

But Nora was firm. "You wear a star, Johnny. There are counties where Pick could be gone a year and nobody'd ask questions."

"I wouldn't want to live in one," Johnny said flatly. "I'd be scared to blow my nose with one hand."

Nora leaned over a little. "Johnny, I'll tell you a true

story. Mrs. McKenzie got home from work late last night.
It was little Jake's birthday, and she wanted to bake him a
cake. She found she was out of sugar, so she thought she'd
run down to the store to get some. She got as far as the
Kiowa Head when somebody threw a bottle through the
door. It missed her, but the men coming out didn't. Before
she could pick herself up, she was in the middle of a street
brawl." She paused and regarded Johnny soberly.

"I heard about it," Johnny said, and the trace of a grin
showed on his face. "That was Leach Wigran and Mickey
Hogan. They was arguin' a little."

"Leach Wigran!" Nora said contemptuously. "Everyone
knows he's a tough. Some say he's a rustler. And Mickey
Hogan is trash. Still, you tolerate them in town."

"I ain't the marshal," Johnny protested.

"Is there one here?"

"Now that you mention it, there ain't. County seat and
all, the commissioners figured the sheriff's office could
police the town," Johnny admitted honestly. He caught the
look in Nora's eye. "Lordy, girl, I ain't an insurance company. That's a natural accident, like fallin' down on a
slippery sidewalk. You want me to guarantee kids' birthday cakes in Cosmos county?"

"You couldn't!" Nora said hotly. "If you can't guarantee them a decent place to grow up, you can't guarantee
them anything!"

"Wa-a-i-t a minute," Johnny said softly, half rising out
of his chair. Just then the dining-room door slammed,
interrupting him.

Johnny looked up irritably. It was Hank Brender, one
of the Bar 33 hands, who was already thumping across the
empty dining-room. "Hullo, Hank," Johnny growled.

Hank, a stocky, mild-looking puncher in work clothes,
made a pass at tipping his hat to Nora, but he didn't even
look at her.

"Johnny, we found Uncle Pick this mornin'."

Johnny didn't say anything, just looked at him, but
he felt something gathering inside him.

"Dead," Hank added. "His face shot off. He was blowed
clean off the Kiowa rim down onto the rocks."

Johnny settled back into his seat, his eyes never leaving Hank's face. He heard Nora gasp, and said, "Go on."

"I reckon they was aimin' to rob him up on top, but likely he fought and they had to shoot him—blew him off. Down below, around his body, there was tracks. He'd been robbed, cleaned out, and left for the buzzards."

"Are you sure it was Pick?" Nora said.

Hank nodded. "It was hard to tell when we got to him, but it was Pick's build and Pick's clothes. Carmody found him. Pick was wearin' that buckskin jacket with the square patch in the back. Couldn't mistake it. His pipe was there and that old flat-crowned Stetson with matches stuck in the brim. He was—" Hank looked at Nora, swallowed, and left his sentence unfinished.

"Pick dead," Johnny said dully. "It can't be, Hank. It can't be true!"

"It's him, all right," Hank said miserably. "Likely he was comin' down from the hills with a little dust when some whippoorwill tried to stick him up."

Johnny's face was white. Something inside him was balled up, cold, and he rose and walked to the window. Pick dead. The man who had found him, raised him, given him a home, counsel, food and clothing, his name—dead.

As he looked over the sordid, shabby town, a hot, murdering rage welled up in him. On these streets, tonight, tomorrow, for maybe a whole year, he would be rubbing elbows with the man who had killed Pick, might even shake the hand that had held the gun. He half turned to look at Nora. She was watching him with those dark, quiet eyes, maybe reading his thoughts. He turned to the window again to try and control his face. He rubbed it with a flat, hard palm, and turned.

"I know," he said coldly to Nora, without her saying a word. "It's what you've been tryin' to tell me." She didn't say anything, but he could see her eyes bright and moist. He said dully to Hank, "You had breakfast, Hank?"

"No. Carmody came in about daylight. I started right off."

"Where's Pick? At the Bar 33?" Hank nodded. "Get some breakfast for Hank, Nora. I'll see you at the stable,

Hank. Take your time."

Johnny's pace up the block to the sheriff's office was swift, but his mind was working even more swiftly.

Sheriff Baily Blue, sixty, solid, slow-spoken, and affable, was seated at the roll-top desk. He had the calm, unruffled manner of a work-worn mule, but his eyes were like a mule's, too—a little veiled and surface-lighted, wary. The few men who had ever seen him in a gun fight afterward treated him with a new respect. He wore a black suit four sizes too big for him, which may or may not have been the reason why he looked so unassuming. His hair was thick and white, his face broad, almost unwrinkled.

Right now he was sheafing a stack of reward posters—they had come in on the morning stage—preparatory to throwing them in the wastebasket.

He looked up as Johnny entered. "Hank told me, son," he said quietly. "It's tough. Besides that, it's filthy. No grudge, nothin' but the robbery of a harmless old prospector."

"But was it?" Johnny said bleakly. "It was a shotgun that killed him, Hank says."

The sheriff looked at him a long moment. "You figger it wasn't a chance meetin'? No man is goin' to pack a greener up in them barren damned hills unless he knows what he was huntin'?"

Johnny nodded. "There was a poke of dust on one of them burros, Baily. Besides, Pick's body was robbed."

The sheriff cut a sizable third of a black plug lying on the desk, licked his knife, closed it, and fondled the plug with his tongue until it came to rest in his cheek.

"You mean," he said slowly, looking up, "that you think Pick had found somethin'—somethin' big, maybe?"

"Sure. Whoever done it could have caught those burros if he'd wanted to. But he didn't. He left them to go down and search Pick. What would he be huntin' for on Pick that was so important he passed up searchin' the burros for gold?"

The sheriff answered promptly. "The directions that would lead him to more gold, likely."

"Location papers."

The sheriff nodded his head. "I know what you're thinkin', Johnny. You figger the man who gulched Pick has got the location papers, and will get the gold. He couldn't sell it here for fear of startin' a rush and givin' hisself away. So he'll mosey over the Calicoes, drift down-country, and get rid of it in little pieces. You want me to send word out to be on the lookout."

Johnny had been watching him quietly, and now he sat on the desk. "That's part of it, Baily. I want the gulcher. The gold or papers don't matter. But there's somethin' else."

"What?"

"Don't it mean anything to you when a harmless old man is beefed on the day he's struck it after forty years work?"

Blue shrugged. "It's his chance. He was unlucky, son."

"Uh-huh. That ain't it," Johnny said softly. "It's us, Baily. If that had happened fifteen years ago when Cosmos was a boom camp and the law wasn't here yet, it would've been different." He paused. "It's because we're runnin' a robbers' roost. Every hardcase that can kill his man and cloud up his back trail good has got fair pickin's in this county. He's safe here and he knows it. You know it. We both do."

"You been talkin' to Nora again," Blue said, smiling.

"No. I just come to my senses, Baily." He leaned forward. "What have you got against cleanin' out this county and Cosmos with it?"

"It don't work," Blue declared flatly. "Look at Ellsworth and Abilene. Look at any of 'em. When the law gets tough, it's the signal for every glory-huntin' would-be tough gun toter to drift in and limber up. It's a dare."

"Other counties do."

"Not with our setup. We're close to mountains no one man can ever know. We got company ranches. We got mines. In other words, we got dynamite. Handle it rough, and not all the deputies I can swear in will stop the hell-raisin'. Our ranges'll be cleaned, and won't an insurance company touch a mine payroll. There'll be more men

in the Calicoes than there are in Cosmos, and every danged
one of 'em will be livin' off the fat of Cosmos county."

"They are now." Johnny counted off on his fingers.
"Friday night, a hundred head of Kennicott's stuff drove
off into thin air. Last month, the Esmerella payroll knocked over. Two weeks ago, a miner found knifed, and thrown
in a *barranca*. Two jaspers with cracked skulls dyin' in
Doc Palmer's back room. Seventy head of horses moved
off that free range out south—to where? And now Pick
beefed after he cashed in on a lifetime's work."

"What do you aim to do?" Blue asked. "We've done our
durndest to settle all these right, son. A man can't do
more."

"When there's a polecat under your shack, you don't
move out, do you?"

"Then you want to clean up the county and Cosmos with
it?"

Johnny nodded.

Blue tapped on the desk absently. "There's an election
comin' up in a week, Johnny. Maybe you'd like to try a
law-and-order platform."

"Are you goin' to run?"

"I reckon. But not on that platform. I meant *you* could
try it."

Johnny slid off the desk. "That's just what I was comin'
to, Baily. I'm goin' to run for sheriff." He watched the
sheriff's face for a tense twenty seconds, but it told him
nothing. "I reckon you'll want my badge," he said finally,
reaching up and unpinning it.

Blue shook his head. "Not unless you want to turn it
in, son."

"It wouldn't look right," Johnny said, his face flushed.
"I'm gettin' out the war paint. You wouldn't like it."

"Did I ever tell you to leave a man go you had somethin'
on?" the sheriff asked gently, and he saw Johnny flush
deeper. "Think, son. Without that star, it may be a sight
harder to make your word carry any weight. With it, people
talk. You know that. And in case anything happens, you
got the whole weight of the law behind you."

Johnny hesitated, for what Blue said was true. He owed

it to Pick to try and find the murderer, and he'd be a fool if he turned that help down. On the other hand, he owed it to Blue not to make a row while working under him. He let his hand fall from the star.

"I'll be campaignin' against you, Baily, with your food in my belly. It don't seem right."

"Go ahead," Baily said. "Nothin' either one of us is goin' to do or say will change folks' feelin's about how they want this county run. You're no liar, Johnny, and we got an honest difference. Tell folks so. Come election time, we'll find what they want."

"But I'm goin' to fight you, Baily. I want to be sheriff."

"And I'm going to fight you, too. I want to stay sheriff." He rose, smiling, and extended a hand. "You stick. Work on Pick's murder. I'll back up any play you make."

"Are those orders?"

"Just so long as you don't stir up the county agin' the law, they are."

"I'll wait to do that," Johnny said, and took the sheriff's hand. "I'm ridin' out to the Bar 33 now."

The sheriff waved careless assent and was sitting down as Johnny stepped out onto the boardwalk. Johnny's sheepishness at having defied an old friend had left him. There was a grim confidence in his walk as he headed toward the stable.

But his purposefulness was mingled with grief, too. He couldn't quite get used to the idea that Picket-Stake was gone. He never would get used to it.

Chapter Three: SOUNDINGS

BY THE TIME JOHNNY AND HANK were in sight of the Bar 33, Johnny was pretty familiar with the details of Pick's death. What Hank, in deference to Nora, had omitted in the original version, was that Pick's body was unrecognizable. What the thousand-foot drop onto rocks below hadn't done, the buzzards had. Before Hank left for town he heard Hoke Carmody, who had found the body, refuse a buckboard and call for a pack horse and a gunny sack.

"Did Carmody get a look at the tracks?"

"He said they was in sand, and drifted bad. You can ask him when you see him."

The Bar 33 lay south of Cosmos some eight miles. It was a big brand, managed by Major Fitz, and included six other ranches reaching down into New Mexico. It had pre-empted the Santa Rita bench, a thirty-mile stretch of grama grass lying eight hundred feet above the desert at the base of the Calicoes. The torrential spring rains of ages past had cleaned the mountains long since of topsoil, leaving them naked rock, while the original foothills had filled in with mountain drift until they were now the vast, rolling three-sided Santa Rita mesa of the bench. In the process, the bench had kept its own plentiful water, and had soaked up the streams from the Calicoes, until the land to the west was parched and arid, while from her height she remained aloof and green and proud. To the west was semidesert, dropping into desert relieved only by the far blue-misted line of the Nation range. South, indifferent grazing-land fought for brief life on the flanks of the Calicoes. Far, far south, the rock let up, and the mountains were crowned with trees and grass. To the north, skipping the deep, sheltering pocket where Cosmos sprawled between a jumble of buttes, the rocks were less hostile, and it was here that ranchers, making the best of a mediocre deal from nature, fought drought, rains, and rustlers, and sometimes prospered. Hard to the east lay the Calicoes, colorful, savage desert of climbing, snarling rock, defiant of man and God, mute watchmen of puny fortunes, the bare cone of Monarch peak its liege lord.

Climbing up to the bench, Johnny's black horse, Soot by name, had smelled green, growing grass. Now, as they swung through the pasture gate, he quickened his pace. Home was where they took the saddle off, but Bar 33 had been the home of his colthood, and these three barns looked just as white and spacious, the corrals as trim and break-proof, and the long, rambling, one-story frame house as cool and white under the interlaced cottonwoods, as ever.

Major Fitz was much smaller than the two punchers who joined him at the bunkhouse door and walked over to greet Johnny. Cavalry regulations would have frowned on his dress—half-boots with a three-inch stockinged gap to his tight army trousers; a hunting-coat of duck over a cotton singlet; and an oversize Stetson—but they would have commended his straight carriage, his bowed legs, his sharp, wind-reddened face, and his air of authority. His voice and his restlessness combined to give the effect of a terrier, but his heart was that of a St. Bernard, Sheriff Blue used to say, and none knew it as well as Johnny.

"He's in the wagon shed, Johnny," the major said harshly, "but you won't want to see him. What a day to live. And what a man he was. And how rotten I feel, how humble before him. Get down." He shook hands with Johnny, and Johnny felt his hand tremble.

"Now what do you want? Dinner? After a while, men? I'll give you every hand on the place. I've got two out where we found the body, but it's no use, Johnny. The tracks are gone. I've got my best man up on the rim, but it's rock, and he won't find a thing unless the killer was a fool. Carmody?" He turned to one of the men beside him, a squat man with a blank, oversize face. "Here, Hoke Carmody, meet Johnny Hendry." He turned to Johnny again, before he could shake hands with the man. "I went out with him to get the body. Nothing. Not a damned thing to work on. Buzzards had almost finished their work. Coyote tracks, buzzard tracks—and man tracks. You could tell that by the deep dent in the sand. He'd been robbed."

"That's what Hank said." Johnny looked at Hoke Carmody. "How'd you come on it?"

"I'd packed some salt out to the rim water hole yesterday. Saw tracks and spent the day cleanin' up strays. I had to camp there last night, and got an early start this mornin'. When I kicked up about a dozen buzzards just off the trails, I took a *pasear* out of curiosity. There he was. I never touched the body, but studied the ground a long while. There'd been a man there, but there was no clear tracks to muss up, so I searched him. I brought back what I'd found along with this jacket. The major knowed it right off, and come back with me."

"Good man," the major said, nodding.

"I want to thank you for what you've done," Johnny said.

Johnny and Major Fitz went into the wagon shed, and came out in less than a minute. Johnny's face was a little pale as they started off to the house. He told the major what he and the sheriff had pieced together about the murder, and the major agreed.

Once in the long, low-ceilinged living-room, the major quieted a little. Back to the cold fireplace, he looked out the window a long time. Johnny idly watched his lean, sharp face and wondered what he was about to propose.

Suddenly, he turned to Johnny. "This has got to stop, youngster. I thought it before Pick died. I know it now. A vigilante committee won't bring Pick back, but it ought to clean out the cause of his death."

"You won't need it," Johnny told him, and he announced his decision to run for sheriff.

"It's no good, son. You'd make a rotten sheriff," the major said bluntly. "You're too easygoing. Does the army cure disease? Partly, but it removes the cause, too."

"I'll run on a law-and-order platform," Johnny continued. The major listened with interest to Johnny's account of his talk with Blue. "If I can get you behind me, and about a dozen of these cattlemen who've been rustled into debt, I'll swing it. You'll pull a dozen votes through your hands, and they'll pull two dozen more through their friends. It'll work that way with all the straight ranchers. I'll pull some of the mine vote, too—the management—but the miners will likely swing to Blue because he's let them do whatever they felt like. I'll get the town, because they want some peace, and if Blue don't liquor up the Mexicans, I'll win them. They're tired of bein' rawhided by every drunk in town."

"And Blue will get the riffraff," the major said, "and don't forget that's considerable. When the word gets out, they'll know that once you're in they're out. It'll be a fight."

Johnny shifted in his seat and leaned foreward a little. "All right. I've learned somethin' from Blue. Will you back me?"

"You know I will," the major said promptly. "I believe you've been burned, Johnny. Not that I thought you didn't do what you could under Blue. But you went at it wrong. Clean up the county and I'm behind you. What's more, my word carries some weight. I'll make it."

Johnny stood up. "Good. I want one thing more now." The major looked at him quizzically.

"I'm not right always—maybe not half the time," Johnny said stubbornly, "but if I get in office I want to be nearly right. I want to know the names of the men you'd like warned out of this county."

The major was about to voice surprised protest, but Johnny held up his hand.

"I know. It could breed a dozen gun fights if it ever got public, but it won't. When you make that list, it'll include the men you suspect but can't prove anything on. You're too fair to make it a grudge list, and I reckon all the rest of our decent ranchers are. I'm goin' to get a list from each one of 'em. When I compare them, it'll give me a pretty good idea of what's right."

"But what if the lists were stolen from you, Johnny? It would take fifty years for the smoke to blow away."

"They won't be. You'll mail them to me. Print them, and don't sign them."

"Then what?"

"The day after I'm elected, I'll give these unwanted hardcases just twenty-four hours to leave town."

"And get blown off your horse for your pains."

"That's my chance," Johnny said stubbornly. "Besides, I owe it to Pick." His voice fell suddenly, and he said in a grim tone, "Major Fitz, as long as I live, I'll be on the trail of the man who murdered Pick. Maybe this list will help to find him."

"True enough."

"Another thing," Johnny went on, "I reckon I was Pick's heir."

"Of course."

"All right. Some way, somewhere, Pick was bound to leave a clue to where he was workin'. The jasper that murdered Pick will know that, and he'll think likely Pick told me the location of his claim. So this jasper will try and beef me, won't he?"

"It's reasonable—too reasonable," Fitz said dryly.

"Then the first jasper that shoots at me will be the man I want. And I'll get him," Johnny said grimly. He rose, about to speak, then paused, as if searching for a way to say what he wanted to. "Reckon you'd turn me loose in your tool shop for a while, Major?" he asked finally.

"I think I know what you want, Johnny. I had the blacksmith make the coffin this morning. I'll have the buckboard hitched and send a driver to town with it."

Johnny shook his head. "Thanks, but Pick wouldn't have wanted that. There's a little patch of young Navajo pines out on one of them rises to the east. Pick liked it. It's on Bar 33 range. Would you give him land to lie in?"

"Of course," Fitz murmured.

Twenty minutes later, Johnny drove quietly from the ranch buildings. The day had turned hot and clear, and the Nations a hundred miles off looked close enough to shoot over. The last fresh whisper of spring was in the air as Johnny pulled the team up on the crest of the knoll and climbed down.

The job was quick, for the ground was soft and the box small. By dinnertime Johnny was back at the Bar 33.

Chapter Four: HARD-CASE DEPUTY

JOHNNY AND THE MAJOR ate with the hands in the cookshack adjoining the bunkhouse. Only a sporadic visitor to the Bar 33 these days, Johnny was nevertheless surprised to see so many new faces among the hands. Hank Bunker and Morgan, blacksmith and water-mason, were the only familiar faces. Johnny asked the major about why the old band was gone.

"Simple," the major said. "How did you feel when you were working here? You resented company rules—like no drinking, pay check every two months, no gun totin', and such. There isn't the freedom here of the old independent spread, and some of the men resented it. I didn't blame them much, but then I'm only the manager. They got fed up and drifted on."

"Speakin' of guns," Johnny said, "I come off without any. Reckon you could lend a pair till I get back?"

The major nodded. "Get back from where?"

"Campaignin'. I'm ridin' over to Crockett at the Stirrup Bar, then I'll drop down and see Kennicott. The whole bunch. I'm puttin' them the same proposition I put you, and I'll use your name for a starter."

An hour later, Johnny and Soot, his black, were headed up for the trail under the Kiowa rim which would bring them to Crockett's spread north of Cosmos by late afternoon. Another hour's ride put him off the lush San Dimas into the rocks and, farther on, into the Snake Pit—this a corkscrew tangle of wind- and water-eroded sandstone, which, when viewed from the Kiowa rim, seemed a tangle of snakes caught writhing and petrified for eternity.

Johnny gave Soot his head and, reins over arm, rolled a cigarette. Pick always liked this stretch, said it had more color in it than his mother's sewing-basket. Pick and color, they seemed to like each other. Color in rock and sky and life, even in mineral. Suddenly Johnny paused, match poised to discard. Color! If Pick had been working on one location and thought it good, certainly he would have packed some ore down to Hugo Miller's in Cosmos. The color of the rock and ore might give a clue to Pick's claim. The Calicoes held a hundred shades of red and purple, sullen grays, rusty orange, blacks, yellow and white sands and quartzes, miles of black malpais, miles more of these bile-tinted sandstone scarps, pinnacles, gargoyles, cattle rocks, and buttes that he was riding through now. Johnny didn't know them all, but he knew a good many of them through his childhood years spent with Pick. It was a long shot, and would take an eternity, but if by some blind chance it should guide him to an encounter with the claim jumper and murderer, then he shouldn't pass it up. If Pick only brought Hugo his—

Whang!

It scorched across his chest, slammed into his arm, and kited him out of the saddle onto the rocks, face down, before he could cry out. *Play dead!* something warned him. His mouth was bleeding, but he lay quietly, kicked one leg twice in a studied convulsion, then subsided.

His back loomed as big as a corral lot to the sky, inviting another shot. It crawled, shrunk, channeled sweat, but he did not move, waiting for that last blast to blow breath and life out of him.

Soot, good horse, stood still, and Johnny could hear his bridle chains jingle. He listened. No other sound. The seconds, loaded with lead, dragged by. Still no sound, and still Johnny did not move.

He's waitin', Johnny thought. *He's got a tip of that Buckhorn rear sight on each of my shoulder blades.*

His ears began to ring until he was sure its rhythm made him move. He opened one eye, hair-width by hair-width— and looked at dirt. The man was on the other side of Soot, that much he was sure of, else why had the shot knocked him off to the left? He was up there in those rocks, and if Johnny stalled long enough, it might toll him down.

So he waited, listening. He waited and waited and waited until he could feel his arm aching painfully and his chest wetting his whole shirt front. He felt the sun hot on his neck and head, and sweat was soaking his hair. Still there was no sound, no noise of a gun being levered, however softly. Soot whickered a little in friendly protest, then subsided, and the quiet of the afternoon flowed over again like still water.

Had the gulcher gone, confident that his first shot had done the work? Johnny didn't know, but he did know that he had to find out, to get off the ground before he bled so much he couldn't make for help.

I'll count sixty slow just fifteen times, then I'm movin', gulcher or no gulcher. The counting helped to pass the time, and he clung at it doggedly, listening meanwhile with the other half of his attention. When he was finished, he had not heard a sound.

He let his head roll over until he was resting on his cheek, and it was done so slowly that it took almost fifteen minutes more. Six feet or so to the side of him was a low, flat sandstone slab that tilted up a little at the far side. It would be enough to shelter him. He gathered himself for the effort, took a deep breath, then rolled over swiftly, and lunged for the rock, sprawling on his face behind it.

No shot, no sound, even, except Soot's slight shying at Johnny's sudden movement.

Maybe he's tollin' me out in the open, he thought. Determined to find out, Johnny first stuck his guns out from behind the rock, and getting no shot, his hand, then both hands, then his arms, then his boots. Finally, disgusted, he decided to take a chance. He raised his head, kept it there for several seconds, then lowered it.

If there was a man there, he had the patience of an Indian. The thing to do was to get it over with.

So, gun in hand, he drew his knees under him, then leaped from his rock to another one. No sound yet. In short zigzags, always keeping to shelter, he worked his way around the stubby butte where he figured the shot had come from. Once behind it, he could see there was no one on the sloping top. Carefully, he walked up to the rim where the man had hidden. One burned match lay on the rock; that was all. Johnny squatted and looked at it.

He couldn't have been here long—not even long enough to smoke down a quirly. And he was so sure of his first shot that he didn't even eject the empty.

His first impulse, colored by a hot, smothering rage, was to ride the Snake Pit until he had found the man, but his judgment told him it would have been futile. The three quarters of an hour he had lain there waiting for the second slug had given the man time enough to lose himself in this mass of twisted rock. Then, strangely, for the first time he wondered who the man might have been. And fast on the heels of the question came suspicion.

"The Bar 33?" Even as he said it, he felt ashamed. No. Simply because several men at the Bar 33, including Fitz, knew where he was going, the blame for the gulching didn't lie with them. Any clever killer could have followed Hank and him out from town, hung back out of sight at the ranch, seen the course Johnny was taking after dinner, and cut across to the Snake Pit to fort up and beef him. Of all the men he knew, Major Fitz was the most friendly and helpful and, looking at it in a cold, practical light, had the most to gain by preserving his life.

Could it have been Pick's killer, skulking in the vicinity since Pick's death and confident that sooner or later Johnny would show up to claim the body? That was more like it.

He took a whole hour out to examine the ground, looking over every inch of it for tracks. In a deep arroyo, forty yards behind the butte, he found what might have been tracks. The sand and rocks had been disturbed, but the arroyo was so rocky that he could tell nothing. It might even have been a stray beef. And all around it was rock, none of it scratched. Evidently, the gulcher had been at pains not to ride a shoed horse.

His face grim and hard, Johnny returned to Soot. This, then, was a foretaste of what he might expect.

"All right, pardner," he said to Soot, his tone quiet. "Just once their luck is goin' to trip. And if mine holds out to then, we'll know a lot of things."

He bandaged his arm, which had only a flesh wound, and mounted. The bullet furrow across his chest smarted a little; that was all.

Between the day Pick's body was found and election, there remained seven days for Johnny to campaign. In three of these, he contrived to see ten ranchers, and they listened to his plan with an open-minded, if dubious, attentiveness. Things were too far gone, they said; there were too many bums in the county to hold an honest election. There was more of this talk, but each man pledged his support, and the support of his men and his friends. Moreover—and this was what Johnny was most concerned with—they agreed thoroughly with his suggestion that they mail in the names of the men they thought should be run out of the county.

Back in Cosmos, Johnny stabled his horse, got a shave, had Doc Palmer put a fresh bandage on the slight flesh wound across his chest and arm, and went over to see his Nora. She was folding napkins in the dining-room, and she greeted him warmly, concern in her eyes.

"I—I thought maybe something had happened to you," she told him. Johnny sat down lazily and rolled a smoke. "You've changed, Johnny," she told him suddenly. "I heard about your talk with Blue."

"He's told it, then?"

Nora nodded. "A few people in this town are going to vote for you—the decent ones."

"And a few more aren't," Johnny said grimly.

"Nothing more about Pick—about his killers?" she asked hopefully, and Johnny told her no. He neglected to mention that he had been shot at. He listened to her chatter about Pick. She was recalling the many things done for her and others that showed Pick had not been the crotchety old man he was thought to be by some. Johnny knew she was trying to comfort him, but that part of him that had to do with Pick was buried deep within him, untouchable even by her. He would never feel he had done right by Pick until several things were squared. So he told her suddenly of what was uppermost in his mind now, but he went at it obliquely, starting with a question.

"If I'm elected sheriff, Nora, what do you think I ought to start out by doin'?"

Nora looked at him, puzzled. "But you said what you were going to do, Johnny—clean up the town and county."

"How?"

"By hiring honest men, incorruptible men for your deputies."

"Know any?"

"Fred McLain," Nora suggested after a pause.

"He's honest. He's also dumb. How long do you think he'd stack up against a handy gunman?"

Nora frowned. "Not long, I'm afraid. He isn't that kind of a fighter."

"Know any of your honest men that are?"

Nora ceased her work and sat back in her chair, her serene face almost scowling. "Outside of yourself, no, I don't."

Johnny leaned forward, grinning. "How would you like to marry a sheriff that had the short end of a ninety-ten chance of livin' a week?"

Nora smiled back at him, but her smile was not without apprehension. "Maybe I will marry you some day, Johnny —after you've proved you're worth it." And she added hastily, "Not because I think I'm a girl in a million, Johnny, but—"

"I do," Johnny said, and rose and walked around the table and kissed her. Nora laughed, flustered, and pulled him into a chair.

"Not because I think that, but because I only want a few things—and I don't guess I can be happy without them. One is a husband who won't stand by and see the innocent trodden on and the decent, helpless people put in the wrong. How would you like to marry a wife and never be sure that she was safe? How would you like to have children grow up in a town like this—at the mercy of any drunken wretch with a gun? My husband's got to be a fighter—and that's the only thing worth fighting."

Johnny nodded, grinning. "You'll get him. Only, how do you expect to marry a saint and have him sheriff and still keep him alive?"

Nora looked worried now. "What are you trying to tell me, Johnny?"

"That I've got to have hardcases for deputies. They've got to be tough and hard to kill—and not pillars of the church."

"I can see that," Nora said slowly.

"Other folks won't," Johnny pointed out. "The day I'm elected sheriff, I'm goin' to appoint some deputies that will get this whole county on my neck. And when I say the whole county, I mean it—good people and bad." He looked steadily at her. "I just didn't want you to get the wrong idea. I'm out to clean up this county. If I do it kinda' rough, it'll be because I have to, understand?"

Nora patted his hand. "You know I do."

With that encouragement, Johnny went ahead with his plan. Out on the porch of the Cosmos House, he surveyed the town with a kind of impersonal criticism. Its wide street, flanked by twin rows of unpainted, weather-scarred, false-front buildings, was always fetlock-deep in rutted dust or mud. Cans and paper littered it. Each of the dozen saloons in town was easily recognizable by the slatternly stack of empty beer barrels on its front boardwalk. Ore wagons, four teams to the wagon, plodded down the street in an almost unbroken line between the mines up the slope back of Cosmos to the stamp mill below the town. Saddle horses, buckboards, and spring wagons helped to clutter up the street. To a stranger unused to a modest boom town, it would have seemed a madhouse.

And to Johnny, his gaze skeptical, it seemed almost that now.

He picked his way across the traffic of the street and turned into the Kiowa Head. It was thronged, as usual, but the man he was looking for was not there. He proceeded down the street, stopping at the Melodian, the Legal Tender, the War Bonnet, the Drum Head, the Dry Camp, the First Chance. That put him at the head of the street. He crossed and went into the Gem, Prince's Keno Parlor, and finally the Palace. Possibly because it was the largest and toughest of all the saloons, the Palace wore its name with a little more splendor than the others. Johnny saw the man he wanted standing over by a poker game in the far corner, watching the players. He was a burly, squat redhead, with a full, square jaw, cold blue eyes, and freckles that almost dyed his face the color of his hair.

Johnny walked up beside him and watched the game and, after a pause, looked up. "Hello, Turk," he drawled, and Turk Hebron nodded curtly.

"Got a minute?" Johnny asked.

Turk looked at him suspiciously. "All day."

Johnny flagged a waiter and ordered drinks, and they retired to a corner bench, well out of earshot of the main crowd.

Turk did not try to hide his skepticism. He drawled, as he sat down, "You must want somethin'."

His blue eyes chilled a little as they looked at the deputy.

"I do." Johnny grinned. "I wouldn't buy a saddle tramp like you a drink if I didn't."

Turk grinned back. If he did not have any affection for Johnny Hendry, he at least respected him as a lawman who was blunt, to the point, and no pussyfooter. Turk said, "Is it about them horses that I stole from Cass Briggs?"

Johnny shook his head and frowned a little. "No, not about that. But now that you mention it, did you steal the horses?"

Turk looked around him and then said, "There ain't a witness here to hear me. Sure I took 'em. I'll take his hide some day and nail it on the fence, too."

Johnny didn't say anything until the drinks were set down before them. He leaned back against the wall and said, "Man to man, Turk, don't you get fed up with this business? You ain't with a bunch. They don't want anything to do with you. The little smidgin of horses and cattle you steal, you got to drive a hundred miles to a market and do it alone. You're tough enough that nobody bothers you, but on that account, nobody'll work with you. I don't savvy it."

Turk said cautiously, "I don't do so bad."

"You do awful bad," Johnny contradicted him. "You know it."

Turk shrugged. "Not much choice, Johnny. I'm tough because I don't want anybody to throw in with me. And I don't want anybody to throw in with me because he'd be bound to get big ideas about stealin' every horse and steer in the county. We'd get away with it for a while, and then we'd get caught. And then you rannies over at the sheriff's office would start lookin' through your reward posters and you'd ship me back over the mountains—if you didn't hang me." He shook his head. "Just a little suits me. You wouldn't bother to run me down and, besides, you couldn't."

Johnny let that pass and went back to what Turk had said.

"I've seen some of those reward dodgers. You used to make big tracks, didn't you?"

"Sort of." Turk grinned.

"Tired of this penny-ante rustlin'?"

"Plenty," Turk said flatly, "but a man's got to live."

"Ever try a job?"

"That's a laugh," Turk said wryly. "Every time I go

near a mine, somebody picks up a shotgun and says, 'The weather'll get some hotter if you come any closer, Turk.' "

"What about ridin' jobs?" Johnny asked him.

"Ranchers claim every one of their steers knows me on sight and will start a stampede when they see me." He added, grinning, "Which is exaggeratin' it a little, but then that's the way they feel."

"Still, you stick here," Johnny pointed out.

Turk swallowed his drink and said mildly, "Thanks to you and Baily Blue. You could run me out if you wanted. You haven't. I try to pay you back by not stealin' the county blind. I don't do half the thievin' anybody else in my line would do."

Johnny drank his whisky then, and set down his glass, regarding Turk with amiable curiosity. "Heard about my runnin' for sheriff?"

"On a law-and-order platform, yeah. You better pull in your neck."

"How'd you like to be my deputy after I'm elected, Turk?" Johnny said.

Turk raised his pale eyes to Johnny's face. "It's been a long time since I heard about Santa Claus. I thought he'd left the country."

"I mean it," Johnny said. "Before you start laughin', think it over. If I'm elected, I don't aim to write to every county in the Territory and ask for a list of their wanted men, then comb over this pack of hardcases and ship them home. I ain't even interested in hangin' the dead-wood on anybody—least of all you. All I aim to do is move them out of here. If they don't want to go, they got to prove they're men enough to stay. That's simple, ain't it?"

"To say it, yeah," Turk admitted.

"I'm sayin' it, and I'm doin' it. But I can't do it alone. I need a deputy—at least one—who's a scrapper and can beat these hardcases at their own game. I don't care anything about his past. All he's got to do is worry about his present. I'll expect him to be honest, impartial, and willin' to risk his neck for somethin' he's fought against most of his life." Pausing, he regarded Turk closely. "It strikes me you've had just about enough of dodgin' reward posters, Turk. Am I right?"

Turk fondled his glass with a square, hairy hand, his eyes musing. "How long will this job last?"

"Forever, if you're on the level and I can work it for you. I won't be sheriff forever, Turk, but I figure if I'm sheriff once, I'll do enough for these ranchers that they'll do me a favor. And one of those favors will include forgettin' the old Turk Hebron and rememberin' the new one."

Turk said quietly, "I've never known you to go back on your word, Johnny. But can you promise that much?"

"I think so. You willin' to throw in with me?"

Turk didn't say anything for a moment. Johnny said softly, "I know what you're thinkin'. You know plenty about the men that are robbin' this county. You wouldn't want to double-cross 'em, even if you did hate 'em. Isn't that it?"

Turk nodded.

"If I get elected, I'm not goin' to try and trap these birds on the first night. I'm goin' to tell them I'll give 'em twenty-four hours to clear out of the county. After that, anything goes. That's fair enough, ain't it?"

"Sure. But how about them that don't take your little message to heart? Most of these birds have been told to get out of places before. But they don't scare easy. If you was elected sheriff with such high notions, they might give *you* twenty-four hours to move on somewheres else."

"I don't scare very easy, either," Johnny said. "And— I'm tellin' you—I aim to *have* to help some customers that don't move easy. That's where you come in. How does it sound to you?"

"Interestin'," said Turk.

"How about it, then? A hundred a month and horse keep—and brawls and shots at your back and gun fightin' and ridin' and plenty other misery."

"You're on," Turk said briefly.

Johnny rose and said, "Come out in back a minute, Turk. There's one other thing to settle."

Turk rose and followed him out in back of the Palace.

There was a bare square of hard-packed dirt between the Palace and the rear alley. Johnny looked around and saw no one in sight, and he reached up and unbuckled his gun belt and laid it on the step. Turk was watching curiously.

"I've had a notion," Johnny drawled, "you think you ride a little higher and wider than me, Turk. In other words, if it come to a showdown, you think you could take care of me pretty easy. That right?"

"Not easy," Turk murmured. "But I could take care of you. Not when it come to guns, though. You'd cut me to doll rags."

"But fists," Johnny drawled.

"I can take you."

"Try it," Johnny suggested. "I'm open to conviction."

Turk laughed and shucked his belt, and they squared off and circled a moment. Then Turk, head down, sailed in, arms flailing. Johnny straightened him out with a blistering hook and stepped back.

"You ain't fightin'," Turk complained, shaking his head. "I can't dance. But I can fight."

"Here she comes," Johnny murmured.

They rushed at each other. Turk hoped to make it a clinch, where his weight and heavily corded shoulder muscles could wrestle Johnny around while he ladled out punishment. But Johnny hacked down on Turk's guard and sent five lashing blows—three in the midriff, two on the shelf of the chin—at Turk.

Turk went down, and on his back. When he got up, he was scowling and cursing furiously.

"Look at my tracks," Johnny murmured. "I didn't back up to do that."

But Turk was mad now, and he wasn't looking at anything but Johnny. He came in, shoulders lowered and rolling, and they collided. This time there was no science about it, nothing but vicious, body-weighted slugging. Toe to toe they stood, weaving a little, trying to dodge the worst blows, but so intent on hitting that each took them and grunted and gave them back. For perhaps forty seconds it went on that way, neither of them conceding an inch, taking the shock of the blows full on the body. But slowly Johnny was working out his plan. Turk's chin was buried in his thick neck, where it was protected, and Johnny was pumping savage blows into Turk's midriff. And slowly, from the pain of it, Turk was hauling his own blows in so that his elbows would protect him. And he was breathing hard. Suddenly, Johnny shifted a little to the right, so that he was at one side of Turk, and then he laced over a left that yanked Turk's chin out of its cover. And then, savagely, putting every ounce of bone and muscle in him, Johnny drove the chin higher, until it shelved clear, and then he slugged hard and desperately, and there was a sound of skin-padded bone on knuckles.

Turk seemed to carom off Johnny's fist into the dirt.

He lay there, absolutely motionless except for a little convulsive movement of his knees. Johnny, dragging in great gusts of breath, stood over him, watching. Then he picked up his hat and went over to a barrel standing under the eaves trough of the Palace and ladled out a hatful of water, which he doused on Turk's face. Turk rolled over and dragged himself to his knees, then shook his head and looked around for Johnny.

"Enough?" Johnny murmured.

"Plenty," Turk muttered, and then grinned. Johnny helped him to his feet, and they faced each other.

"Brother," Turk said ruefully, "I've seen the hind legs of a mule that couldn't do that."

Johnny grinned and touched his ribs gingerly. "You've got five of my ribs between your fingers, it feels like."

They both laughed, and Turk stuck out his hand. "By thunder, you *will* make a sheriff," he said slowly.

Johnny stuck out his own. "With a hardcase, redheaded deputy, how could I help it?"

And then and there, behind the Palace, the pact was sealed.

Chapter Five: STRAWS IN THE WIND

IF JOHNNY DID NOT SET UP DRINKS for the whole county in each of the dozen saloons for a week, he did other things designed to offset Baily Blue's whisky buying. On the quiet, he managed to see every merchant in town and point out the advantages of a law-and-order term. To them he promised a deputy who would act as marshal. Then he went to the mine owners and operators, and to them he promised he would stop holdups, or anyway cut them down to the place where insurance rates on the bullion shipments were not prohibitive. It was a busy week, but in the midst of it he took the time to go down to Hugo Miller's assay office and talk with him.

Hugo was a quiet man, a graduate engineer, middle-aged, not given to talking much about his past. But Pick had found him thoroughly honest and he had often spent evenings in the back of Miller's workshop talking over ores and minerals and mines, and Johnny sometimes listened. He, too, liked this pale, sensitive-faced man who forever had a pipe in his mouth, and who minded his own business.

Miller was working at his scales; at Johnny's entrance he quit and pulled up two chairs. After a few minutes of small talk, in which Miller bitterly lamented Pick's death, Johnny said, "Did Pick have any samples with you, Hugo?"

"About ten." .

"Anything good show up?"

"They weren't worthless," Hugo said carefully. "Pick knows too much about the game to lug rock down to me that isn't good. But on the other hand, they were run-of-the-mill samples for him. They all assayed about the same."

"No one better than the others?" Johnny asked hopefully.

"We'll see," Hugo said, rising. He got his reports and glanced over them briefly. "Here's one that's better than the others. Not much, though."

Johnny's heart sank. He had hoped Hugo could show him a rich assay, something that would indicate Pick had struck it and had been murdered by claim jumpers, but there was nothing here pointing to it.

"Know where any of these claims were located?" he asked glumly, and then he went on to explain. Surely

Pick had been murdered for his gold—it was certain that he had found gold, for some of it was found on his burros. In view of this, it was almost certain that he had the location papers on him when he was murdered. "Maybe he found this gold at a place he'd been workin' a long time. I thought maybe he'd told you of a place that looked good."

Hugo shook his head. "He never told me."

Johnny sighed. "That's out, I reckon."

"Maybe not," Hugo said quietly. "He's brought me a lot of ore to assay, Johnny. Most of it lately has been a peculiar kind of ore—what a geologist would call volcanic breccia, and my guess is that it's in a long dike, or fault. Every one of his last thirty samples has been of this ore. Maybe he struck gold in this volcanic breccia dike."

"That's a lot of help," Johnny said dryly. "What do I do? Hunt the Calicoes for volcanic breccia?"

"There isn't much of it," Hugo said.

"I know. But it may be only a mile long. It'd take years to find it."

"Let someone else do it for you," Hugo said calmly. Johnny was about to protest, when he closed his mouth and looked hard at Hugo. "What do you mean by that?"

Hugo took his pipe from his mouth and pointed it at Johnny. "Each one of these samples Pick has brought in is higher-grade stuff than the one before it. That argues that Pick was following this breccia dike to its head, doesn't it? He was getting closer and closer to a really good thing. All right, if the man who killed him did it because Pick had something, the chances are he'll bring in this ore to be assayed. It'll have this volcanic breccia in it. And I'd know the looks of that anywhere, because in ten years of assaying for this town and the Calicoes, it's the first I've run across."

Johnny turned this over in his mind. "Then if a jasper brings in some samples with volcanic breccia, you'll know it come from Pick's workings?"

"More than likely it will. Prospectors don't usually work near each other unless they've already found good color and staked claims."

"That'd be it," Johnny murmured. "It wouldn't be a

sure thing, but it might be." He rose. "You'll let me know, then, Hugo, if anyone brings in samples that jibe with Pick's?"

"Gladly."

Johnny left then. Here was something to work on; slim enough, it appeared, but nevertheless something. It would take patience and a lot of it. He stopped in at the sheriff's office and found Baily Blue loading his pockets with half dollars. He grinned up at Johnny and said, "That's my ammunition. Fifty cents a drink. You ought to take a tip from an old campaigner, son."

Johnny shook his head. "Got the mail yet?"

"Uh-uh. I'm on my way."

"Don't bother. I'll pick it up," Johnny said. He turned down toward Bledsoe's Miners' Emporium, where the post office was. A section in the front of the store had been partitioned off to make the post office. This partition consisted of a rack of pigeonholes, opened at both ends. The mail had been brought in on the stage only a few minutes before, and Bledsoe, the fat postmaster, who always waited to rack up the local mail with that brought in on the stage, was busy behind the partition. Most of the waiting crowd had already received its mail and was reading it.

Johnny looked in his pigeonhole and saw that it was vacant and stuck his head through the wicket. "Nothin' for me, Bledsoe?"

"A lot," Bledsoe said, and reached up to haul it out. He withdrew his pudgy hand, looking surprised. "Why, you had a whole boxful not ten seconds ago, Johnny," he said slowly.

Johnny wheeled to confront the crowd. Miners, punchers, men, and women were standing in small clusters in the front of the store, most of them reading, some conversing. They had not heard Bledsoe's conversation with Johnny, for they were paying no attention to him—all except one dirty and unshaven puncher. Johnny's gaze whipped past him, and the man turned down-store. As he wheeled, Johnny saw a sheaf of envelopes peeping out of his pocket.

Johnny started toward him, and then stopped. It would

look mighty foolish to go up and accost the puncher and ask to see the letters. If that story got around, Baily Blue would turn it into a laugh, and no one knew better than Johnny how easy it is to laugh a man out of office. But still, he wasn't sure, and he loafed back through the store keeping a good distance between the puncher and himself.

The puncher stopped down the counter and asked the clerk for a box of shells, then turned and glanced obliquely at Johnny, who was pretending to examine a gun lying on the counter.

When he looked up again, the puncher was walking rapidly toward the rear of the store. Johnny, his suspicions thoroughly aroused now, took after him.

Outside, the puncher turned up the alley and out of sight, and Johnny ran to the back door, yanked it open, and raced out into the alley. Ahead of him, the puncher was running as fast as he could. Johnny lit out after him, drawing his gun. He shot once into the air and yelled, "Better pull up, fella."

For answer, the puncher stopped abruptly, whirled with gun in hand, and started to shoot. Johnny cut off to his right for the shelter of a shed, and he emptied his gun in swift *rat-a-plan*. He saw the puncher go down, and he stopped, then loaded his gun and walked carefully toward him. He hadn't expected this, and he cursed himself for losing his head. What if the man had only been trying to get out of the way of what he thought was an officious lawman? One look at him and Johnny saw he was dead. One of the slugs had caught him in the neck, and he lay on his back, head twisted awry. And Johnny remembered that it was himself who had shot first.

Men started to collect in the alley. Swiftly, Johnny knelt down and rolled the man over and pulled the letters out of his Levi's pocket. A glance at them brought a wave of relief over him, for they were his.

To the first few men around him—hardcase loafers at Prince's Keno Parlor—Johnny held out the letters. "Stole them," he drawled calmly. "When will these tinhorns learn they can't hooraw everybody in this town?"

He could see the dislike in the eyes of these men. One

of them said, "You couldn't've asked him for 'em, I don't suppose?"

"If you see a man ridin' off on your horse, you don't ask him to get off, do you?" Johnny drawled.

"It ain't the same thing," the man countered.

Another said, "This a sample of that law and order you're talkin' about?"

Johnny picked out the speaker and walked over to him. "It is. Don't you like it?"

"Not much."

"This is a wide country, friend," he said gently, ominously. "If you don't like it, there's lots of roads out of here."

"I'll stick," the speaker sneered. "We ain't worried much about your gettin' in. Even if you do, we ain't exactly frettin'."

Johnny said, "Saturday night, I may start to worry you." He indicated the dead puncher. "Any of you know him?"

None of them did. They had seen him, they said, but they didn't think he worked here or was known except to maybe a few barkeeps.

"Just a harmless pilgrim," Johnnly drawled dryly. "Like so many rannies I could name around here. In a couple of weeks maybe these pilgrims will decide it's a little safer to ride on through Cosmos." And with that he left them to hunt up a teamster who would deliver the corpse to the coroner.

When that was finished, he went down to the hotel. In his pocket were the letters—and they were the ones he had been expecting today from the ten ranchers he had consulted. In them would be the names of all the undesirables the honest ranchers wanted run out of the county. Obviously somebody knew what these letters contained and wanted to destroy them.

Nora wasn't at the Cosmos House, but Johnny went into the deserted dining-room, shut the door behind him, and pulled up a chair, spreading his letters on the table.

He opened all eight of them, for two of the ranchers were not represented. The lists were all printed, giving no clue to their writers.

With a stub of pencil and a sheet of paper, Johnny tabulated the names, and when he was finished, he sat back in his chair, amazement in his face.

"So Major Fitz heads the list!" he murmured. "Well, I'll be whupped! I'll be double, triple hog-whupped!"

It didn't make sense, yet there was the evidence. Six of the eight ranchers put Major Fitz's name at the head of their lists. Johnny pulled out a sack of tobacco and thoughtfully rolled a smoke. He'd got more than he bargained for here, but what did it mean? Originally, he had wanted to give these men a chance to express their honest beliefs without having to present inadequate proof and explanations. But Major Fitz? In cow country, no company outfit is ever loved, but to accuse the manager of the Bar 33 of rustling beef was another matter. Of course they would seize this opportunity of telling it, for they wouldn't dare say so in public. And it couldn't be one man's grudge; too many had hit on Fitz's name.

He heard the door open and he swept the lists into one pile as Nora stepped into the room. She looked at him accusingly as she walked over to him, peeling off her coat.

"Hiding something?"

Johnny only grinned, and then, on that chance that two heads might be better than one, he decided to tell her. "Remember that scheme I told you about—having the honest ranchers send in the names of the bad hombres?" Nora nodded. "Guess who's the most unwanted jasper in this county."

"Johnny Hendry," Nora said, and then became serious. "Who?"

"Major Fitz."

Nora's face fell. "Let's see." When she'd looked over the lists, she put them down and said flatly, "Honest ranchers, nothing! Who all did you go to, Johnny? The bums and cattle thieves?"

"Ten men you like."

"But I like Major Fitz!"

"So do I. What do you make of it?"

Nora said hotly, "I just think it goes to show that some men will do mean and underhanded things if they don't have to sign their names to them!"

Thoughtfully, Johnny struck a match and touched off the lists and shoved them in the fireplace. "Mebbeso," he said slowly, but he couldn't help thinking about that puncher who had attempted to steal the letters. Had he been sent by Major Fitz, who might have guessed that his name would lead the list of undesirables? Johnny didn't know. "But whatever it is," he told Nora, "it's a secret between us."

Chapter Six: GOLD SHIPMENT

HANK BRENDER WAS CLEAR OUT beyond the fourth corral when the Bar 33 triangle clanged for breakfast, so that he was the last man to the cookshack. As he entered he felt, without being able to pin it down, that a subtle change came over his fellow punchers. The talk didn't stop, the usual number started to ride him about not being hungry, but he had the uncomfortable impression that the subject of conversation had been suddenly switched, and that the cameraderie was forced. This wasn't the first time he had noticed it, and it made him feel an outsider.

Sitting down, he noticed a stranger at the table, and like all these strangers lately—men who rode the grub line and could not be refused a meal—this one was shifty-eyed, furtive, and silent. Nobody knew him, or said they didn't, but Hank had the feeling that they did. Somehow, things were different lately. Hands never stayed here long any more, and there wasn't that old loyalty to the Bar 33 that used to make it a pleasant and secure place to work.

As Hank sat down, Major Fitz rapped his tin cup with his knife, and the table fell silent.

"No work today, boys," the major announced. "As you all know, this is election day. As soon as you've finished the work around the place, you can ride into town. Blake, at the bank, will pay you at two, not a minute before. If you haven't all voted before that time, you'd better not let me find it out." He paused, and glared around the table at his men. "And if you don't get down there—all of you— before you see a pay check or any whisky, and vote for

Johnny Hendry, you needn't bother to come back here. Understand that?"

They did. The talk turned to the election, and although there was a long ticket of offices, nobody discussed anything but the election of the sheriff. Hank listened closely, but he could not hear one dissenter from the major's opinion. Johnny Hendry was liked here, it seemed.

After breakfast, as Hank stood outside the cookshack rolling a toothpick in his mouth, Major Fitz and Carmody, the foreman, came up.

"Hank, I've got a favor to ask of you," Major Fitz said bluntly.

When Hank inclined his head, the major said, "I picked you because you're the steadiest hand here and probably won't feel this is such a burden. The rest of the men are anxious to get to town and vote and start drinking. It won't matter to you if you're an hour or so late, will it?"

Hank said no.

"Well, Art Bodan rode past that north pasture last night on his way home and he said there was a hundred foot of fence down. He rode around and made sure the horses were pushed up to the far end, but he couldn't fix it because he didn't have any tools. Would you mind ridin' out today and stringin' that wire back?"

"Not a bit," Hank said obligingly. He was a little surprised at the politeness of the major's request, since he usually didn't ask a man to do a thing; he simply ordered him.

Carmody, the foreman, said, "Better get goin' now, Hank. The boys can clear up the work here in short order."

Hank went over to the bunkhouse to get a pair of heavy gloves. No one else was in the place. Prompted by something he could not immediately define, Hank tucked a pair of glasses in his hip pocket and went out to saddle up. When he had his wire wrapped in gunny sack and slung over the saddle horn, and the hammer and some staples, he mounted and rode south up the ridge. Once over it, he turned sharply and headed for some trees that saddled the ridge. Dismounting, he worked his way up the hump and bellied down in some brush, training his glasses back on the ranch house not a half mile away.

Out in the yard, the whole crew was gathered listening to Major Fitz. Something stirred Hank's anger at the sight. It was as if Major Fitz didn't want him to be in on this parley. And suddenly Hank knew that he had been sent on this errand so that the major would be rid of him. Passionately Hank wanted to hear what was being said by Major Fitz down there. The hardcase stranger stood at the major's right, listening. Then the gathering broke up, and Major Fitz joined the stranger, and they both walked toward the trim white house.

Hank drew back into the brush and squatted on his haunches, rolling and lighting a smoke. He was an even-tempered sort, but for the first time in his life he felt sulky. He cuffed the battered Stetson back off his forehead and thoughtfully pulled the lock of gray-shot hair that licked down on his forehead. He'd worked under Major Fitz longer than any man down there—twice as long as Carmody had worked for him. And now they thought they had to send him away so they could talk among themselves. But why? Funny things were going on down there and had been for a year—secret things that a man could only guess at.

He smoked his cigarette down until it burned his fingers and then he dropped it and stepped on it, his homely face set in a stubborn cast. That fence up there could go straight to hell as far as he was concerned. He was going to get at the bottom of this.

Back in the brush, he trained his glasses on the house and kept them there. Presently the stranger came out alone, went to the corral, snaked out his horse, and saddled up and rode north, toward town.

Hank didn't waste a minute. Back to his pony, he cached the wire and tools and swung down along the ridge west until it petered out.

Riding an arroyo bottom, he swung north, keeping out of sight until finally he was a mile or so away from the house, and then he cut back to the road. The tracks of the stranger's horse showed plainly in the dust of the road. He followed them at a leisurely pace. Just before the road

topped the ridge south of town, the tracks turned off to
the left. This time, Hank used more caution. The tracking
was difficult in this broken and rocky terrain, but he saw
that the man was keeping to this side of the ridge until
he was below the town. Hank dismounted then and went
ahead, carefully scanning the broken country ahead of
him.

Rounding a jut of rock, he saw the man's horse ground-
haltered by a screening piñon. He drew back, circled wide,
and crawled up on a small, flat-topped butte. There, on
the lip of the ridge under a piñon, the man was bellied
down watching something below. Hank shifted his position until he also could look into the canyon.

Below them, in the bottom of the canyon below the
town, lay the stamp mill. Hank watched it for a few moments, his face puzzled.

Suddenly, he saw a flash of reflected sun, and then he
understood that someone was signaling to the stranger.

Tip Rogers, superintendent of the Esmerella mine, was
at work a little early on election day, so as to be at the
shaft mouth when the night shift came off duty. The men
of this shift he called into the big freighting-shed and
told them to wait a minute. The day shift of miners was
just collecting at the shaft mouth, and he told these men
to come into the freighting-shed, too. Once they were all
collected, Tip mounted a piling and looked them over.
He was a young, high-shouldered man with crisp, curly
brown hair, dressed in breeches and lace boots and with an
engaging, serious face that was more sober than usual
today. These men were his seniors, most of them, and he
did not like the task set him, but he cleared his throat and
raised his hand.

"What I've got to say is mighty short," he told them.
"If Baily Blue is elected sheriff of this county again, the
Esmerella will have to shut down. I don't have to tell you
that means you'll lose your jobs."

"How come that, Tip?" one of the miners asked.

"Because the insurance companies are asking such high
rates to insure our bullion shipments that we can't make

any money. And if we can't insure the stuff, we'll be cleaned out in a couple of months. And if we're cleaned out you won't have any employer to work for any more—no pay checks. That's simple enough, isn't it?"

The miners looked at each other. A voice carried over their murmur. "First time I ever knowed a outfit to make its workers vote the way it said."

Tip nodded. "We don't like it, either, Bill, but that's how things stand. Unless there's a law-and-order sheriff put in here, we can't operate. We're not tellin' you how you have to vote. We're just saying that if you want to keep your jobs, you'll have to help put Johnny Hendry in office."

"You think he'll clean it up?"

Tip's jaw muscles corded a little. "You really want to know what I think? I don't think he will. I don't think he can. But he's the only hope we've got. Get behind him and give him a try." Then he told them that the day shift would get two hours above ground at noon to vote, and dismissed them.

Inside the Esmerella office, he passed the door of Sammons, the manager, and went into his own neat cubbyhole. He drew some papers from his desk, put them in his pocket, and went outside to a saddled horse waiting at the tie rail.

His ride into town was slow and thoughtful. The streets of Cosmos were in an uproar, and there was much drinking already at this early hour. Tip looked at the scene contemptuously, and picked his way down the thronged street to the Cosmos hotel.

In the dining-room, Nora was serving the late breakfasters, and among them was Johnny Hendry. Tip scowled, but Nora smiled and waved him over to where she stood talking with Johnny.

"Sit down, Tip," Johnny invited, and Tip did, ordering his breakfast. He and Johnny regarded each other with a wary neutrality, for when Johnny wasn't with Nora, Tip usually was. But Tip knew that hard-faced, grinning Johnny had the inside track with her and he resented it with all the heat his good manners allowed him to show— which wasn't much.

"You don't seem worried about the election," Tip observed as Johnny went on with his breakfast.

"I'll win it. Why shouldn't I?" Johnny countered arrogantly.

"What if you do? Do you think you'll be able to clean up the place?"

Johnny looked at him swiftly. "I do. You don't, do you?"

"No."

"Want to bet?"

"Sure," Tip said, smiling crookedly. "What?"

Johnny laid down his fork and stared at Tip with speculative interest. "What is it you think I can't handle?"

"You won't calm down these hardcases, let alone drive 'em out. You won't solve the rustling or the robberies or the murders any more thañ you did under Blue."

"You think I can expect trouble soon, then?" Johnny murmured innocently.

"Right away," Tip said flatly.

Nora came back now with Tip's breakfast and sat down at the third chair. Johnny said to her, "Tip thinks I can expect trouble right away after I'm elected." He looked at Tip grinning. "How soon?"

"If you're elected, you'll get it tonight or tomorrow."

Johnny grinned broadly now. "And you're willin' to bet I can't handle it? Furthermore, you're willin' to bet I can't solve all this stuff that Blue don't pay any attention to?"

"That's right."

Johnny leaned back and drawled, "Nora tells me as soon as you heard about this election dance Monday night, you asked her to go."

"I did," Tip admitted, and looked down at Nora. "You're going with me, aren't you?"

"You asked me first," Nora said.

Johnny cut in. "Are you willin' to bet the chance to take Nora to the dance that I can't handle any trouble that comes up between now and Monday?"

"Sure," Tip said flatly. "But I already had the date. That's what I'm putting up. What are you putting up?"

"My resignation," Johnny replied, eying Tip steadily.

Tip leaned forward in his chair and said, "You're crazy, Hendry. Even I wouldn't expect you to put that up for a stake."

"It's up," Johnny murmured, and rose, looking down at Nora. "I'll leave you love birds to yourselves," he said, grinning. "Me, I'm goin' out and elect myself. I'll see you Monday night, honey," he said to Nora, and laughed at Tip's glare of anger.

Tip regarding Johnny's receding back with a wry expression. "Some day, somebody's going to work that cocky puncher over," he growled.

Nora giggled. "It'll take a good man."

"But look!" Tip protested. "His stepfather was killed only a few days ago. You'd think he'd be a little more considerate of his memory, quiet down a little, and stop his swaggering. Instead, you wouldn't ever know he'd had any hard luck. You'd—"

"Stop that!" Nora said sharply. "Johnny loved Pick! But does he have to go around moaning in public to prove he's sorrowing?" Nora's eyes were dancing with anger. "Everything he thinks or does now is planned to help in getting Pick's killer. Don't criticize something you don't know anything about, Tip Rogers!"

Tip smiled a little. "All right, I'm wrong. But don't scratch my eyes out."

Nora flushed a little, and her eyes lost their anger. She even smiled forgivingly. "All right, Tip, but don't ever try to knock Johnny to me. He's all right."

"I suppose he is," Tip agreed wryly. "I might even like him if he didn't like you so much."

When Tip was finished eating, he went out to his horse again, mounted, and rode west out of town toward the stamp mill. Approaching it, he could hear the earth-shaking thunder of the stamps as they crushed the ore in the reduction process. The mill itself was a series of red-painted, corrugated-tin-roofed sheds tipping up the slope of the canyon side. The offices were down in the valley bottom at the very end of the building. A dozen ore freighters waited their turn at the scales and hoppers, and the place buzzed with activity. Tip saw a bent old prospector drive his buckboard onto the weighing-platform. He had a half-dozen sacks of ore in the back of his buckboard. Tip smiled a little as he regarded the man. Then he stepped into the building and was shown into the manager's office.

Kinder, an officious, sandy-haired little man, greeted him, and they shook hands. Kinder had been watching out the window, and now he returned to it.

"His outfit is pretty clever, isn't it?" he said to Tip.

"Is he the one?" Tip asked, laughing. "I thought he was an old desert rat."

"Here he comes now," Kinder said.

In a few moments, the prospector was ushered into Kinder's office, and Kinder shook his hand and indicated Tip. "Reese, this is Tip Rogers, the Esmerella super." To Tip he said, "Believe it or not, this is Reese, your insurance man. He doesn't look like an insurance man, but he is—in more ways than one."

They shook hands. Reese, under his week's growth of stubble, was a tough, wiry man of middle age. His soiled and tattered clothes seemed more incongruous when he spoke to Tip in cultivated English.

"The bars are under the sacks in the back of my buckboard," he announced to Kinder. "Your man contrived to unload my sacks of ore and put the bars in without even seeing it." He laughed softly. "Well, do you think we'll get away with it this time?"

"I hope so," Tip said fervently. "One more holdup and you people will quit insuring us for good."

"That's right," Reese said crisply. "If this fails, the only alternative is a good-sized army to guard the shipments. And that, I'm afraid, is a little too expensive all around."

Kinder laid out some papers in front of Reese. "Here's the weight. Four pigs at twelve thousand dollars' value each. That's forty-eight thousand. Here's the ounces and weights, checked and rechecked."

"I'll take your word for it," Reese said. He in turn drew papers from his pocket, as did Tip. When everything was signed, Tip retained the insurance papers.

Again Reese shook hands all around. "Wish me luck."

"I do," Tip said solemnly. "It's a rotten shame that this is the only way gold can be got out of the country. Maybe a new sheriff will help, but I doubt it."

"We'll see," Reese said.

Outside, Reese went over to his buckboard and waved to the checker, who stood by the scales.

"Good luck, dad," the checker called, and he watched while Reese turned the buckboard around and took the road west away from the mill.

Then the checker turned to his assistant. "Take this over, Frank. I want a drink."

He walked over to the huge watering-trough away from the buildings. A pipe funneled water into it, and the checker leaned over to drink from its mouth. But at the same time, he drew a small mirror from his shirt, and while he was pretending to drink, he held it out in the sun and turned it toward the opposite rim of the canyon. He could see its reflection on the cliff side. Finally, he focused it at the base of a gnarled lone piñon on the canyon rim. Then, by dragging his hand across the mirror, he conveyed a simple code in dots and dashes. It only took a half minute. When he was finished, he drank and returned to his work, whistling.

Chapter Seven: ELECTION NIGHT

WHEN THE STRANGER WITHDREW from the rim, Hank stayed where he was. He saw the man get his horse and ride west, past the very butte on which Hank was lying. For a long moment, Hank regarded the vanishing horseman with puzzlement. None of this made sense—or very little of it— but Hank was a stubborn man.

He got his horse and started to follow. In an hour's riding, he was off the ridge and down in the shallow canyon. Presently the tracks crossed the dusty road, and Hank pulled up to investigate. Here the stranger had also paused to look at tracks—buckboard tracks—but instead of clinging to the road, he crossed it, heading northwest. Now Hank could see that the man had put his horse into a steady trot. Hank followed suit. The country was so broken and up-ended here with shale hills and clay dunes that the going was slow and tortuous. It was also dangerous, for if it once occurred to the stranger that he was being followed, it would be simple to pull off behind a dune and wait for his pursuer. But that was a chance Hank was willing to take.

Trying to figure out the rider's destination, Hank recalled the country as best he could. He remembered the road continued west for a few miles, then turned at right angles north to skirt the edge of this dune country and the desert. In other words, the rider must be taking a short cut.

As he approached the edge of the dunes, Hank went on with a little more caution, his hand riding close to his gun. And then, rounding one of the dunes, Hank saw the man's horse ahead of him. Shuttling his gaze to the peak of the tallest dune, Hank saw the stranger bellied down, facing the far side. Even as he watched, the stranger raised a rifle to his shoulder and sighted it. For one full second, Hank was locked in indecision, and then his hand swept down toward his gun. The stranger's rifle crashed sharp and loud in that stillness, and on the heel of it, Hank's six-gun roared. The stranger made a move to rise, to push himself erect, then fell down on his face, slacked over on his back, and continued to roll down the side of the dune until he lay stretched in the powdery clay at the bottom.

Hank regarded him with sober distaste, then urged his horse forward. He did not stop at the man's body but circled the dune until he could see beyond. There the road snaked along paralleling the dunes only a hundred feet away. Up the road, a buckboard was traveling at a smart clip, and Hank could see the shapeless form of a body on the seat.

Spurring his horse, Hank overtook the buckboard and pulled alongside the off-horse. Leaning out, he got a short grip on the reins near the bit and pulled the team to a stop. Dismounting, he walked back to the buckboard and examined the man lying face down on the seat. He was shot through the chest and must have died immediately. To Hank he looked like an old desert rat, dirty and unshaven and tattered.

"But he can't be," Hank mused. "Why'd this jasper want to kill an old hard-shell desert man?"

The gunny sacks on the floor of the buckboard beneath the seat caught Hank's attention, and he clawed down among them, hoping for something to give a clue to the killing. And there, just beneath the sacks, Hank discovered the bars of bullion. He whistled in exclamation, admiring their rich sheen, and then turned back to the dead man. In his pockets, Hank found the insurance papers, and immediately he understood. It was Esmerella gold, and the insurance company had tried to sneak it safely out of the country. Some hardcase at the stamp mill had given this bushwhacker the tip-off, and he had followed the agent to kill and rob him of the bullion.

Hank rolled a smoke and considered all this. Whether he wanted to deny it or not, he couldn't escape the fact that this bushwhacker had been in conference with Major Fitz only five hours ago, and that he had come from the Bar 33 straight to this killing. Was Fitz behind it? Hank couldn't believe it. He thought he knew Fitz well enough to feel sure that he would never be a party to a cold-blooded killing, but on the other hand, Hank remembered that conference he had witnessed through the glasses only this morning.

And suddenly, Hank thought of Johnny Hendry. By nightfall, he might be the new sheriff. Why not take the matter to him? For Hank knew without having to be told that his days with the Bar 33 were over.

It was nearly dark when Hank pulled in the alley behind the sheriff's office with his strange burden of forty-eight thousand dollars in gold and two dead men. His entrance was practically unnoticed, for he chose the side streets. Besides, the town was too busy with election hilarity to pay any attention to him. He slipped the bars into a gunny sack and hoisted them on his shoulder. The sheriff's office was locked and dark, and he could not leave the bullion here in the alley.

On the street, he picked his way through the milling

crowds looking for Johnny, stopping to rest occasionally. He found Johnny seated on the porch of the Cosmos House in one of the deep chairs in a dark corner. Just as Hank dumped his load beside Johnny, there was a fanfare of shots and chorus of yells upstreet. That would be another demonstration for Blue.

Johnny said, "What's that? The Bar 33 votes?"

"Take a look," Hank advised.

Johnny dragged out a bar and looked at it, noting the Esmerella stamp, and then shifted his somber, questioning glance to Hank, who told him what had happened. But Hank neglected to mention that the murderer had stayed the night at the Bar 33.

When he was finished, Johnny said shrewdly, "How'd you come across him, Hank?"

"I was ridin' in from the spread, and he was ahead of me," Hank said carefully. "He kept lookin' around. Finally I didn't see him on the road. Then I noticed where his tracks turned off. I pulled off the road, myself, farther on, and hid, and pretty soon he come along. I was curious, is all."

"You liar," Johnny murmured calmly, smiling a little. "Where did you really pick him up?"

Hank grinned sheepishly, and then the grin died. "At the Bar 33." He told Johnny the true story, and Johnny did not comment immediately. Hank took a chair beside him, and they sat there in silence, rolling smokes. When the match flared, Hank could see Johnny's face, and it was stamped with a somber scowl.

"What do you make of it, Hank?" Johnny asked quietly.

"I dunno. I ain't even tryin' to make anything out of it. All I know is what I told you. Did Fitz want to get me out of the way so he could talk to that hardcase?"

"It looks like it."

"It does. It looks enough like it that I'm quittin' the Bar 33. I don't like the feel of it."

Johnny considered a long moment. What Hank had told him was more than significant in the face of those six notes naming Fitz as an undesirable, and the bushwhacker who tried to get him the other day. But proof! Nothing was any good without proof. Besides, Johnny wanted to be fair. Setting aside his own real affection for Major Fitz, he wanted to make sure of his facts before doing anything —providing the election put him in a position to do anything. None of it made sense—or rather it did make sense, but the wrong kind.

While he was sitting in silence, the hotel door opened and Tip Rogers came out. Johnny called to him, and Tip walked over. Johnny pointed to the bars. "Those yours?"

It was so dark Tip could not immediately make out what he was pointing at, but he stopped and examined them. Then he took one bar over to the light and checked the stamping. Back beside Johnny, he said quietly, "Yes. Where did they come from?"

"Your agent was killed," Johnny murmured. "Hank Brender here killed the man who did it."

For a moment, Tip said nothing, and then he turned his attention to Hank, asking for details, and Hank told him. When he was finished, Tip thanked him, and then was silent a moment.

"Well, Johnny," he said finally. "It rests with you whether or not the Esmerella shuts down. If you clean out this riffraff, we can operate. If you don't, we're closing."

"I've done all right so far," Johnny murmured.

"You?" Tip asked, surprise in his voice. "What did you do?"

"It was my deputy who got your gold back for you."

Tip peered at Hank, whose face was as surprised as his own. Luckily, the dark hid Hank's expression. "Deputy? Is he your deputy?"

"He is. Unofficially right now. Officially when I get elected."

Tip said resentfully, "I suppose you're going to claim that you're entitled to take Nora to the dance, now?"

"Not at all," Johnny murmured. "I'll earn that on my own hook."

Tip grunted and said, "Will you watch this gold until I can get hold of Turnbull to open the bank for me?"

Johnny said he would, and Tip left. When he was gone, Johnny looked over at Hank. "How about it, Hank?

Would you like the job?"

"I couldn't handle it, Johnny," Hank said gravely. "I don't know anything about the business."

"So much the better. The only thing you need is honesty. You've got that." He told Hank about hiring Turk Hebron, and the circumstances which prompted him in his choice, and Hank agreed with him. "What I want now is a deputy to police this town in place of a marshal. It'll take a tough man and a scrapper, and a man that this wolf pack of hardcases will respect." He grinned. "I don't want to give you a swelled head, Hank, but you fit that bill pretty good. You've quit your job. Furthermore, it'll make it easier for you to quit Fitz, since I'll be offerin' you twice what he's payin'. What about it?"

Hank, after a moment's thought, said dubiously, "All right." Johnny felt pleased now; he had acquired his deputies. All he needed now was the election, and that was out of his hands.

Chapter Eight: ULTIMATUM

COSMOS, NATURALLY, DID NOT GO TO BED election night. At ten o'clock the ballots were brought in from Lynn's Ford, the only other settlement in the county which could be dignified by the name of a town. There was shooting and shouting as the election officers retired to the courthouse to count them; because, except for one far corner of the county, Doane's Trading-Post, which at best would only muster a dozen or so votes, the election would be decided when the votes now in were counted.

Johnny and Hank picked up Turk Hebron at the Palace, and the three of them stood out on the sidewalk watching the crowd. It had collected now in front of the courthouse, an ordinary store building next to the sheriff's office. It had once been a saloon, but now its interior was partitioned off to allow for a half-dozen offices in the front part of the building and the courtroom behind. The street was blocked now with the milling throng, half of whom were drunk.

Turk, observing it with a wry expression on his hard

face, grinned crookedly. "If we get in, gents, we've got our work cut out." At Prince's Keno Parlor, they took a corner table and ordered drinks. Turk heard Hank's story of the attempted holdup of the Esmerella gold and he only grinned with pleasant anticipation at what this signified.

Hank had scarcely finished his story when suddenly the noise in the street started to fade.

Johnny said quickly, "They're announcin' the vote."

Out on the sidewalk across from the courthouse, they leaned against a store building. Bledsoe, one of the commissioners, was on the steps, his pudgy hands raised high in the air for silence. Slowly the talk died down, until there was utter quiet along the street.

"The results of the election for sheriff are as follows," Bledsoe bellowed. "Baily Blue—three hundred and seventy-three votes." A mighty shout rose from the crowd, and Bledsoe waved his arms again to quiet it. Johnny looked bleakly at Turk, but said nothing. When Bledsoe had silence again, he said, "For sheriff, Johnny Hendry— four hundred and one votes."

For a moment, there was a stunned silence, and then a scattering of applause which was dimmed by a disgusted muttering. Again Bledsoe raised his hand. "If Johnny Hendry is in the crowd, will he come forward?"

Johnny said to Turk and Hank, "Come along," and elbowed his way through the crowd to Bledsoe's side. A few people called congratulations on the way, but Johnny did not fool himself that he was popular on this night. If he was not openly hissed and booed, it was only because the hardcases would need a little time to brood on the injustice done them.

Bledsoe, a stout, bald merchant, head commissioner, led the three of them back into the courtroom, where several men in shirt sleeves sat idling at a table littered with ballots. Four of them rose, took Johnny aside, and swore him into office. Once that was finished, Johnny came back to the table. Hank and Turk were sitting unobtrusively in chairs against the wall.

"Well, Hendry," Bledsoe said, his round face beaming. "We did it for you. Are you going to pay us back by cleaning up the town and county?"

Johnny was irritated a little at Bledsoe's assumption that it was the merchants who had elected him, but he only nodded gravely. "That's what I promised."

"Then we've all got in mind a couple of good men for your deputies. The statute provides for two of them, one to police the town in case of necessity. We've got your men for you."

Johnny looked long at Bledsoe, his face expressionless, and finally said, "I've got my deputies."

Bledsoe seemed disappointed and a little suspicious. "Who?"

"The two you see sittin' right over there," Johnny said. "Turk Hebron and Hank Brender, Hank to be the marshal."

It was Turk's turn now to look uncomfortable as every man in the room looked over at him. Finally Bledsoe said to Turk, "Would you mind leaving the room, Hebron?"

"He would," Johnny cut in flatly. "What you've got to say about him, you can say to his face—and to mine."

Bledsoe looked at his colleagues with obvious discomfort, and at a nod from two or three of them, he sat on the table and faced Johnny.

"All right, boy," he said seriously, "I will say it to your face. You've been elected by us on a law-and-order platform. Three minutes after you've taken the oath of office, you announce that you've appointed an outlaw and an unknown puncher for your deputies. Does that look like you're keeping your word?"

"Who did you men have in mind for deputies?" Johnny countered.

"Frank Salem and Les MacMahon are two men you couldn't beat. Honest, incorruptible, and industrious."

"True enough," Johnny drawled, walking over to Bledsoe and facing him, hands on hips. "But if I recollect right, Bledsoe, Frank Salem is a man who's never worn a gun, or has he?"

"No. So much the better."

"And Mac is studyin' law while he's counter jumpin' at your store. That right?"

"That's right. Nevertheless, they are both honest men."

"True," Johnny murmured. "Supposin' there was a quarrel over at Prince's Keno Parlor—you know, the usual kind, with somebody goin' for a gun, somebody else shootin' out the lights, and the rest of them takin' sides and wreckin' the place. What would Mac do in a case like that?"

"Stop them," Bledsoe said.

"How?"

"By being there—by demanding law and order and threatening the lot of them with arrest."

"We've got a four-cell jail," Johnny said dryly. "I saw one of those hardcases toss Mac clear over the doors of the Palace one night because he didn't like Mac's white shirt." Johnny leaned both fists on the table and looked around at the commissioners. "Wake up, you men. A man has got to be a gun fighter to lay down the law in this man's town and county. He's got to be a little handier with his fists, and a sight quicker with his guns, than anybody else in sight if he wants to live long. I appreciate that honesty is somethin' my deputies have got to have. But I also know they've got to be tough enough to cram that honesty down the throats of these men that are makin' this county impossible to live in." He straightened up. "Turk Hebron and Hank Brender stay. And if you'll give me a pencil and a piece of paper, I'll show you why."

In silence, one of the commissioners handed him paper and pencil. Johnny printed in big letters across the paper:

BY MIDNIGHT TOMORROW, EVERY MAN THAT CAN'T SHOW ME HE HAS GOT A FULL-TIME JOB WITH A RESPECTABLE EMPLOYER HAD BETTER BE CLEARED OUT OF COSMOS AND THE COUNTY.

(SIGNED)
JOHNNY HENDRY, SHERIFF.

He shoved the paper at Bledsoe and said, "How far would Frank or Mac get enforcin' that?"

Bledsoe read the paper and handed it to the other commissioners. Each, in his own way, expressed disapproval. "You'll never make it stick, Hendry," Bledsoe said flatly. "You've got more sense than to stir up a hornet's nest." Pausing, he regarded Johnny with outright suspicion. "In fact, I think it's a bluff."

Johnny ripped the paper out of his hand and strode down the hall. Outside, the crowd was still collected in the street. Johnny ignored them, turning to the bulletin board. He hung the paper over a nail, and then turned to face the crowd. "You want me to read it to you?" he asked, and they could tell by the timbre of his voice that he was angry.

"Sure," somebody called.

Johnny said, "It just says that every one of you hard-cases who can't show you've got a job with a genuine employer had better clear out of here before midnight to-morrow night."

He listened for any protest. There were a few quiet laughs, considerable muttering, but no open defiance. He was surprised at this, and half suspected a conspiracy to ignore him, when an insolent voice drawled, "And who says so?"

Johnny leaped down into the crowd, but Turk and Hank were already ahead of him. Violently, they shouldered their way through the crowd until they got to where the speaker stood. It was one of Leach Wigran's men, and nobody in that crowd had to be told that Wigran was one of the most successful and insolent rustlers in the county, and that his spread, the Running W, was a robbers' roost.

Neither Turk nor Hank wasted words. The man who had called was behind four other hardcases who made a solid rank in front of him. He was grinning over the shoulder of one.

Hank simply flipped out a gun and slugged one man of the four. He went down like a shot quail, and Hank stepped back then, covering the other three with his gun. It was Turk who stepped over the fallen man into the breach in the ranks, put out a hairy, hard fist, grabbed the grinning man's coat in a tight ball of his fist and yanked. The man came out sailing, to land squarely on his feet in the circle that had been cleared for the scuffle.

Then Turk, holding the man erect by his coat, hit him once in the face. Then, for that whole crowd to watch, Turk finished the job. The man was fighting now, but Turk ignored his blows as if they were not not even aimed at him. With the spaced precision of a ticking clock, he hit the man twelve times in the face. After four of them, the man's knees buckled, and Turk had to hold him up. But he kept on, until each sodden punch smacked over the hushed silence of the crowd. At the twelfth blow, Turk rolled his shoulder under and heaved the man off his feet and then threw him at the other Wigran men. They caught him, and let him slide to the ground.

"Anybody else want a taste of what's comin'?" Johnny drawled from behind Turk. Nobody did, it seemed; but if ever hatred was a living and tangible thing, it was then. It would only take a spark, a word, a voice lifted in anger to turn the crowd into a lynch mob.

Johnny said quickly, "Then break it up. The other offices won't be announced for an hour yet."

Slowly the crowd started to mill, and then tension eased off. The Wigran men, without a word, took their two casualties and disappeared in the throng.

Turk turned to Johnny and said, "That was close, wasn't it?"

"There'll be closer," Johnny replied grimly.

Suddenly, he felt a hand on his arm, and turned to confront Nora. Her face was paler than he had ever seen it, and he had his mouth open to speak when Nora said passionately, "Johnny Hendry, that was the most foolish thing three men ever did!"

Turk only grinned, and Hank looked sheepish, while Johnny smiled broadly. "We've got to make our brag good now."

Nora shook her head in earnest bewilderment. "But Johnny, nobody can get away with a thing like that twice! You were lucky tonight!"

"I know it."

"What about next time, though?"

"Wait till it comes, Miss Nora," Turk said gently. He

looked quizzically at Johnny. "You know," he said slowly, "somehow I feel better for doin' that than I'd feel if I'd won a couple of thousand dollars."

Johnny looked swiftly at Nora to see if she had understood, for Turk had spoken with the simple honesty of a man who has had a chance to make good, and who is thankful.

Nora said gently, "You three will have to stick together from now on. Let me change your room, Johnny, so that nobody will know the number. And whatever room Mrs. Jenkins gives you, I'm going to have three beds put in it. From now on, you'll have to hang together or be shot separately."

And all of them, without saying anything, knew it was true.

As they turned to go, Major Fitz approached and held out his hand to Johnny. "Damn glad, " he said bluntly, and then, turning to Turk, observed, "Once upon a time, Hebron, I would have said that you were about the least choice trash I ever had the misfortune to know. Mind if I take it back now, in public?" and he held out his hand to Turk.

To Hank, he said, "How did you get in on this, Hank?"

Johnny put in quickly, "I've got a favor to ask, Major."

Major Fitz looked at him and then back at Hank and said, "What is it? I think I know."

"I need a deputy. Hank fills my bill. Do you think you could spare him from the Bar 33 until I get this mess cleaned up?"

"Certainly," Fitz said with surprising abruptness, and smiled at Hank. "He's wasting his time with me. Keep him as long as you like. And, Hank, there's always room at the Bar 33 when you've done."

Hank, inarticulate at his best, only nodded gravely, and Major Fitz turned away, after saying good night to Nora. Hank looked over at Johnny, his eyes asking a question, and so did Nora. Johnny knew that both were wanting to ask him now about Major Fitz. If possible, Nora would have asked him if he still thought Major Fitz was the guilty party, after such a gracious acknowledgment as he had made to Turk. And Hank would have asked if this didn't fit in pretty well with what he had felt was coming. But Johnny, more puzzled than both, could not have answered either question yet.

The room Mrs. Jenkins provided for them at the Cosmos House was in the attic, with the only entrance a ladder and a heavy trap door. Johnny, Hank, and Turk went to bed while the town was still drowning its sorrow.

Johnny was first up next morning, and he dressed quietly, thinking over the incidents of the night before. At last he had the chance and the position to enable him to get at the bottom of Pick's murder. Whoever it was had murdered Pick, they would not get out of the county while they had a chance to get Pick's gold. One of these men fighting him would be Pick's killer. Of that he was certain.

Dressed and yawning widely, Johnny moved over to the trap door and shoved away the trunk which he had dragged over it the night before. Leaning down, he had almost grabbed hold of the ring ready to heave, when he noticed a tiny scattering of shavings around a knothole that was just to one side of the ring. Gently, then, he drew his hand away from the ring and backed off. Lighting a match against the permanent twilight of this room, he knelt down to examine the knothole. In the light it turned out to be not a dark knothole, but twin holes bored close together in the wood of the trap door. Gently Johnny put two fingers in these holes and felt cold steel. He had looked at the business end of enough shotguns to recognize those twin holes. Somebody, during the night, had drilled holes right by the ring, over which a man would have to lean in order to move the heavy trapdoor. In these holes had been inserted two barrels of a shotgun.

Johnny pondered this a long moment. Then he went back and woke up Hank and Turk and brought them over to the trap door.

"That's it, all right," Turk murmured. "Let's see how it works."

They lighted the lamp and brought it over beside the

ring, and Johnny knelt down to examine it closely. There was another, smaller hole right under the ring, and over the shank of the heavy ring was a tiny fishhook. From it, a tight wire stretched down through the hole.

Turk whistled in exclamation. "You pick up the ring to heave, that pulls the wire that sets the shotgun off, and the next thing you know, your head is plastered on the roof."

"Let's try it," Hank suggested.

"And blow a hole in the roof?" Johnny grinned. "Let's don't. We got a landlady here."

They compromised by prying the trap door up without touching the ring. As they had suspected, there was a shotgun underneath. The hole had been drilled so expertly that the gun barrel was wedged tightly in position. The wire was drawn down tautly over the butt and up to the trigger, so that the slightest pull on the ring would have set it off.

After it was dismantled, Johnny said grimly, "There's no sense in anybody else knowin' this. We'll settle this by ourselves when the time comes."

But that was the only incident of the day. The town was quieter than usual, and Johnny and his deputies did not molest anybody. They spent the day cleaning out the sheriff's office and getting it ready for their own occupancy. Ex-Sheriff Blue appeared at midday and was entirely amiable. He tendered no advice to Johnny, and Johnny, on his part, asked for none. But as evening drew on and dark fell, there was a noticeable tension in the town.

Little groups of men clustered in the saloons, engaged in a conversation which they were at pains to keep private. Hank, on his rounds, was met with sullen, defiant stares. Nobody offered to buy him drinks. The saloonkeepers, members of a usually wise profession, did not bother to set up drinks and toast the health and long life of a new marshal. Hank had the growing conviction that the town, for once in its mushroom career, was co-operating—and in a way which was merely a gang-up.

He reported this to Johnny late in the evening. Turk, a

few moments before, had reported the same thing. Johnny almost wished that he had set the deadline so that it would expire in daylight. It was not reassuring to know that a hundred men, all willing and able to shoot, had the protection of night behind them. But a stubbornness in him would not let him admit it to Turk.

Their plan was simple. It would consist of swift raids after midnight. There would be no orderly schedule; suddenness would be the secret. Johnny realized that it was within his authority to deputize as many men as he wished, but if he did that, the hardcases would fade away until the deputies were dismissed, then return again to plague him. No, it would have to be a swift and sudden showdown. But he took one precaution.

Along in the afternoon, he drifted down to Hugo Miller's place, and to Hugo made this proposition. The three of them could take care of the trouble in the saloons, but what about the street? It would be open, and at the first ripple of excitement would fill with hardcases. Would Hugo, then, consent to being conscripted as a shotgun guard?

"Shotgun guard where?" Hugo asked, with all good humor.

"If you fort up on the roof of the place we raid, then you're in a position to keep the streets clear if any trouble comes up."

"Sure," Hugo said immediately, so it was decided that he would cover them while they were engaged in their own kind of disciplining.

As midnight drew near, the streets began to empty, which was pretty unusual, because night in Cosmos was hardly different from day. Johnny, watching it from the window of the darkened sheriff's office, said to Turk, "They'll be ready for us."

"Where first?" Turk said.

"Prince's Keno Parlor, I think."

Turk faded out into the night, Hugo beside him, a shotgun in his hand. And then that careful silence settled on the town, and it lasted until midnight, when Johnny murmured to Hank, "Come along."

A man lounging in the doorway of Prince's Keno Parlor faded back into the room at sight of them. At the swing door, Hank leaned his shotgun against the building, and, shoulder to shoulder, they pushed through the doors— to confront the strangest sight either of them had ever seen.

In a line across the room, from bar to sidewall, a row of chairs had been drawn up facing the door. And on each of these chairs a man sat, hands folded on his lap, staring innocently at Johnny and Hank.

In the middle of the group, bulking large and dominant, was Leach Wigran. He was a black, scowling man with a shovel beard down to his collar. His clothes were incredibly dirty. Above a small hooked nose, he had deep-set black eyes that never lost their mockery. His great hands, folded loosely around the six-gun in his lap, gave him the ridiculous appearance of a peaceful child on a chair—which was exactly what he had intended. To Leach's right, his tough face wearing a mocking smile, sat Mickey Hogan, Leach's foreman.

As Johnny let his gaze rove the crowd, Leach Wigran piped up in a falsetto voice, starting a tune which every school child uses to greet his teacher. Only the words were changed, and the whole row of men lifted their mocking voices to join him.

> "Good morning to you,
> Good morning to you,
> Good morning, dear Sheriff,
> To blazes with you."

As the song ended, a mighty chorus of laughter roared through the room. Tim Prince, the sour and cynical owner of the place, allowed himself a spare smile, which Johnny did not miss.

Johnny walked forward a little to stand in front of Wigran.

"Why, Leachie," he said in mocking tones, imitating the inflection of a schoolteacher. "You haven't washed your hands or wiped your nose this morning." Slowly, so that his movement wouldn't be misunderstood, he reached in his hip pocket and drew out a handkerchief, and walked slowly over to the bar. There, he picked up a half-drained schooner of beer and stalked back to confront Leach.

"Well, Leachie?" he drawled.

Leach's eyes flickered faintly. He could also see Hank Brender closing the weather doors and leaning against them, shotgun in hand. But Leach Wigran was not a man to be bluffed. He answered in a mincing voice, "Why, teacher, I had my mind so set on bringin' you an apple this mornin' that I plumb forgot. You want to see the apple?"

"Wash your face first, Leachie," Johnny said gently, ominously.

Here was the challenge. Leach said just as gently, "Suppose you try to do it, teacher."

His last word was not out of his mouth before Johnny's foot shot out and kicked Leach's chair. It tipped over, and Leach, arms sawing wildly, shot once at the ceiling as Johnny dived on top of him.

Then, inevitably, someone shot out the lights, and there was a wild tangle on the floor. Johnny, knowing instinctively that no one would risk gunplay at these close quarters, grappled with Wigran and rolled under him, just as half that milling, shouting, kicking, and screaming mob got into action, tangling men and chairs and even women.

Then, over this uproar, came the mighty, deafening blast of a shotgun, and the bar mirror simply collapsed in a jangle of glass. Another spot, and the front door boomed hollowly. Here was real panic, for not a man or woman in that room could mistake the message of that shotgun and what it meant. A sudden clangor on the piano, as if a man was stamping on the keys, crashed through the room, and then Turk Hebron's voice lifted above every other sound.

"Prince, light a lantern up there or I'll bust this wall lamp and fire your place!" Turk bellowed. The fighting ceased abruptly.

In a very few seconds, Prince struck a match, then another, and finally a trembling barkeep came out into the middle of the room and pulled down an overhead lamp and lighted it. The disorder had ceased now. Johnny was in the midst of a dozen of Wigran's men, and he still had a hold on Wigran's collar. Now everybody turned to look for Turk. He was sitting on top of the piano, hat pushed back on his head, his shotgun slacked just away from his shoulder.

"Anybody want to try and knock me off here?" he inquired in the sudden silence.

"Or me out of here?" Hank asked. He was planted against the closed doors, a shotgun in his hands.

Johnny laughed quietly. "Line forms at the bar, gents. Put your hardware on it, then get these chairs untangled and take your seats again. I'll give you about twenty seconds to get back to school again."

There was no choice, and Leach Wigran was the first to see it. Cursing sulphurously, he put his guns on the bar. In a few moments, the whole room was crowding to the bar. After that, the chairs were pulled upright and a sullen, surly, and sheepish crew of men took their seats. Johnny had a smear of blood on his face, and an eye which was rapidly swelling shut, but he was grinning broadly.

"So you bunch of tinhorns thought you could laugh the law out of this town, did you?" he asked, when they were all seated.

No one answered. Johnny addressed himself to Leach now. "Never give a ranny you want to kill an even break, Leach. Haven't you learned that?" Leach didn't answer. "If I want to kill you, Leach, I will. And I'm loco enough to give you an even break." Pausing, he let his hard gaze rove the room and then settled it again on Leach. "What'll it be, Leach? Guns? I'll fight you now, here."

Leach's gaze shifted. He was motionless. "Well, well," Johnny drawled. "You don't like the idea of sassin' teacher back with old man Colt's language. How would you like to settle it with fists, then?"

Leach only shifted faintly in his seat, and did not answer. Johnny looked over the rest of the hardcases. "Anybody else want to make it guns or fists with teacher?"

Still he got no response. He was carrying the room now

in a magnificent, mocking bluff. He ran a hand through his hair and scowled. "Maybe you'd like a kickin' contest, Leach. No? Let me see." He pursed his lips. "Get up, Leach," he said finally. Leach hulked out of his chair.

"You, too, Mickey," Johnny said to Hogan. Hogan did. Johnny walked over and yanked Hogan's chair out into the middle of the floor and grasped the back of it. Then he said to Leach, "Pick up your chair, Leach. I'm goin' to see if you've got a sign of a brain in that skull of yours. I'll crack it wide open with this chair if I have a chance—and I will."

Leach hesitated for a moment, then picked up his chair and circled out into the cleared space. Johnny, grinning now at the absurd weapons of this fight, came at Leach with chair outthrust, jabbing. Leach raised his chair up and swung it viciously at Johnny's, but Johnny drew his own back and the momentum of the swing carried Leach half way around, exposing his back. Johnny put the legs of his chair in Leach's back and shoved with all his weight and strength and Leach went off balance to sprawl across his chair on the floor. There was a scattering of subdued laughter throughout the room.

Leach rose with a growl of fury and threw his chair at Johnny, who caught it in his own chair. Then Johnny picked it up and threw it back, and Leach, dancing to escape its low sweep, got his feet tangled in the rungs and crashed to the floor again. There was a howl of laughter through the room.

"Give him your chairs," Johnny called to the seated men. He was laughing delightedly now. But Leach could see nothing funny in all this. Impotent, he was cursing in bitter fury, and as each chair skidded out to him, he picked it up and threw it at Johnny. Johnny stopped two of them, ducked the third, and then, still on his knees, saw the spittoon beside the bar rail. Without hesitating a moment, he picked it up and sailed it at Leach. It crashed on the wall behind Leach, and all its contents were dumped over Leach's shoulders and clothes. Before Leach could collect his wits, Johnny had vaulted behind the bar and was leveling a barrage of bottles at him. They came fast and furious, breaking on the wall and splashing over Leach, who could not get out of the way. The room was in an uproar of laughter.

When Johnny had hit him a half dozen times, Leach picked up a chair to use it for a shield. Johnny sailed five bottles over Leach's head, and as each one broke, Leach got a fresh bath of whisky, brandy, gin, and rum. Finally, when Leach was cowering against the wall in the front corner, Johnny called to Hank, "Open the door, Hank."

Hank did, and Leach made a dash for it. Johnny had a waiter's tray in his hand, and as Leach was almost to the door, he sailed it, flat, at Leach's head. It hit him a glancing blow, just as he was in the doorway, and the last that laughing crowd saw of Leach Wigran, bully and bucko rustler, was a flash of his boots as he sprawled out onto the boardwalk.

Johnny turned now to confront the rest of the hardcases. He had a bottle in each hand. "Make a run, boys," he invited. "My aim's improving."

Three of them made a run for the door, and Johnny, laughing himself now, let them have the bottles. They were clean misses, as he had intended, but that did not lessen the stampede for the door. In a very few moments, under that barrage of glassware, the room was cleared of the hardcases. Only the townspeople and punchers and miners were left. Johnny waited until he heard the pounding of horses' hoofs in the streets, and then Hugo, up on the roof, sent a peppering of buckshot at the retreating riders.

Johnny's grin died as he faced Tim Prince, who was regarding the wreckage of his place with a dour poker face.

"How do your bad boys stack up now, Tim?" he asked quietly.

Tim only shook his head.

"Still think they're worth backin'?" Johnny asked him.

"They never was," Tim said dryly. "I don't give credit."

"But as long as you thought they had a chance to lick me, you were on their side. Wasn't that it?"

"Pretty close," Tim said, and spat at a spot where the spittoon had been.

Johnny looked at the mess across the room, the broken chairs, the broken mirror, the shattered door, and then he smiled narrowly. He walked over to Prince. "How would you like to be put under bond to keep the peace, Prince?"

Tim regarded him levelly, and did not speak for a long moment. "I don't think you could do it, Sheriff. You don't *own* the town."

Without turning, Johnny said to Hank, "Go get Stevens, the J. P., Hank."

Hank started for the door when Prince raised a hand. "All right, you could," he said calmly. "I guess this is your town, now, Johnny. What you say goes."

"You guess right," Johnny said. "I'm givin' you your choice, Prince. You hire a bouncer tough enough to keep these hardcases from makin' trouble in your saloon. When one of that gang comes in—and they'll try it—throw them out. Either do that or I'll put you under bond to keep the peace. And once I do that and one of my deputies walks in here and sees one of these tinhorns in your place, I'll shut you down for good and all. What about it?"

Prince threw up both hands and said, "I got a livin' to make here, and why—"

"What about it?" Johnny asked.

Prince shrugged and said, "All right. I'll hire the bouncer. You're the boss now."

Johnny rapped the flat of his palm on the bar and it echoed in that silence. "You will!" he said bluntly. "If you don't I'll run you out of town, Tim. I first laughed Leach Wigran out of town. When you go, nobody'll laugh —not even me—because it won't be a laughing matter."

With that, he signaled to Turk and Hank and walked out the door. The street was ominously quiet.

"Let's make it the Gem next," Johnny said.

They approached the Gem in the same way they did Prince's, but their reception there was different. The games and drinking were orderly. Only one known hardcase was in the place and he was playing solitaire at a lone table.

Johnny approached him and said, "The curfew's rung, fella. Clear out. Go home to bed."

The man only nodded and rose and went out, and Hank reported that he had ridden out of town. At the bar, Johnny asked the barkeep, "What happened to the bad boys, Jim? It's sort of quiet in here. Quiet's awful noticeable in your place, ain't it?"

"They cleared out," Jim said, and grinned.

The three of them went down the long line of saloons, not skipping one of the twelve. And each one was orderly, with not a known hardcase in the whole crowd. To each saloonkeeper, Johnny made the same proposition that he had made Tim Prince. He said he was going to try and keep the hardcases out of Cosmos, but he wanted co-operation. They could either hire a bouncer to keep order or be bonded to keep the peace. And one and all, they agreed to his proposition. They had no alternative.

Back at the office, Johnny and Turk and Hank and Hugo looked at each other and grinned.

"Well?" Johnny said.

"They ain't out of the county yet," Hank told him.

"They will be," Johnny said quietly, and that was a promise that he planned to keep.

Chapter Nine: VOTES FOR BAILY BLUE

MONDAY IN COSMOS was the quietest day anyone could remember. Not one gunshot sounded over the busy street clatter; not once did the long line of ore freighters have to stop while a street brawl blocked traffic. Business was good everywhere except at the saloons. Turk, on the north end of the street, had a six-minute argument with an undesirable who hadn't heard about Johnny's new regime. It was Cass Briggs. Turk was gentle with him, didn't even bother to hit him, and Cass rode away without ever having reached town. Hank spent the day whittling. Johnny roved the saloons and streets on the watch for trouble that never came.

He saw Tip Rogers at noon just as he passed the bank, and Tip grinned self-consciously at him.

"Goin' to the dance?" Johnny drawled, reminding him of his wager.

"Alone," Tip said, nodding, and laughed a little. "That's all right, Hendry. You win. I'd go to dances alone for six months if it meant cleanin' up this place."

"You watch."

"I am," Tip said.

The afternoon was calm as the morning. After supper, Johnny, up in his attic room, dressed for the dance that was to be held in the courthouse that night, and then came down to sit in the lobby while Nora completed her dressing. When she came out, her tawny hair combed back into a loose knot at the base of her neck and her rich green dress full and sweeping, Johnny knew that no woman had ever looked so beautiful. The first thing he said was, "Marry me tomorrow?"

Nora laughed with pleasure and looked at him. He stood tall and clean-looking in his white shirt and red neckerchief and hand-tooled boots. Nora was almost tempted to say yes, but then she remembered. "Clean up the county first, Johnny."

The orchestra—a piano, violin, and accordion—was in full swing when they arrived at the courthouse. Bledsoe, having deposited his mountain of a wife at a wall chair, was calling the dances from the platform. The whole town had turned out. Turk, true to his resolve to reform, was struggling manfully but politely to dance with a little restaurant waitress as shy as himself. Hank had on a boiled collar and worked at pushing Mrs. Jenkins around as if her two hundred pounds of very active flesh were at least eight hundred. Over in the corner opposite the orchestra, Major Fitz, in a neatly tailored black suit, was joking and making himself popular with half a dozen laughing girls.

Johnny soon lost Nora to one of the many men who clamored for a dance with her. He felt a hand on his arm and wheeled to confront Hugo Miller, who said, "Let's find a quiet corner, Johnny."

They walked over to a window, and Hugo lighted up his pipe. "I've got what you wanted," he said, and blew out his match. His deep eyes were watchful as he observed Johnny's face tighten and lose some of its good humor.

"The volcanic breccia?"

"Yes. A man brought it in tonight while I was dressing for the party."

"Know him?"

"Nope. He didn't look much like a hardcase, either. Clean-shaven, tall, a puncher about my age. He said he was in a hurry for a report. Wanted me to stay in tonight and turn out the assay report for him."

"Give any name?"

"Lemrath. I told him I'd leave the dance a little later and come back and work on it. I told him I'd have it tomorrow night."

"Is he still in town?" Johnny demanded.

"Possibly." Hugo smoked in silence a moment. "It's just occurred to me, Johnny—if you wait around till he comes back and arrest him then, you're going to have a hard nut to crack. He won't talk, and you'll get no farther. Why not try another way?"

"What?"

"Let me fake his report. I'll give him such a wild assay that the first thing he'll do will be to dash for the claim recorder. That way, you'll find out not only who owns the claim but where it is. If you want him, all you'll have to do will be to go out to his workings and get him."

Reluctantly, Johnny agreed to this idea. Almost surely this Lemrath was the man he had been waiting for. He must be Pick's killer, and Johnny's impulse was to go after him this very moment. But there was wisdom in Hugo's suggestion. Let Lemrath lead him to the ore deposit, which would be the additional proof needed. Not, Johnny swore darkly, that Lemrath would ever come to trial; he would die before Johnny's guns. But still proof would be needed to vindicate himself, Johnny thought. He looked over the dance floor, took a deep breath, and said quietly to Hugo, "Did you check up to see if Lemrath had filed any claims?"

"Yes. He hasn't."

"Then we'd better wait," Johnny said glumly.

"I thought you'd see it that way," Hugo said, and walked off.

Just then, Bledsoe called a Ladies' Choice, and Johnny

was almost mobbed by girls. Tonight, as always, he was the most popular man on the dance floor, and the engaging thing about it to Nora was that Johnny didn't seem to know it. She watched him dancing with a half-dozen girls, feeling a little jealous, when she heard Major Fitz addressing her. He was standing beside her, watching the dancers.

"Not hard to see who's the man most in demand tonight, is it, Nora?"

Nora flushed a little and laughed. "Yourself, Major Fitz."

"Nonsense. I'm a relic. I mean your Johnny."

"That's because he's the new sheriff and this is an election dance."

Major Fitz, smiling a little, asked her to dance. As he swung her out on the floor, they saw a rider in dusty Levi's and Stetson make his way through the dancers to Bledsoe's side and begin talking in a low, urgent voice.

"Wonder what's up?" Major Fitz asked. Then pretty soon Bledsoe excused himself, sought out the three other county commissioners, and retired to one of the offices in the front of the building.

Nora had forgotten all about it when Johnny came over to claim her first dance. Halfway through it, Bledsoe again appeared, and this time he hurried to the platform and waved the orchestra to silence.

"Folks," Bledsoe said. "I've got news." Everyone stopped dancing and waited. "The votes were just brought in from Doane's Trading-Post over in the corner of the county. It seems there were fifty-six votes cast in that corner of the county. Unfortunately, this changes the result of the election." He paused. "Since all fifty-six of these votes were cast for Baily Blue, that puts him ahead of Johnny Hendry by some twenty-eight votes."

Notwithstanding the fact that Baily Blue and his wife were right there among them, the dancers raised a storm of angry protest. Bledsoe raised his hand for silence, but it was awhile before he got it. When he did, someone called out, "That's plain ballot-stuffin'! Why weren't them voters registered?"

"They were," Bledsoe assured him glumly. He looked over the crowd and then raised his voice to call to a man at the rear. "Doane, come up here."

The dusty rider came forward. He was an ordinary-looking man in rough clothes, unshaven, a little stiff from his long hours in the saddle. When he stood beside Bledsoe, the merchant announced, "This is Morg Doane, the election judge over there. Tell them, Morg."

"Like he said," Doane began, "it looks legal. Last registration day I was out at one of my line camps. Had been for a week. I left the registration book with one of my clerks. I never even thought to look at it when I got home. Come this election, I took out the book. There was somethin' like fifty-six men registered. I couldn't ask my clerk about it because he'd left. But them fifty-six men voted, and I guess they had a legal right to."

"Did you know any of them?" Bledsoe asked.

"Not me. They claimed they'd had a wild-horse camp up on the edge of the Calicoes for somethin' like two years now. Mebbeso, but I never saw it."

Johnny left Nora and elbowed his way through to the front of the crowd. "Did you bring that register with you, Doane?"'

"It's up front, there."

Johnny went up to one of the front offices, where the other commissioners were gathered, their faces solemn as owls. One glance at the book showed the fifty-six names registered. Johnny looked up at Bledsoe. "That ink looks mighty fresh to me, Bledsoe. Maybe it was put there in March, but I'd say it came closer to bein' only a week old." He swiveled his gaze to Doane, whose eyes were untroubled, fearless.

"You say this clerk of yours left a couple of weeks ago, Doane?"'

"That's right."

"And he never mentioned to you when you got back from your line camp last March that fifty-six voters had registered?"

"Nary a word."

"Don't that strike you as a little queer?" Johnny persisted. "If there were fifty-six men up in your end of the county, wouldn't you mention it to folks?"

"I would. But then there's always wild-horse hunters up where we are."

"But fifty-six—that's a lot. Wouldn't it naturally be mentioned?"

"I reckon so," Doane said slowly. "Howsomever, it wasn't. I never even looked at the book all year. Election day, I'd 've forgot it if all these men hadn't come in and wanted to vote. Then I dug up the book, and sure enough, the names was there."

Johnny watched him all the while he was talking. If any man looked honest Doane did, but the fact remained that the whole setup seemed crooked. "Answer me this, then," Johnny said mildly. "Wouldn't it have been possible for a man to watch your place until you went away, then go in and talk to your clerk? Maybe he could have slipped him a hundred dollars or so, and the clerk would have given him the registration book. Next day, he would bring it back to the clerk with fifty-six extra names registered. Your clerk, knowing questions would be asked, just picked up and left. Why shouldn't he? He had a stake."

"It could be," Doane admitted. Here he allowed himself a spare smile. "Lord, son, it surprised me more'n it did you."

Baily Blue shouldered his way forward. He said gently, "Johnny, you ain't a very good loser. This all looks legal to me. You're huntin' excuses instead of acceptin' facts."

"Why haven't we seen or heard of these fifty-six horse-hunters?" Johnny drawled.

"That's danged easy to explain," Baily said. "They're a good sixty miles from Cosmos, right on the very edge of the county. When they want to go to town for a drink or for grub, they just drift down over the Calicoes to Bowling county. It's only a short fifteen miles over the Calicoes—nothin' for a man that knows the trails. And they'd know 'em." He smiled amiably at everyone in the room. "Me, I never kicked when Johnny was elected. It was the mandate of the people. I don't see any reason why he should kick now. Tough luck, that's all."

Johnny's mouth came shut with a click, and he straightened. "I'm not kickin', Baily, providin' it's fair, and decidin' that is in the hands of the election board, which is the county commissioners. I'll leave it up to them." He turned and stalked out of the room.

Outside, Nora came up to him. "What did they decide?" she asked breathlessly, and Johnny, stony-faced, only shrugged.

The orchestra made a halfhearted attempt to put the dance in full swing again, but people had lost their enthusiasm. Major Fitz, Hank and Turk, and Nora and Johnny, along with Hugo Miller, all gathered at one side of the room to wait. Johnny told them quietly what had happened.

Major Fitz appeared the most indignant of all, and Hank watched him covertly, a little puzzled. A good half hour passed before Bledsoe, his face flushed and harried, made his way up to the orchestra platform. He didn't have to raise his hand to command silence this time.

"I—I don't know how to announce this," he said. "But when it comes down to brass tacks, it's a question of the legality of the registration. All right, but what about our registration in this town? We know that maybe a tenth of the voters here did not register. Nevertheless they voted. Are we going to draw the line when it comes to those outside of Cosmos?" He shook his head. "I don't see how we can. At any rate, these men were better registered than a tenth of our voters. So the votes stand—and Baily Blue is re-elected sheriff of Cosmos county."

Johnny's heart dropped, to rest in a sodden unhappiness. Only Nora's look of sturdy courage and faith in him made this minute bearable. To Turk and Hank, the news was like a blow across the face. Turk grinned wryly and murmured, "Well, it was a nice two-day vacation from business."

Nora turned away from the dozen people offering Johnny their sympathy and took him by the arm. "Shall we go, Johnny?"

Outside, in the silver-pricked blueness of the night,

Johnny didn't say anything for a long while. They walked along instinctively drawn close together. Then he felt Nora squeeze his arm.

"I guess I'm soft," Johnny murmured huskily. "But I hate to get a rookin' when I'm lookin' it right in the face."

"Who did it, do you suppose?"

Johnny looked at her in the dark. "What do you mean?"

"Why somebody sent those fifty-six men over to vote, didn't he? Whoever it was knew that the election would be close; he didn't want to take any chance of losing."

Johnny didn't answer for a moment. Of course that was it, but who was responsible? And was Johnny Hendry going to let him get away with it?

At the hotel they went out into the kitchen, where Nora made them sandwiches and coffee. Soon a little of the anguish was gone from Johnny's mind, and it was done through Nora's skilled argument.

"But Johnny, you're not vain, are you?" she began.

"No. Not much."

"And you didn't want to be sheriff just to wear the star?"

"You know I didn't," Johnny growled.

"Then why did you?"

Johnny smiled sheepishly. "Two reasons, honey. The first was because I thought it would lead me to gettin' Pick's killer. The second was because you said you'd marry me if I did a good job of cleanin' up this county."

"All right," Nora said. "You forget what I said. It's not possible now. You did your best, and you were doing a good job when the chance was taken away from you. All right, now about Pick's killer. Hasn't Hugo told you enough tonight to give you the chance you wanted?"

Johnny nodded.

"Then why care about the sheriff's office, dear? It's got you what you wanted—information about Pick's murder. As for me, I'll marry you when you bring that killer to justice, just as I promised in the first place."

There was only one thing to do then, and Johnny did it;

he kissed her. After a cigarette, he said good night and went up to his attic room. Turk and Hank were undressing glumly, and it sort of hurt Johnny to watch them.

Hank announced grimly, "Me, I've wore this country out. I'm clearin' out tomorrow. Maybe in a month of ridin', I'll have the taste of it out of my mouth."

"And me," Turk said, "I haven't wore this county out. It's the only place they'll leave me alone, so I reckon I'll go back to my old business."

Wisely, Johnny said nothing. He unbuckled his holster belt and hung it over its peg, taking out the pearl-handled Colts, wrapping them in their flannel and putting them in his war bag. He looked around for his everyday, cedar-handled guns, but he could only find one of them. The room was in a litter of clothes and blankets and gear, and he was too tired to finish the search. He blew out the light and tumbled into bed.

Sleep was long in coming. And he couldn't estimate how long he'd been asleep when a low rumble awakened him. He said, "Turk," softly, and Turk grunted.

"Hear that?" Johnny asked.

"Yeah. What was it?"

"Thunder? Blasting?"

"Probably Baily Blue turnin' over in bed," Turk growled. "He makes big enough tracks now to do it. Whatever it was, it ain't any of our business, is it?"

"I guess not," Johnny said, and turned over. He slept.

Chapter Ten: IN THE CANYON

IT TOOK OLD PICKET-STAKE HENDRY one full day of tireless walking to get back to the canyon he had cited on the false location papers planted on the bushwhacker. The next morning, he summed up the situation. It would probably take a couple of days for the body to be discovered. It would take at least two more for the discoverer—who would undoubtedly be a partner of the bushwhacker—to find this canyon. One day had passed; that left at least three days before anyone would appear in the canyon, time enough for him to hunt and gather berries and stock his cave with provisions.

Pick had discovered this cave a long time ago. It was high up the canyon side, just a few feet below the rimrock, and from the bottom of the canyon, it was invisible. Its only entrance was by a length of rope anchored to the rimrock. He knew it would be a perfect place of concealment.

Satisfied, Pick left the canyon to go to a salt lick higher up in the Calicoes. Two days later he returned with his pack full of partially dried deer meat. The next day, he went back to the salt lick for the rest of the meat and the berries he had picked.

On the morning of the fourth day he left the cave at sunup and made his way down into the canyon. Choosing a small butte screened with thick brush, he pushed his way into it, and by full day he was on the watch, invisible to anyone in the canyon or on the rimrock. During that long day, Pick did a lot of wondering. Would the bushwhacker's body, under the belief it was Pick's, be turned over to Johnny? Maybe then Johnny would be the one to find the false location papers. If so, Johnny would come up here.

But Pick didn't think so. He knew two men had been following him. Up yonder and over south where his real strike was, where the mother lode was, he knew that he had not been seen. Neither was it down here, where he had dug fruitlessly for months and sunk a dozen test pits, that the two men had picked up his tracks. It had been farther over toward the north, where he had been puttering at a couple of test pits off and on for the last two months before he moved up the mountain. There were two of them, and they were careless with their tracks, he thought. That had cost the life of one. Surely this man's partner would be the one to find the body and to get the false papers.

Afternoon came and passed, and Pick did not see a living thing the whole day but a jack rabbit. At dark, he went back to his cave. Next morning, with the patience of an Indian, he was back in the brush.

Around nine o'clock, he saw a man enter the canyon on

foot, and a dry smile of satisfaction crossed Pick's face. The man's movements were cautious; he had a rifle slacked under his arm and a pack of miner's tools on his back. When he had climbed a pinnacle rock and scanned the canyon for a full half hour, he came down and pulled a paper from his Levi's pocket. Those would be the location papers, Pick thought.

Pick lay there a long time, watching. The man paused perhaps three hundred yards away, down on the floor of the canyon, and soon was working at a shallow test pit Pick had dug. He was filling small ore sacks with a short-handled shovel. The clang of his pick and single jack were loud in the morning stillness.

Pick debated. He wanted a good look at this man. He also wanted to talk to him, but after a few minutes of watching, he knew that it would not be easy to capture him here. The pit stood in the midst of a barren space that afforded no cover at all. He would be a perfect target for the man's rifle. Pick knew that the old trail was the only logical way out of the canyon. *Why don't I drop down there and stop him? He won't be half so spooky if he gets his work done and thinks he's alone.*

His mind made up, Pick backed quietly out of the brush, and, keeping the big boulders of the canyon floor between himself and the man, worked his way to the canyon side. Halfway up it, he heard the ring of the single jack cease, and he hurried a little. It was a good mile to the place he had in mind. Still, the man would have to tote the heavy ore sacks, and that would slow him up. Even if he missed him, Pick thought, it wouldn't be hard to overtake a man afoot packing forty pounds of ore on his back.

Just the same, old Pick hurried. The place he chose was so similar to the one in which he had lain in wait for the bushwhacker that a wry smile pulled up the corners of his mouth. Crouched behind a rock, gun drawn, Pick waited—and waited and waited.

When he could stand it no longer, he took to the trail and worked carefully back toward the mouth of the canyon. When he got a view of it, he saw it was empty. Dismay struck him, and immediately he searched for tracks. Back in a little *rincon* he saw the reason why he had missed the man. Here, in the drifted dust, were the tracks of a horse.

Pick squatted on his haunches and cursed himself with blistering venom. He had been taken in like a child, like any simple fool. Just because the man had entered the canyon afoot, it had not occurred to Pick to look for a horse. And while he was making his laborious way afoot to the trail, the man had escaped on horseback.

But Pick remained standing there only a moment. Then he started out trailing the horse. He could do it at a fast walk, but it was nerve-straining work, and when darkness fell he had to admit defeat. He could not overtake the man; but maybe he could track him to the end of his journey.

But next day, at noon, Pick knew he really was licked. The tracks petered out in the gravelly bed of a stream, and four hours spent in searching for tracks went unrewarded. Pick glared at the horizon, cursing himself and his luck and life in general.

"But hogtie me," he swore darkly, "if this isn't the last time I get caught."

Next night, down at one of the foothill water holes, Pick helped himself to a Bar 33 horse. In four more days, he was over on the other side of the county, where he was sure he wouldn't be known. He was there for a reason. He wanted to find out if Johnny Hendry was doing anything about cleaning up the mystery. To Pick, this was more important than finding the man who had tried to bushwhack him.

Pick met a puncher near Doane's store. And, talking with him, learned many things, among them that Johnny Hendry had been elected sheriff, that he had run the hardcases out of Cosmos, and that there had been an election dance held for him last night.

The puncher, seeing Pick's grin, said, "What's the matter, pop? Anything funny about that?"

"Nary a thing," Pick answered. "I was just wonderin' when it was goin' to happen."

"Brother, it has," the puncher said fervently.

And Pick, satisfied, headed back for the Calicoes, his patience a bottomless thing once again. In a few more days, if Johnny's success in dealing with these hardcases continued, Pick could come back to life. Just a few more days.

Chapter Eleven: KILLER'S GOLD

AT THE FIRST GRAY DAWN, Johnny was awakened by a soft noise. Almost instantly, he realized that last night he had neglected to haul the trunk over the trap door. He reached out for his gun, pulled himself back in a dark corner of the bed, and trained his gun on the attic's only entrance.

And Nora appeared.

"Johnny," she whispered, and when Johnny answered her, she came over to him. Her hair was down around her shoulders, and she held a gray wrapper close around her. Johnny could not see her face, but he could tell by the timbre of her voice that she was frightened.

"What is it?"

"Are you awake enough to get this straight? The bank was blown last night and the Esmerella gold taken from the vaults. The robbers escaped. But Baily Blue is down here—in the hall right below—waiting for you. He—he found something of yours in the bank."

Johnny sat bolt upright. "Mine? What?"

"I don't know. He wouldn't tell me. Dress and come down. And, oh, Johnny, do keep your temper. I know it's all right, that you weren't in it, but be careful what you say."

Nora went back down the ladder, and Johnny dressed hurriedly. Turk and Hank were breathing deeply, and he did not think they had awakened.

Baily was waiting down in the hall below. Johnny stepped off the lower rung of the ladder to face him. "What is all this, Baily?"

Baily's chill blue eyes belied the amiability of his face. "Nora tell you about the bank?"

"Yes, that it was blown. What about me, though?"

For answer, Baily held out a worn Colt. It was cedar-handled, its butt scarred with use. "We found that in the alley just outside the back door of the bank. It fell out when a man jumped on his horse and it bucked." He looked at Johnny. "It's yours, ain't it?"

Johnny nodded, not taking his gaze from Baily's face. So that was why he hadn't been able to find his other gun when he went to bed.

Baily extended his other hand. It held a worn spur. "We found this, too. You got any idea whose it is?"

Johnny looked at it and then shuttled his gaze back to Baily. "You know whose it is, don't you?"

"I got a good idea. You tell me," Baily said.

"Turk's."

"That's what I thought." There was a little silence, during which Nora came and stood by Johnny's side. They were both watching Blue, waiting for him to make a move. He lounged erect from the wall, took off his hat, mopped his head with a handkerchief, and said, "Son, heaven knows I hate to do this. But I got to take you and Turk in."

"You believe it?" Johnny said softly.

"It ain't that, and you know it. But you've worked around my office long enough to know how we run things like this."

Johnny had his mouth open to answer hotly when a dark form hurtled down from the trap door above and crashed on top of Baily Blue, carrying him to the floor. It was Turk and, straddling Blue, he pinned both his arms to the floor.

"I heard," Turk said angrily. "Wake Hank and get your bedroll, Johnny. We're gettin' out of here."

"No!" Johnny said angrily, his voice sharp above the sucking and gasping that Blue was making in his effort to recover his wind.

Turk's face was dark with fury. "You fool! Don't you see what kind of a frame-up this is? We'll be strung up by a lynch mob if we give ourselves up! All those hardcases—Wigran and his outfit—will be in town in the mornin'! Once we're in jail, they'll see us swing higher'n a kite!"

"It's true, Johnny," Nora said.

"Get your stuff! Get mine! Wake Hank and tell him to dress and come along. If you don't, we're dead, and you know it!"

Johnny looked at Nora, and she nodded bleakly.

When he was gone to wake Hank, Nora looked down at Blue. He had his breath, and he was observing Turk with placid friendliness. "Well, now, Turk, that was a giveaway, wasn't it?"

Turk growled, "Shut up."

Baily looked up at Nora and said sadly, "It's pretty tough on you, girl. Johnny's the last man I ever thought would do that."

Turk's open palm smacked sharply across Blue's mouth. "Say that again, and I'll show you how your teeth taste when they roll loose in your head."

Baily only smiled. When Hank and Johnny returned, Turk took Blue's guns away from him and let him get up. He said nothing; his smile was still only amiable, and a bit pitying.

"Baily," Johnny said gently, "I don't know if you're behind this or not. I don't think you are. Anyway, you were at least partly behind that election steal. But if you are mixed up in this, heaven help you. I don't like a frame-up!"

"I'm sheriff and I done a sheriff's duty," Baily answered.

"A sight too well," Turk growled. He took the rope from Hank, and in a moment Blue was tightly trussed on the floor.

"I just wanted to tell you the rest," Blue said. "There was three men robbed the bank. One of 'em held the horses. Would the third man be you, Hank?"

Hank said nothing. Johnny turned to Nora and took her in his arms. "It'll be a long time before I see you again, honey. But I'll be back. And when I do come back, I'm goin' to have plenty scalps in my belt. All right with you?"

"You know it is," Nora murmured.

Twenty minutes later, the three of them were riding south out of town. At the rise above Cosmos they pulled up and looked back at the grimy, slatternly town that they had tried to save. "Still want to hit the grit, Hank?" Johnny asked.

Hank only shook his head.

"And you, Turk?"

"You couldn't blast me out of this county," Turk said savagely.

"Nor me," Johnny murmured. "Looks like we're all here. Want to stick together on it?"

They nodded.

They pulled off the road and headed cross country for the shelter and solitude of the Calicoes. To Johnny, these were the bitterest hours of his life. To see success within his grasp and then to lose it was enough to dishearten anyone. But had he really lost? After all, the election didn't matter, and the fact that he was an outlaw wasn't much more important. He had a clue to Pick's killer. That alone was worth all the hard luck he had suffered. "Let's don't ride too far," he said, toward noon. "I'm goin' back to Cosmos tonight to talk with Hugo Miller. And not even Baily Blue had better try to stop me."

Miller was deep in his report when the door opened and Lemrath came in. It was seven-thirty. Hugo had been working all day.

"Evenin'," Lemrath said pleasantly, and he took the chair Hugo waved him into. He was an ordinary-looking man of middle age with a square, alert face. His least movements were slow and entirely controlled. There was no nervousness in him at all. His clothes were worn but clean; he looked at Hugo with a frank and steady gaze.

"Knowing anything about minin' and assayin'?" Hugo asked by way of conversation.

"Never saw a place like this before," Lemrath said. Hugo glanced at Lemrath's hands. They were not soft, but neither were they the horny hands of a man who has swung a pick all his life. Hugo was certain he was a cowman, not a prospector, and that puzzled him all the more.

Hugo put down his last notation, *Silica—006*, and glanced over the faked assay report. Then he looked up at Lemrath and said carefully, "You have a mighty good thing here, friend."

He was observing Lemrath closely, but he could see no sign of excitement or exultation. Lemrath's face changed not at all. He simply said, "That's good."

"Take a look yourself," Hugo said, and gave him the paper.

The assay, of course, had been doctored up to make the gold content of the ore look phenomenal. Lemrath glanced at the paper and nodded imperturbably. Folding it, he held it in his hand. Hugo was confounded. Was this the way a man greeted fortune?

To cover up his confusion, Hugo said, "If there's much of that ore around, I'd advise you to keep it quiet. That'll start a rush anywhere, any time."

"I reckon that's right," Lemrath said idly.

Hugo's intentions began to falter. If this man was a crook, dishonest, then Hugo was willing to admit that he did not know an honest man when he saw one. And Hugo was a shrewd judge of character. Then something else occurred to him. This plan of his and Johnny Hendry's risked a reputation for honesty that had taken him a life-time to build. Once the news got out that he had faked an assay, his business and name would be ruined. He wouldn't have minded if he saw a chance to catch a crook and a killer, but Lemrath was definitely neither. The whole thing puzzled and angered Hugo. He said impulsively, "You've filed on your claim, of course."

"No."

"Don't you know where it is?"

"I got a paper that shows it," Lemrath said quietly.

Hugo was more bewildered than ever. He said, "You mean you've never been to your location?"

"No."

Hugo took a deep breath of relief and walked over to confront Lemrath. "Do you mind if I stick my nose in busi-ness that doesn't concern me?"

Lemrath regarded the spare, gray-haired man before him with mild concern. "Why—go ahead," he said.

Hugo said, "The man who registers the claim this ore

was taken from will brand himself a murderer. And he'll be killed."

Slowly Lemrath came to his feet. "A murderer?"

"Yes. Because the real owner of this claim was murdered, and the location papers were stolen from him before he had a chance to file. Naturally, the only man who would file on that claim is the man who killed the rightful owner."

Lemrath regarded Hugo with blank surprise. "You know where the claim is, then?"

Hugo told him about the volcanic breccia. "That stuff could only come from one place, the place Pick Hendry was working. And there's volcanic breccia in your sample. Figure it out for yourself."

Deliberately, Lemrath drew out his pipe and packed it and sucked the blue smoke into his lungs while Hugo watched him closely.

"I'll tell you how it was," Lemrath said slowly. "I'm a rancher down in the next county. I've been havin' hard luck. My wife died, my place burned down, and my kid is sick. Then a man rode up to my tent a week or so ago and offered me five hundred dollars if I'd bring this ore to you, have it assayed, and then register the claim. I jumped at the chance."

"Did you know his name?"

"No."

"Remember his looks?"

"No. He looked like a saddle tramp. Hadn't shaved, his clothes were dirty, and he looked shifty—but that didn't matter. I needed the money."

"How much did he give you then?"

"Two hundred." Lemrath smiled a little. "It just about saved my life, too. I squared up with the doc, got a nurse, and got help to rebuild my shack."

Hugo nodded. He could understand that, and he believed the man's story because it jibed with what he had already observed. "What did this jasper say to you?" Hugo persisted.

"Nothin', except what I told you. And he said I wasn't to make any fuss at all about registerin' the claim."

"So you've got the location papers on you?"

Lemrath patted his pocket. "Right here."

"Are you going to register it, knowing what you do about the claim?"

"I reckon," Lemrath said slowly. "I don't see how that'd change things much, and that's what I was paid to do."

"Do you mind showing me the location papers?" Hugo asked mildly. "I'd give plenty of money to see them—not, understand, because I want the gold, but because I want to locate the place where I can find Pick Hendry's killer."

Lemrath took his pipe from his mouth and scowled. "That wouldn't be livin' up to my word, because I promised to keep this quiet."

Hugo said coldly, "You're workin' for a murderer," and let his hand move toward the drawer where he kept his gun. He was going to see this through.

Lemrath did not answer for a moment. He studied Hugo and then scowled down at his pipe. Finally, he said, "Tell you what I'll do. The claim-recording office closes at eight, don't it? It's a few minutes to eight now. We'll both go over, and I'll register the claim. You can copy it down from the book and find out what you want to know. And that way, I'll be keepin' my word to the man who paid me. That all right?"

"It's perfect," Hugo said, relieved, and reached for his hat. Lemrath folded up the assay report and tucked it in his pocket.

The claim-recording office was a small shack at the very end of the town. Hugo and Lemrath hurried, for it was within a few minutes of eight o'clock, the closing-time. They could see the lamps of the office still lighted. Stepping off the boardwalk, they went past a dark warehouse.

Hugo felt a gathering excitement in him.

He turned to Lemrath and said, "Friend, when you've registered this, you'd better—"

Crash!

The bellow of a shotgun pounded right beside Hugo, and he saw Lemrath driven down on his face. Whirling, Hugo turned just in time to see the dark figure of a man leap from the corner of the warehouse. And then something rapped down over Hugo's skull and a blanket of stars blossomed and burst in his head. He didn't even remember falling.

When he regained consciousness, he was lying on his own bed in the back room of the assay office. His head ached abominably, and it was a long time before he could focus his eyes on the figure beside him. When he did, he saw the sturdy figure of Baily Blue.

"Well, well," Blue drawled. "For a minute, I thought they'd done it, Hugo."

"Is Lemrath dead?" Hugo murmured.

"A hole shot through him as big as a washtub," Blue said cheerfully. "Who was it?"

"Did you search him?"

"Sure."

"Find anything on him—any papers?"

"Not a thing," Blue said. "Not even a cigarette paper. His pockets were turned inside out."

Sick at heart, Hugo turned his face to the wall. The location papers were gone before he'd had a chance to see them. The claim would never be filed now, or if it was, he would never be able to identify it as the one containing the volcanic breccia. The only sure thing was that, since the faked assay report was stolen, too, the claim would be worked. But that would be meager consolation to Johnny Hendry.

Hugo heard Baily go out. He lay there a long time and finally, when his headache calmed down a little, he struggled out of bed and fixed himself something to eat. He'd nearly finished when he heard the back door open and, turning to look, found Johnny Hendry standing there.

Hugo plunged into the story of Lemrath's murder. Johnny listened to it with an increasingly morose face. When Hugo was finished, Johnny tilted back in the extra chair, rolled a smoke, and lighted it.

"Well," he observed to no one in particular, "it seems when I take a beatin', I take a good one. What is there to do now?"

And Hugo, who had asked himself that same question, didn't answer, because he couldn't.

Chapter Twelve: THE FINEST MAN IN THE COUNTY

MAJOR FITZ'S OFFICE REFLECTED, as did everything else in this clean, white house, a military neatness. It held a roll-top desk, a safe, three chairs, and a book-shelf filled mostly with copies of the *Stockman's Gazette*.

Major Fitz was there examining a small ledger. Before he took it out of the safe, he carefully pulled down the blinds and locked the door. He didn't spend much time over the ledger, for he knew its contents almost by heart. When he was finished and had the ledger back in the safe again, he allowed himself a thin smile of satisfaction. Then, because he was waiting for someone, and idle time always hung heavy on his hands, he pulled out some back issues of the *Gazette* and leafed nervously through them, glancing often at the wall clock.

He waited almost twenty minutes before he heard a soft knock on the outside door, and he crossed the room to open it. Carmody stepped in, followed by a smaller man, a puncher. The look on this man's face made Major Fitz frown. "Well?" he said.

"It went all right," Carmody said in a businesslike tone, following Fitz across to his desk. He laid down two sheets of paper, which Fitz picked up after he sat down at his desk.

"Did he get to the claim recorder's?" Fitz asked.

"We left him stretched out almost on the steps of it," Carmody said.

Fitz looked at one of the papers and handed it to the puncher. "That's the same location paper, isn't it, Barney?"

The puncher came over and glanced at the paper. "Sure, that's the one I give him."

Fitz, his hands trembling ever so slightly, deliberately opened the other paper, which was Hugo's falsified assay report. He read it swiftly, and Carmody heard him sigh a little.

Carmody said, "What is it?"

"Better than I had hoped for," Fitz said softly. He stared

at the paper a long moment, then raised his eyes to Barney. "Barney, you did a good job. I thought maybe old Pick was onto something, but I never dreamed it would be this good."

"I did," Barney said, his voice bragging and arrogant. "I could tell by the way he acted up there in the Calicoes when we was followin' him. When a man's got a strike, everything he does gives him away—even an old tough jasper like him."

"Well, he had a strike, all right," Fitz said dryly. "Describe this canyon to me again."

Barney did. He obviously knew something about minerals and mining. He described the dike at some length, guessed at its probable length and depth, while Major Fitz took careful notes.

"How many claims would it need to cover it?" Fitz asked, looking up from his writing.

"Six would blanket it."

"You're sure Pick didn't register it before he was killed?"

"I looked through the register this mornin'," Barney asserted. "There ain't a thing registered in that canyon, not a thing."

"How do you explain all his test pits?"

"Why, Pick was like any other prospector. He dug around, puttin' in a lot of pits and gettin' no color at all, or maybe just a little. He didn't go deep enough. There wasn't no sense in payin' good money to locate a worthless claim. On the other hand, he might have knowed that the gold was there, or somewhere close. He wanted to make sure of the best claims before he recorded anything. That's natural enough, ain't it?"

"I suppose," Fitz said, rising. "Well, Barney, you've earned a nice cut out of this. One of those claims—the best one in fact—will be yours."

"It ought to be," Barney bragged. "If it hadn't been for me, you wouldn't 've known anything about it."

"That's right," Fitz said. "Good night, boys."

Barney turned to the door and went out, Carmody swinging in behind him. As Carmody was about to step out, he shuttled his gaze to Fitz, and it was questioning.

Imperceptibly Fitz nodded, and Carmody closed the door.

Major Fitz stood utterly still, his hand traveling to the breast pocket of his coat, from which peeped the tips of five cigars. He drew one out, his head cocked as if listening, and bit the end off it. Striking a match, he held the flame to the tip of the cigar, just as the muffled explosion of a gunshot sounded out in the night. Major Fitz paused long enough for the corners of his mouth to turn up in a slight smile, and then he lighted his cigar.

He was sitting at the desk when Carmody returned. "Where do you want him?" Carmody asked quietly.

"I don't care. Get rid of him on your way over to Warms. Did the boys wake up?"

"I told them I shot at a dog nosin' around the corrals." Slowly Carmody walked over to Fitz's desk and looked down at him, his slack face thoughtful and grave. "I didn't like that much, Fitz," he murmured.

"Did you want him getting drunk in Cosmos and babbling the whole thing?" Fitz inquired.

"It isn't Barney. He'd 've got it in the back sooner or later." Carmody paused, his face still grave, his eyes meditative. "It's you, Fitz. When you're through with a man, you throw him away—like you'll throw that cigar butt away."

"I don't deny it."

"I wonder if—" Carmody's voice died, and his face settled into an unpleasant hardness. Leaning both hands on the desk, he put his face close to Fitz's. "Don't try it with me, Fitz. I'm a careful man."

"Hoke, you're a fool!" Fitz said angrily. "You've been with me almost since I took over the Bar 33. We've built ourselves a nice stake by trusting each other. If your cut doesn't suit you, say so. If you want to pull out of here, saddle up and ride out—only I'd hate to see you go."

Carmody straightened up. "I'll stick," he said briefly. "I just wanted to make sure."

"Are you sure?"

"Sure as a man can be when he's runnin' with a man like you," Carmody murmured. "What do you want me to do about Westfall over in Warms?"

Fitz indicated the papers before him. "Take those over and tell him what I want. He's to take his crew to the canyon and put up his monuments. Then he'll go down and file on these six claims, buy his supplies, and start work. Once he's operating, I'll expect to see his books once a month. The expense funds, all cash, have been deposited in the Warms bank. If he ever mentions my name, either in public or private, tell him what he may expect." Here Fitz smiled thinly. "Also, you might impress upon him what he's to expect if I even suspect that his books are crooked. Have you got all that?"

"Sure, but he's honest, right enough." Carmody cuffed his Stetson off his forehead and drew out his sack of tobacco dust. Fitz relighted his cigar and sat scowling at his desk.

Presently, as they both smoked in silence, the old feeling of close camaraderie returned. But Fitz was drumming on the desk with his fingers.

Then he said abruptly, "You know, Hoke, there's only one thing in all this business that I can't explain."

"What's that?"

"Barney and Tohill were sent to follow old Picket-Stake Hendry. Barney comes back with the news that Pick has been shot, blown off the rim. By whom? Presumably Lee Tohill. But where is Tohill?"

Carmody studied his cigarette. "My guess has always been that Pick Hendry tagged him, and that he died up there."

"But we searched the country."

"No man can cover that country like it should be covered. Besides, a man that's shot bad ain't so careful about directions."

"But how could Pick shoot him when he got a load of buckshot right in the face?"

"Maybe Pick got first shot at Tohill."

"That could be," Fitz said. "However, my mind's not at rest on that point. Where is Tohill? If I knew that, I'd feel a lot better."

"What difference does it make?" Carmody said. "You've got the location papers. And they're the true ones, because they're in Pick Hendry's own handwritin'. If they weren't, maybe you could accuse Barney and Tohill of double-crossin' you, of fakin' the location papers, and keepin' the real ones Pick had with him. But you can't do that. That handwritin' checked."

"So it did," Fitz said quietly. "Well, get along, Hoke. And good luck."

When Carmody was gone, Major Fitz rose and blew out the light. On the way back to his room, he let the memory of this evening filter through his mind, and it gave him pleasure. Once he had something tangible like this gold mine, he would be fixed for life. It pleased him, too, to recall how neatly he was cleaning up all the evidence that pointed to him. Pick had found the claim, and he was dead. Lemrath was dead, for Fitz had not wanted the claim recorded; he had only wanted the assay. And Barney was dead, too, now. That left only himself and Carmody—and Westfall, a legitimate mining man. Sooner or later Carmody and Westfall would go the way of the others.

It was all working smoothly. Soon no one could touch his back trail. And in a short time, he would be a man of wealth and power, not just a salaried manager of a cow outfit. Yes, life was good. But to Barney, slacked over the saddle of a horse out in the night, he did not give a thought. That was over.

Next morning Major Fitz rode into Cosmos. He went first to several stores and ordered supplies. Major Fitz had a gift for making storekeepers talk. They valued his advice as well as his trade, and he gave both impartially.

Standing with legs outspread, big sombrero on the back of his head, duck coat over his singlet, he was talking to Bledsoe about Johnny Hendry in the Miners' Emporium when he caught sight of Nora at another counter. He left Bledsoe and walked over to Nora, who greeted him with gravity, taking his hand. The major's foxy face was carefully gloomy.

"I've heard about this deal they shoved off on Johnny. What's behind it?" he asked bluntly.

"A frame-up," Nora answered simply.

"Of course, but whose?"

"Baily Blue found the gun."

Fitz eyed her keenly. "You think he planted it?"

"I don't know, Major Fitz. Johnny didn't, either."

Major Fitz rapped on the counter and bellowed, "Bledsoe! Bledsoe!"

A clerk called the storekeeper, who hustled over to Fitz and Nora. Bledsoe looked harried, as if he had spent a sleepless night, and his manner contrived to be both ingratiating and defiant.

"You're a commissioner here, Bledsoe. Why can't you do something about clearing Hendry?" he snorted. "You know as well as I do that he didn't do it!"

Bledsoe shrugged. "What can we commissioners do, Major Fitz?"

"Get a decent sheriff!" Fitz answered sharply. "You had one and let him go."

"Please," Nora said, putting a restraining hand on Major Fitz's arm. "He did what he could, Major Fitz."

Fitz scowled, and drummed on the counter top with his fingers. "Do you think it would do any good to give Baily Blue a dressing down?"

"It never has, has it?" Bledsoe asked.

Suddenly, a gleam of inspiration appeared in Major Fitz's eye. "I'm going to talk with that gentleman," he declared firmly. "Maybe he'll change his tune. You wait until I get back and you'll hear something," he promised, as he tipped his hat to Nora and walked out of the store.

Baily Blue was in his office. Fitz stomped in and closed the door, and immediately he relaxed.

"Take a chair," Baily said amiably. "It ain't often you pay me a call in broad daylight."

Fitz chuckled and sat down. "Are we alone?"

Baily nodded.

"That was a nice job at the bank," Fitz said. "Where'd you cache the stuff?"

"Two bars are in this bottom drawer here," Baily drawled, indicating his desk. "The other two are under a bunch of junk in the closet."

"Tell me about it," Fitz said. "How'd Hendry take it?"

"Just like we thought he would. The girl kept him from flyin' off the handle, Turk Hebron jumped me, and then they decided to run. They had Leach and his hardcases figured pretty good. It was Turk that said Leach would likely breed a lynch mob."

"Did they suspect you?"

"I don't think so. They think I crooked the election, all right, but Hendry said he didn't think I framed this bank robbery on him." Baily grinned slyly. "I'm quite an old duffer, Fitz. They got me down for a little bit of a fox, but that's all. Johnny don't think I'm crooked. Leastways I never give him cause to while he was my deputy."

Fitz nodded. "I've got an idea. I was just talking to the girl, and to Bledsoe. Of course, they believe it's a frame-up. I sided in with them, naturally. But I want to make my sympathy look plenty real now, Baily. We've got too much at stake for them to suspect me."

"That's right."

"I'm supposed to be in here now, arguing with you. When I go out, I'm going to tell them I've offered a thousand dollars reward for the capture of the real bank robbers —not Hendry and Hebron and Brender. That'll leave you in the clear, since you only did your duty in trying to arrest them on the evidence found. You haven't put a reward on their heads. This bounty I offer for the bandits will be with your full knowledge. You can say in public that you approve it, providing anybody can prove to you that it wasn't Johnny and those other two." He paused, regarding Baily. "How does it sound?"

"I dunno. There's a lot of feelin' against me."

"All right. That's a way to show you're open-minded, isn't it?"

"I reckon. Only don't say we've had a row about it. Say I was reasonable and agreeable, that I was only doin' my duty."

"Fine." Fitz shifted in his chair and pointed a finger at Baily. "Here's something else that will give it weight, Baily. Tonight have Leach Wigran steal a hundred head of steers off that south range of mine. They'll be along the creek, with no one riding herd. I'll have them pushed over today. It'll make it look like the robbers—just to mock my reward offer—are beginning to raid my stock."

"What'll the company say about that?" Baily asked.

"I'll take care of the company. I haven't showed them any losses so far. Besides, once the excitement has blown over, the steers can be returned, can't they?"

"Sure." Baily plucked at his lower lip. "You don't want anything planted, do you, like somethin' of Temple's or Hart's or Kennicott's—anything from one of them honest ranchers?"

Fitz shook his head. "Not a thing. All I'm interested in doing is showing the girl and Bledsoe and anybody else who's apt to make trouble that my sympathy is with Johnny."

"What are we goin' to do about him?" Baily drawled.

Fitz made a wry face. "That young man has a charmed life. First he managed to survive that shot of Carmody's. Next, he discovered that trap-door set-gun. I'm beginning to believe he can't be killed."

"I could have told you that."

"Well, he's taken care of now. At least, he can't harm anybody where he is. And if we ever get a try at him again, we'll make it stick."

Baily nodded, and Fitz rose.

Baily said, "I'll get those two bars up to you tonight. I'll give the other one to Leach, like you said. Tip Rogers was in here all day rawhidin' me to take a posse out. That all right with you?"

"Go ahead." Fitz started out, and suddenly turned and asked, "Has the Esmerella got a reward out?"

"Two thousand."

Fitz only grinned and stepped out on the walk.

Back at Bledsoe's, he found Nora still talking to the storekeeper. They looked at him expectantly as he approached.

"Well, I found him reasonable," Fitz said briskly. "I've offered a thousand dollars reward for the capture of the real bank robbers—the reward not to apply to the capture of Johnny or Turk or Hank, because I don't believe they did it."

"You darling!" Nora cried, and her voice was tight with gratitude.

"What did Blue say?" Bledsoe asked.

"Oh, he was reasonable. He said he'd only worked on the evidence he found, which was inescapable. He admitted the gun and spur might have been planted by the real robbers, but he said he only did his duty in acting on the evidence at hand." He snorted loudly. "The fool!"

"Let's hope your offer will make the Esmerella officers change theirs, too," Bledsoe said, shaking his head.

"Three thousand dollars is a lot of money," Fitz said wisely. "Many a man has sold out his companions for less. I believe these robbers will."

He chatted a moment longer, then left them. Watching his trim figure mingle with the crowd, Bledsoe, as if voicing Nora's own thought, said, "There goes the finest man in this county—or any other county."

Chapter Thirteen: STUBBORN JOHNNY

JOHNNY REMEMBERED a little-known water hole high in the foothills of the Calicoes that Pick had told him about long ago, and it was here they decided to make their camp. It was a long, silent ride, for all of them were disheartened at the news Johnny had brought from Hugo. It meant that every clue they had to Pick's killer had vanished. And of the three, Johnny was the most downcast. Outlawry would have meant nothing so long as he had a chance to even Pick's score, but now that this was gone, these long and aimless days on the dodge would be intolerable. He resolved grimly not to remain idle, waiting for chance to free him of these outcast bonds. And he had the wisdom to sense that Turk and Hank, good men that they were, would fret at idleness until one or the other of them would decide to pull out. He must have a plan, something to keep them all busy until they could pick up again the trail of Pick's killer.

The camp did not suit him, but in the circumstances it was the safest. Tucked in a fold of a gaunt and up-ended field of malpais, the trail to it was devious and rocky. To cross the malpais would have meant that the horses' hoofs would be cut to ribbons, so that it was necessary to follow a thin ribbon of arroyo which angled down through the malpais field to strew its pebbles over the glass-sharp terrain. Wood had to be hauled; there was no grass; but there was a tiny spring of good water seeping out of a crack in the black rock, and the jagged, up-thrust sides of a canyon afforded them the shelter they needed. If it was hard to get to, then it was all the safer, Johnny reasoned.

They spent the first day making the camp livable. They raked the sand and stones out of the arroyo into a small pocket of the canyon, so their horses would have a place to move around. Wood was hauled.

In midafternoon the work was done, and it was now, Johnny knew, that the tedium of passive waiting would begin. Turk had looked at him several times today with a question in his eyes. Hank was more phlegmatic, but Johnny knew they were both thinking the same thing.

Squatting on his haunches against the steep side of the canyon, Johnny rolled a smoke and contemplated the camp. To Turk, who was sitting beside him, he said, "Well, it ain't much, Turk, but then we won't have to be in it much."

Turk looked at him swiftly. "How come? We're hidin', ain't we?"

Hank strolled across to join them now. Johnny waited until he, too, was seated, then said, "Hidin'? Maybe you could call it that. But if you keep movin', you're harder to find than if you sit still, aren't you?"

"But what can we do?" Hank growled. "Hunt the whole Calicoes for that claim jumper that killed Pick?"

"Remember the proposition I made you when I thought I was goin' to be sheriff?" Johnny countered. "Well, that still holds. We're goin' to clean up this county."

"How?"

"Rustle from rustlers," Johnny declared. He paused, waiting for them to comment. When they didn't, he said, "Me, I'm not goin' to let anybody drive me out of this county. I aim to live here. Also, I aim to be sheriff of it some day. And when I am, I'm goin' to drive these hard-cases out, just like I promised. Well, maybe that day's far off, but I reckon I can start in to work right now." He grinned. "Also, since I ain't sheriff yet, I won't be bothered by all the laws a sheriff is bothered with. I'll fight these jaspers their way."

Turk looked fondly at him and laughed. "I could show you some tricks, fella."

"Good! That's what I want. And Hank can learn 'em, too—just in case he's hard up for a job some day. How about it, Hank?"

Hank grinned and nodded. They were with him, Johnny knew.

"When I thought I was goin' to be sheriff," he went on, "I went to Major Fitz with a proposition. It was this." And he told them about the lists the ranchers had given him of the men they believed should be driven out of the county.

"I got the answers," Johnny finished. "Who do you think got voted the most unwanted man in Cosmos county?"

"Me?" Turk queried.

Johnny grinned and shook his head. "Major Fitz."

Turk was surprised, but Hank, remembering things he'd seen while working under Fitz on the Bar 33, was not; and Johnny, seizing on Hank's lack of surprise, questioned him. "You're not surprised, Hank. Why not?"

"I dunno," Hank said, after a moment's thought. "There was a time when I thought Fitz was a broad-gauge hombre, a man to ride the river with. Now I dunno. I think he puts up a good front. But somethin' goes on in his head that we don't see."

"You think he could be a rustler?"

"I don't see how," Hank murmured. "I worked on the Bar 33 for a long time. None of them boys was doin' any considerable night ridin'. On the other hand, they wasn't a good crew, about what you could expect in a company outfit."

"Then if Fitz doesn't steal cattle, how'd his name get at the head of this ranchers' list?"

"Maybe they just got a feelin', like I have," Hank replied. "Remember that jasper that tried to get away with the Esmerella gold? I can't prove it, but I feel like Fitz had somethin' to do with that."

Turk said reminiscently, "I knowed a bank president once. He was the most pious son of a gun in the world. He prayed longer and louder than anybody in church. Come to find out, he was makin' too much money out of the bank. He was tied up with a cattle-stealin' ring. He'd pass on the word to the rustlers about who was borrowin' money to save their places and their cattle. Then those folks would be stole blind, and the bank would foreclose on the place. He had a good thing out of it—and he never wore a gun." He looked at Johnny. "That's what you're hintin' about Fitz, ain't it?"

"About," Johnny said.

Presently Hank said, "Then if somebody's doin' his rustlin' for him, who is it?"

"What do you say, Turk?" Johnny asked. "You know all those boys."

"There's only one man doin' a real business cattle stealin'," Turk replied. "That's Leach Wigran. The rest of them—me, too—wasn't swingin' an awful wide loop. We'd take a dozen head here, and a dozen there and then quit for a month until we'd drunk it up. Once in a while some of us'd get together, but Leach was the only broad-gauge cow thief."

"Then Fitz would be backin' him?" Johnny asked.

"I never said so."

"He'd have to be. If not, these honest ranchers wouldn't put him ahead of Leach Wigran on those lists, would they?"

"Why don't you ask 'em?" Turk drawled, grinning.

Johnny's lean face showed disgust. "Ask 'em? If they're scared to sign a name to those lists, they're scared to say it out loud, aren't they?"

Turk and Hank nodded.

"All right. My plan is danged simple," Johnny said grimly. "I think Fitz is behind Leach. I aim to get proof."

"How?"

"I dunno. But I'm goin' to saddle up in an hour and try to find out. You ridin' with me?"

They were. It was decided they would ride over to Leach Wigran's spread. Perhaps by watching Leach's movements, observing as well as they could whom he talked to, who his visitors were, and how he worked, they might turn up a clue to his tie-up with Fitz. Johnny doubted it, however; it would be too easy for Leach to ride into town and receive his orders, either from Fitz or, more likely, from somebody sent by Fitz. Even by letter. Nevertheless, he couldn't afford to pass up any bets.

But first Johnny had another errand. Hugo had promised to deliver Johnny's message to Nora last night. She was to meet him east of town tonight, above the road to the Esmerella mine, just after dark. This would be on their way to Wigran's, and Johnny timed their ride so that they approached Cosmos just as dusk was settling into night.

The meeting-place was a huge old cedar on a sloping butte, from whose top the lights of Cosmos could plainly be seen. Johnny approached the place cautiously. He saw a horse tied under the tree and dismounted and walked slowly over.

A voice said, "Johnny!" and in another moment, Nora was in his arms.

Johnny laughed huskily as she buried her face against his chest. "I'm a better outlaw than you think, honey," he said gently. "They haven't got me yet."

"Oh, when will this be over, Johnny?" Nora asked despairingly. "Today, Baily Blue got a posse out hunting for you."

"That's queer," Johnny murmured, trying to see Nora's face in the dark. "He never bothered to do that before."

"Tip Rogers insisted."

"Tip?" Johnny asked softly. "So he's leadin' the pack now."

"He was responsible for that gold that was stolen."

"Does he think I took it?"

Nora only nodded, and Johnny's jaw set a little more grimly in that darkness. This was the way things went, then. Your friends, like a pack of snarling dogs, only waited until you were down to jump on you.

He led Nora over to the tree, and they sat down, and Johnny asked for more news from Cosmos.

"Yesterday Major Fitz posted a thousand-dollar reward for the bank robbers," Nora said quietly, "with this provision—that the reward should not apply to the capture of you or Turk or Hank." She paused. "You see he does believe in you, Johnny."

Johnny said dryly, "Does he?"

"Why do you say that?" Nora asked swiftly.

"Remember the ranchers' list?"

"That's foolish!" Nora said vehemently. "Do you still believe that?"

"Eight men out of ten—all honest—can't be that far off."

"But what evidence have you?" Nora cried. "Are you going to believe all the gossip you hear about a friend? You're bitter at Tip, I know, because he believes the worst of you. And now you're doing the same cruel thing to Major Fitz!"

Johnny had no answer to that. Still, he couldn't change his convictions. It was useless to tell Nora anything his judgment was based upon; it wouldn't convince her either. So he remained silent, feeling her anger against him but stubbornly refusing to try to justify himself.

Nora was stubborn, too. "I'd like you to explain a little, Johnny. You seem to doubt that Major Fitz believes in you."

"He may believe in my ability," Johnny said carefully. "But I doubt if he believes in the same thing I do—and you do—that this county deserves to be cleaned up."

"What cause have you to say that?" Nora demanded angrily. "Just because eight sneaking ranchers who hadn't the courage to accuse a man to his face did have the courage to do it behind his back?"

"Among other things."

"What other things?"

Johnny said wearily, "Darlin', you wear long spurs. Let it go. Let's talk about the weather."

"What other things?" Nora insisted.

"They don't matter," Johnny said stubbornly. "This vote of the ranchers is good enough for me."

Nora got to her feet, and Johnny rose to face her. "Major Fitz is my friend," Nora said coldly. "He is yours, too."

Johnny did not trust himself to speak. "First, he offered you the foremanship of the Bar 33 last year," Nora went on accusingly. "Then he advised you to run for sheriff. His men all voted for you. He was the first man to approve your scheme of this poll of undesirables. He gave you his best man to act as your deputy. He tore up heaven and earth for you when he heard you'd been framed. And to top that, Johnny, he has offered a thousand dollars reward for the real bank robbers." She paused, and Johnny could almost feel her contempt. "And now, in your deep gratitude, you believe what eight cowardly ranchers have to say against him without giving the least bit of proof!" She paused, waiting for Johnny to speak. He didn't. "Haven't you anything to say for yourself, Johnny?"

"You've said it all, I reckon," Johnny replied huskily, stubbornly.

"Then—then I don't want to see you again—not until you've changed your mind," Nora said haltingly. "I—I hate—yes, *hate*—ingratitude more than crookedness or stealing or lying or—" Her voice broke, and she turned away.

Johnny, standing motionless under the tree, watched her mount and ride off, and he could do nothing. But deep inside him, he felt a wave of bitterness and anger and unhappiness that was almost blinding. Automatically he reached in his pocket and brought out his tobacco and rolled his cigarette. The smoke helped to calm him, but his hands were shaking so that he could scarcely hold the cigarette.

It was many moments before he could trust himself to turn and walk over to where Hank and Turk were waiting. And, he reflected, the heart gone out of him, all excuse for his staying here had vanished—except one. Pick. When that score was wiped off the slate, he would ride away. Even now, he couldn't blame Nora, but he couldn't understand, either, why she had forced herself to choose between their love and the casual friendship of Major Fitz. For a moment, panic almost seized him, and he was ready to mount his pony and overtake Nora and apologize. But even while he thought it, he knew that honesty would not allow him to do it, and that he was forever a slave—and a willing one—to that conscience Pick Hendry had bred into him.

When he was mounted again, Turk said, "Any news?"

Johnny told him of what Nora had said about Fitz's offer. Turk and Hank did not comment until they had put their horses up the slope and headed north, toward Wigran's.

"That makes us look like three prime saddle tramps, don't it?" Turk observed.

"Look what's behind it," Hank said, and Johnny saw that Hank agreed with him.

"What?"

"If he's goin' to play out this hand he's dealt himself, he's got to have a front, don't he?" Hank argued sanely. "He knew Nora would bring this news to us and that we'd think he was our friend." Hank spat.

Chapter Fourteen: BAR 33 STEERS

LEACH WIGRAN'S RUNNING W OUTFIT was placed deep in the timbered foothills of the Calicoes. Johnny remembered that it was a big frame place built in the dead center of a grassy valley so that no one could approach it without being seen. While Leach had not built it, it seemed as if this place were designed for a man of his shady business. Remote, inaccessible, in the heart of a wide, good range, with a thousand canyons behind it, it was a perfect headquarters for a cattle thief.

They had left the road long since, and were now making their slow way through the tall lodgepoles when Johnny spotted a light off to the right and below them.

"That's the Runnin' W," Turk said.

"We can't move till daylight," Johnny said, "so we might as well pick a comfortable spot."

It was just breaking dawn when they had settled on their place of observation. It was on a high, wooded ridge which afforded perfect cover, yet allowed them a good view down through the tall avenue of trees to the valley below.

While they were not close enough to identify individual riders going into the Running W, they were near enough to the road to ride down for a closer view.

Slowly color began to bloom over the gray landscape, and day marched forward. Smoke began to rise from the chimneys of the Running W, and Johnny settled down to watch, while Turk and Hank rolled up in their blankets for an hour of sleep.

Soon, a strange and distant noise came riding down from the south on the faint wind. Johnny listened, head cocked. In another moment he identified it. The sound of a herd of bawling cattle cannot be mistaken for long. They were being driven up the narrow valley to the Running W.

Johnny moved over to Hank and Turk, about to wake them, and then decided to let them sleep. He could do this job alone, and they were in no danger of discovery.

So, putting the bridle back on his horse which was grazing with its saddle still on, he mounted and worked his way down the slope. He hurried, for the sound of the driven cattle was becoming plainer every minute. When he came to a sprawling thicket of scrub oak, he rose in his saddle and looked down through the trees. Here he could get a good view of the road. He tied his horse in the screening oak, then went forward and down the slope a way and hid himself in the brush.

Presently, the point rider appeared, the cattle strung out in a long bawling line behind him. Johnny caught the brand on this rider's horse, and it was a Running W.

Then, through the cloud of dust that the shuffling herd was kicking up, Johnny tried to read the brands on the cattle. He saw one he thought was a Bar 33, but knew he might be mistaken. He could not be sure because these cattle were branded on the right hip, and he was on their left side. But he was patient, knowing that sooner or later he would have the chance to make sure.

And he did. One of the weary steers angled out of the herd and began to graze, turning back to get some fresh bunchgrass, and Johnny saw with amazement that he had been right. These were Bar 33 steers! Still he could not believe it, for this did not fit in with his theory. But when a calf, pushed ahead in the crush, finally broke loose and turned around and started bawling for its mother, Johnny was certain. Bar 33 cattle!

When they were past, he walked back to his horse, mounted, and turned up the slope, his face thoughtful. Hank and Turk had been awakened by the noise of the herd, and they had guessed where Johnny had gone.

"Whose were they?" Turk asked sleepily.

"Bar 33, believe it or not," Johnny said grimly. Hank sat bolt upright in his blankets.

"Well, I'll be sunk in sheep dip!" he said slowly, looking at Johnny. "Leach is s'posed to be workin' for Fitz. Where does that put us?"

"In the wrong," Turk ventured.

Johnny squatted on his haunches and sifted gravel through his fingers, staring thoughtfully at the ground. "Does Leach bring all his rustled stuff up to this place?" Johnny asked Turk.

"Mostly he drives it over to Warms. It's too easy to track up to here. He ain't got enough rock and rough weather and wind and rain and hard goin' here, and that's what you need to steal cattle."

"Then why is he doin' it?"

Turk shrugged. Johnny was silent for a full minute, and then he rose and savagely threw down his handful of gravel.

"This don't make no sense at all!" He looked up at Hank. "You reckon Fitz sold or give him those cattle?"

"Might be—in payment for a job, or somethin'."

"I'm goin' to find out."

"How?"

"Backtrack, and see if the boys even tried to hide the tracks of this herd. If they did, it might be they stole the beef. If they didn't, it'd mean Fitz knew about them bein' moved."

An hour later, the three of them rode down off the slopes to the valley bottom, and picked up the sign of the cattle. An hour of following the tracks showed them that the Running W men had taken no pains to cover up cattle signs. A two-hour drive to the east, in the rocky, mountain going, would have afforded the Running W men a terrain which would make the tracking of the beef less easy. Apparently, then, they were making no attempt to conceal the drive, although they had been careful to avoid the roads.

It was only when they did not find a bed ground, or place where the riders had camped, that Johnny became suspicious again. "If they were drivin' bought beef, they'd've stopped to make a camp, wouldn't they, and rest the stuff?"

"Sure," Turk said. "It's a two-day drive from Fitz's place, if they didn't push 'em."

"Let's go on," Johnny said. "They looked pushed."

In midafternoon, Hank, riding ahead as a sort of scout, wheeled his horse and rode back. "Pull off in the brush," he said. "Somebody else has the same idea as us."

They turned off behind a ridge into the brush, and dismounted. Johnny mounted the ridge and bellied down to see who was coming.

A lone rider came into sight—Kennicott, one of the ranchers Johnny had seen some days ago. He was riding at a fast walk, eyes on the ground.

It wasn't his beef, Johnny mused. *Why is he cuttin' sign for it?*

When Kennicott came to the place where Johnny and Turk and Hank had pulled off the trail of the cattle, he reined up. For a moment, he stared at their tracks, then up at the ridge, and suddenly whirled and spurred his horse off into the brush. A minute later, Johnny caught sight of Kennicott's horse heading back in the direction from which he had come.

Johnny returned to the horses and told what he had seen.

"Kennicott?" Hank exclaimed. "It ain't his beef."

"Maybe he was as curious as we was," Turk offered.

Johnny remembered that Kennicott might be one of

the eight who accused Fitz. More evidence. He turned a thoughtful face to the south. "It's about time I talked to Hugo Miller," he murmured. "I've got to find out what's goin' on in town."

They stopped on the outskirts of Cosmos just after midnight. The town, as in the days before Johnny Hendry's brief spell of sheriffin', was roaring wide open. The saloons were a bedlam of noise; occasional gunshots racketed down the street. A ranny, dead drunk in his saddle, galloped past without even seeing them.

Johnny made his way carefully down the back alleys until he arrived at Hugo's. A pencil of light lay under the rear door; Johnny moved over to the window and looked in before he knocked. Hugo, his feet tilted on his desk, was deep in a book.

At Johnny's entrance, he rose and frowned. "I've been worried," Hugo said, regarding Johnny with fond seriousness. "Blue was out this morning lookin' for you with a posse."

Johnny grinned and sat down. "He'll never find us. We've got a safe hide-out."

"That's what he said when he came back," Hugo observed dryly.

"Came back?" Johnny echoed. "You mean he only looked for us one morning?"

"Oh, Tip Rogers is still out, but Blue was called back to town by business. Major Fitz had a herd of beef stolen."

"Ah," Johnny said. "Did he?"

"He and his men rode into town this morning and started yelling for Blue. It seems a herd of his just vanished." Hugo shook his head. "The hardcases will start working on Fitz now, since he put up that reward money. Fitz thinks that's what's behind the rustling."

"Does he, now?" Johnny murmured.

Hugo looked sharply at him, his curiosity awakened by the tone of Johnny's voice. For a moment, Johnny was tempted to tell Hugo what he suspected of Major Fitz, but he refrained. If he was wrong in his guess—and he was sure he wasn't—it would not be fair to Fitz. Besides, a secret can be kept only by a few. He said quickly to Hugo,

"Did Blue go out with Fitz?"

"Out and back. The rustlers drove the stuff into the mountains, Blue said, and didn't leave a sign." Hugo smiled wryly. "It's the old excuse."

"Into the mountains," Johnny murmured, smiling privately. "So Blue give up?"

"He did. Fitz was helpless."

Johnny looked at Hugo with some curiosity. "Has anyone claimed that it was me and Turk and Hank that stole Fitz's stuff?"

Hugo shook his head. "Fitz killed that story right off. He said it was five men. Besides, he said you'd be the last man in the world to touch a head of Bar 33 cattle."

"Well, well," Johnny drawled.

Again Hugo looked at him sharply. He said suddenly, impulsively, "What's got into you, Johnny? You're changed."

A slow flush darkened Johnny's lean and browned cheeks. He cuffed his Stetson back on his forehead. "Changed?"

"Are you lettin' this frame-up sour you, boy?"

"No," Johnny said stubbornly. "Why?"

"Just a look in your eyes. Like you don't give a tinker's curse any more." He paused, as if wondering how what he was about to say would be received. "This is none of my business, Johnny, but have you had a row with Nora?"

"Have you asked her?"

Again Hugo shook his head. "No, but she's got the same look in her eyes that you've got—a nothing-matters-now look. Besides, when I asked her what you planned to do after she saw you last night, she didn't say a word." Hugo grinned disarmingly. "Maybe that's all right, but I've got an interest in your career, too, boy."

"Maybe you better ask her, Hugo. As for me," Johnny said slowly, "you know how I feel about Nora—how I always will feel. No, that hasn't changed." He rose and hiked up his Levi's. "Nothin' new about Pick's claim?"

Hugo only shook his head. At the door, Johnny turned and said briefly, "It'll be some time before you see me again, Hugo. Take care of Nora, will you?"

And with that, he slipped out into the night. Back at the horses, he said to Turk and Johnny, "Fitz had a herd of beef stole. Blue went out to take a look and come back with the story that the herd got clean away."

"Ain't that too bad?" Turk murmured sarcastically. "A jasper that couldn't track a ten-horse freight hitch across an alkali flat could have followed that herd." Pausing, Turk waited for Hank to say something.

Hank said only, "Well, don't that prove that Fitz wanted Leach Wigran to get away with the stuff?"

"So it would look to the town like the hardcases was fightin' Fitz now," Johnny put in grimly. "That's what he wants. And"—here his voice took on a tone of quiet savagery—"that's what's goin' to happen."

"Us bein' the hardcases," Turk murmured.

"Right," Johnny said. "And when we end up, Fitz won't know whether he can trust his own mother."

Chapter Fifteen: TRAIL DRIVE

JUST AFTER DARK TWO NIGHTS LATER, Johnny was sitting in the dark doorway of one of the Bar 33 line camps, smoking. The night was quiet about him, the only sounds were those his saddled pony made cropping the grass out in the dark. Johnny had been there an hour, during which he had smoked eight cigarettes. Lately he had found himself restless and impatient, and time and again he had to put a check on his temper, which had always been quick. Deep within him, he knew why he was edgy, but he wouldn't admit it. Right now he was fuming inwardly at Turk and Hank's tardiness, forgetting the fact that the Running W was many miles from here and that they would have to be careful in covering their movements.

When he heard the sound of approaching riders, he faded back into the doorway, drawing his gun. Then Hank's low and cautious whistle came to him, and he stepped out to meet them.

"Get it?" he asked Hank.

Turk answered instead. "Sure. And he's lame now. What luck did you have?"

"They're spread out below us right now, without a man ridin' herd."

"Then let's get to work," Hank said briefly.

It was a horse branded Running W that Johnny had referred to. The three of them mounted, hazed the extra horses and the lame one ahead of them, and rode the short distance down to the flat. Over the rolling, tilting upland of grass, a big herd of Bar 33 cattle were grazing, some of them bedded down.

Out of this bunch they cut a hundred and fifty head and then turned and pushed east toward the mountains. The lame Running W gelding, along with the three other ponies, was pushed in with the cattle.

It was Turk giving orders now, for he knew every one of these devious trails and could pick out the few water holes they would need on their way over the Calicoes. At dawn next morning, they paused to let the herd drink at one of the high mountain springs.

Before they pushed on toward the pass in the gaunt peaks, the gelding was cut out and left behind. He seemed willing to drop out, for he was limping badly. Johnny reasoned that he would rest here by the spring until hunger drove him down on the flats.

All that day they prodded the cattle into the face of a gathering storm that broke in midafternoon, half blinding them with sleet and hail and rain. For an hour they worked furiously to keep the cattle headed up the mountains into the storm, and just when the exhaustion of their ponies was ready to defeat them, the rain slacked off into a steady drizzle.

His eyes red-rimmed and bloodshot, Turk rode back to Johnny, who was riding drag. Both of them were drenched, even through their slickers, and the cold, driving wind that poured down from the peaks had their lips blue.

"It'll be dark before we make the pass. You want to try it?"

"If we let these critters stop, dynamite couldn't keep 'em from goin' back," Johnny said. He raised his eyes to the sky, which seemed almost low enough to touch. They

were far above timber line now in the boulder fields of
the peaks, and all nature here seemed merciless, bent on
breaking them. He shouted into the wind, "Can we do it,
Turk?"

"Sure. You'll lose some of the stuff, likely, and be pretty
doggoned miserable, but we can do it."

"All right. Let's change ponies."

They took turns cutting fresh mounts out and dropping back to saddle; the herd was not allowed to stop.

As night settled down on them, they knew they were in
for it. The rain held on, increasing the misery of man and
beast. A dozen times that night, the cattle were on the
verge of stampeding. Every time they rounded a fresh bend
in this tortuous trail and the wind drove at them with
the force of padded hammers, Johnny and Hank were
driven to a fury of activity. Johnny never knew where
they were going, what the country looked like, or if Turk
was lost. It was his job and Hank's to keep the herd moving—and somehow they did it.

Toward morning the wind died down and the rain
lifted a little so that Johnny almost drowsed off in the
saddle. He could tell by the ease with which his horse
walked and by the increased pace of the cattle that they
were through the pass and on the gentle downslope of the
eastern side of the Calicoes.

Dawn broke cold and clear, and in another hour they
reached timber line. Already behind them, the thunderheads were gathering for a new downpour. When they
got to the green belt of trees, they conferred and decided
to rest the cattle and let them graze on the hardy upland
bunchgrass if they could. Pursuit was hardly probable,
since a fresh storm would be almost certain to blot out
the tracks.

A half day of sleep and dry clothes lifted their spirits.
At noon, after a quick lunch, they got the cattle moving
again. Turk, with the experience of many such drives behind him, took them down the slope through the thick
timber until, when dark fell, they were in the foothills.

Warms, Turk said, was off several miles to the right.

They were heading for the railway station and stock pens that Turk had used in his rustling days. A crooked agent, no brand inspector, and a split of the rustled beef would allow them to dispose of it without so much as a trace to indicate where it had gone.

Close to midnight, they saw the lights of the way station. Turk had ridden ahead, to confer with the agent. When Johnny and Hank arrived with the beef, the pens were open, ready to receive it.

"There'll be a train out of Warms tomorrow morning," Turk informed them. "It'll pick the stuff up." He grinned up at Johnny. "I signed Leach Wigran's name on the way-bill. That all right?"

Johnny nodded. Next morning, in the mining town of Warms, Johnny opened an account at the Warms bank in the name of Leach Wigran. He arranged for the deposit of the money from the sale of the cattle shipment. If Fitz got curious and searched for his herd, Leach Wigran's name would be dark with guilt.

A few moments later he joined Hank and Turk on the main four corners. They looked at each other and smiled. They each needed a shave, clean clothes, and rest. Johnny, in spite of his bone-weariness, felt something driving in him that would not let him rest. His eyes were hard and mocking, as he said to Turk, "You *work* for what you get in this rustling business, Turk. I didn't know that."

"Where now?" Hank asked.

"Cosmos. This has only begun."

In place of Barney, who had been *segundo* under Carmody, Fitz had appointed a silent, surly puncher named Art Bodan, who was years younger than he looked. Fitz didn't know much about him except that Carmody said he was to be trusted.

So that morning, when Bodan had finished his story in Fitz's office, the major regarded him with some curiosity and a little suspicion.

"You say you found the horse down on the flat, grazing. How do you know he was the one whose track you saw?"

"I know," Bodan said stubbornly. "Rain or no rain.

That's the same horse. He's not only crippled in the same foot, but the other tracks tally." He paused, his dark, smooth-shaven face sullen. "You can't track an animal for ten miles without you learn somethin' about his tracks, Major."

Fitz said nothing for the moment, his face scowling and unpleasant to look at.

"Running W. It couldn't be a changed brand, could it?"

"Come out and look for yourself."

"I'll do that," Fitz said, and rose.

Outside, he paused at the corral while Bodan cut out the lame gelding and led him over to Fitz, turning him so that Fitz could investigate the brand.

"That's real, all right," Fitz said. He straightened up. "You're not to say anything about this, of course."

"Three of the men know it a'ready."

"Saddle up my bay," Fitz said, and turned to the house.

An hour later, he rode into the main street of Cosmos and dismounted at Baily Blue's office. He did not need to cover up his visits now, since it was known that, as a victim of rustlers, he had legitimate business with the sheriff. Blue was not in, but Fitz sat down and smoked his pipe, staring thoughtfully out the window.

When Baily finally did come in, "Is Leach in town?" Fitz asked. When Baily nodded Fitz said, "Bring him here."

Blue's eyebrows lifted. "That ain't very cautious, Fitz."

"Bring him here. And do it in a hurry."

Blue vanished; ten minutes later he was back with the hulking Wigran in tow. Leach Wigran seldom talked to the major, never recognized him in public, and that Blue should call him to an open conference with Fitz was a surprise to him. His face, almost hidden by that thick shovel beard, showed a surprise which he could not entirely disguise.

"Sit down," Fitz said abruptly, when the door was shut.

Leach sat down facing him, holding his hat in his hand. Blue leaned on the desk, watching.

"This morning Bodan, my *segundo*, came in with the news that I've been rustled of a hundred and fifty head of cattle. He cut for sign and found where they'd been driven up the Calicoes. The rain had washed away the sign there, but he saw enough to know that whoever stole those cattle had a lame horse. That horse was finally turned loose, up by a spring in the Calicoes, and it drifted down to my range." He leaned forward and regarded Leach with careful eyes. "We found the horse. It was branded Running W, Leach."

Leach stopped fiddling with his hat, his great hands still. "Running W?" he echoed. "There's some mistake. We're missin' no horses."

"I saw it, and it's branded Running W," Fitz said sharply.

"Then somebody stole it."

"Where've you been these last four nights?" Fitz asked him coldly.

"Why—a couple of 'em I reckon I was here in Cosmos."

"Your men were—where?"

Slowly, Leach heaved himself to his feet and regarded Fitz with hot eyes. "So you think I took 'em, Fitz?"

"I didn't say so. I want to know who did."

"I dunno. But I know I didn't and none of my men did. I can account for the whole crew."

Fitz said nothing, and Leach, after holding his gaze for several seconds, turned to Baily Blue, as if for help. Blue, however, kept his face carefully blank.

And then Leach started to get red. "Fitz," he said hotly, "I've danced to your tune for two years now. I've had many a chance to hang the deadwood on you, but I've not been a hog. I've kept in line and taken your orders, and I aim to from now on."

"Then where'd the horse come from?" Fitz said gently. "He was being ridden by the men who took that beef."

"I tell you he could have been stole!"

"By whom, then?" Fitz drawled. Now his voice got ugly. "When I hired you, Leach, you promised me that you'd keep these small rustlers in order, and have them let me alone. Apparently"—and here his voice was dry, thrusting —"you're losing your ability to keep on top in this county, Leach. Maybe somebody has an idea that you've got a little soft, a little easy. What do you think?"

"I'd like to see 'em claim it!" Leach said uglily.

"What do you call this, then? They stole a herd of my cattle and put the blame on you. Either that, or your men think you're soft, too. Do they?"

Leach took a shuffling step toward Fitz, his face dark with anger. "They do what I tell 'em!" he said thickly. "They aren't crossin' me. They know it'd be worth their life if they did."

"Then who is? These smalltime rustlers you thought you could kick around?"

"I still can!"

Fitz rose now. He came scarcely to Leach's shoulder, but there was a look of hard and implacable command in his eyes and on his face that told Blue that Fitz was the stronger man, always had been, always would be.

"Leach," Fitz said mildly, "I can't use a second-rater. I've made money for you, and I'll make more. But not if you can't keep your men in line. If you're through, get out while you still have a chance. If you aren't licked, then straighten this out. Get back my cattle for me and see that the man responsible is punished." He paused. "And Leach, if you're considering stepping into my shoes, don't. I've taken care of a dozen like you in my day, and it wasn't any trouble—only a little messy."

He stepped past Leach and out the door, closing it gently behind him. For a long minute, Leach stood in the middle of the floor, clenching and unclenching his fists, his face hard and savage and entirely readable.

Blue shifted his weight on the desk and cleared his throat.

"Don't get any ideas, Leach," he said softly.

Leach looked at him now, and there was bewilderment in his eyes. "But I ain't. I know when I'm well off. But I don't have any idea who took them cattle, not a one."

"Find out."

"I aim to."

Blue smiled faintly. "But don't ever get any ideas about Fitz, Leach. He goes with good people here. His credit is good, he's polite, the decent women like him, and he acts considerable like a dude sometimes. But don't let that fool you." He jerked a thumb over his shoulder. "Out there at the Bar 33, he hasn't got what you'd rightly call a crew of punchers. Once, just for fun, I added up how much reward money I'd collect if I'd take that Bar 33 crew, nail 'em up in a boxcar, and ship 'em back to where they were wanted. The reward money came to over a hundred thousand dollars."

Leach was listening, his eyes veiled.

"Fitz sends for them. He gives them protection, work, and good wages, until things have cooled off for them. Nobody knows their right names except him—and sometimes me. They ain't common gun fighters, Leach—they're killers. Tested, wanted, gun-slick, hair-trigger killers. So don't get any ideas. And if I was you, I'd see that them cattle was back at the Bar 33 in pretty short order."

"I will."

When Leach stepped out onto the street, he was considerably chastened—and he was angry, too. He knew that what Baily Blue told him about Fitz was true. Without ever raising his voice, Fitz could put more genuine fear into Leach than an army of ordinary men with guns.

Leach went into the bar at Prince's Keno Parlor and downed a stiff drink. Then he walked to the gambling-tables, where four of his men were playing an idle hand of poker.

"Come along," he told them.

One puncher, young, tall, with several days' growth of reddish stubble on his face, threw down his cards and looked up at Leach. "More work?"

Leach nodded grimly. "Plenty, Mick."

Chapter Sixteen: RUSTLERS' WAR

ONCE ON THE ROAD TO THE RUNNING W, Leach motioned Mickey Hogan to drop behind the others. Mickey was Leach's foreman, his top hand and gun fighter. It was Mickey who enabled Leach to keep peace among his twenty hands—saddle bums and saloon riffraff.

"How much time did Fitz give us?" Mickey asked when

Leach had finished.

"He never said."

"I'll need a couple of days, anyway. You got any ideas?"

"Well, there's them Winkler brothers up in that old Ophir mine. They're a tough crew and they don't like us much."

Mickey shook his head. "Maybe not, but they're plumb scared of us. They're out."

Leach named a list of men known as rustlers, but at each name, Mickey shook his head. Nevertheless, when they reached the Running W, Mickey took only the time to change horses before he rode off with five of his men. For Leach, the rest of that day and the next was intolerable. The longer Mickey stayed away, the more certain Leach grew that he was having no luck in tracking down the rustlers.

And that was true in the beginning. Mickey's first visit was to the Winkler boys up in the old abandoned Ophir mine. They were insolent, but they offered an alibi which Mickey had to accept; three of them were down sick. With their blankets pulled around them, rifles slacked in their arms, they stood in the doorway and faced Mickey and his five riders.

"All right," Mickey said. "I reckon you're tellin' the truth. But if I thought you wasn't—"

"You'd blow our heads off," Winkler said. "Well, ride on, Hogan. You've come to the wrong place. When we steal anything you want, we'll admit it and be ready to scrap for it. You can tell that to your boss."

"I believe you," Mickey said mildly, and wheeled his horse out.

So Mickey made the rounds. On the afternoon of the second day he and his riders pulled up at Cass Briggs's place in the bottomlands of a creek over on the west edge of the county.

Cass was drunk and belligerent. "Steal Fitz's stuff?" he said thickly. "Why, why shouldn't a man? His beef will walk just as good as another man's, won't it?"

Mickey regarded him thoughtfully. "Take a *pasear* around the corrals, boys," he said to his men.

Cass straightened up. "Wait a minute," he said loudly. "You'll find tracks over there, but no beef. I had five head here until last night."

"Whose beef?"

"Kennicott's," Cass answered sullenly.

Mickey said, "Look around, boys."

While they were gone, Mickey watched Cass, whose increasingly furtive air he could not quite understand. Mickey, in the course of his business, was pretty well acquainted with these shifty, closemouthed men who practiced on a small scale what Leach Wigran did on a large one. He knew their hide-outs, their markets, their methods, their needs, and their characters. It was another world remote from the brisk and businesslike air of Cosmos, but one in which Mickey was thoroughly versed.

The Running W riders returned. "There's been cattle out there all right."

"How many?"

"I dunno."

Mickey returned his attention to Cass. "I haven't seen you in town much lately, Cass."

"I been here."

"You couldn't have been somewhere else—say over on Bar 33 range—with George Winkler, could you?"

"I tell you, I been here," Cass said irritably.

"Or over the Calicoes in Warms," Mickey went on idly. "Maybe these bad rains up in the Calicoes is what stove up those Winkler boys." Mickey was talking idly, hit or miss, giving little attention to what he said. But he saw now that something he had said had touched Cass. Cass tried to look him in the eye, but failed.

"I was here," Cass said sullenly.

"But with the Winkler boys, though."

Cass spat. "All right, what if they was over?"

"So they were?"

Cass straightened up defiantly. "Anything wrong with asking your friends over to have a few drinks?" When Mickey said nothing, he added, "They got drunk and slept outside. I couldn't help that, could I?"

Mickey didn't answer immediately. Presently, he said,

"That's funny, Cass, that you five should have been together just for a parley." He paused. "So you did drive the beef over to Warms?"

"We did not!" Cass said hotly. "I sold 'em my share for the price of a couple of bottles."

Mickey said quickly, "Your share of what beef?"

"Kennicott's."

"I thought you said you only got five head."

"That was my share, I said. We worked it together."

"I hadn't heard anything about it in town," Mickey said gently. "Usually Kennicott squawks the loudest."

"He don't know it," Cass mumbled.

Mickey let his hand fall to his gun. "Cass," he said gently, "you're lyin'. What did you do with that Bar 33 beef? Drive it over to Warms?"

"I dunno what you're talkin' about," Cass said earnestly. "Don't get so quick, Mickey. Come in and have a drink. I tell you it wasn't no Bar 33 beef. I dunno whose it was. I was drunk, and so was they. We just took it from over west of town and drove it down here in the breaks, and then we come home and we was drunk for a couple of days. I sold 'em my share."

Mickey drew his gun, raised it. "Cass, you and the Winklers took that Bar 33 beef. None of you've been around Cosmos for a week now. The Winkler boys are stove up from that mountain rain. Nobody's missin' beef except Fitz. Are you goin' to tell me you stole it?"

"I didn't!" Cass cried.

Mickey smiled and leveled his gun. Cass made a lunge to get inside the house, but Mickey's gun roared before Cass could make a move.

Slowly, Cass started to claw at his chest and then he sat down abruptly, and his head sagged down on his chest.

Mickey regarded him coldly. "I never thought he'd have the nerve," he said mildly. He shrugged. "Well, the beef's gone. Let's go back to the Winklers'."

It was midnight before Mickey rode into the Running W. He and his riders had a little trouble with the Winklers, had had to burn them out, which took a little time. However, Mickey had a feeling of a job well done as he lifted his saddle on the corral poles and walked toward the house.

The front room of the Running W was bare and cluttered with gear and filthy with dust and papers. At Mickey's entrance, Leach jumped to his feet, his hand traveling toward his gun. By the light of the single lamp Leach looked deathly pale.

Mickey, puzzled, closed the door behind him. "What's the matter, Leach? You're spooky."

Leach regarded him with red-rimmed, bloodshot eyes. "An hour after you left, one of the boys rode in with word that the herd of beef we was holdin' for Fitz is stole, too."

Mickey said softly, "Stole?"

"Drove over the Calicoes. I been out trackin' it. But it was took to Warms, sure as hell."

"How long had it been gone?"

"A couple of days."

Mickey sank into a chair, and he and Leach looked at each other. "Then I must've made a mistake," Mickey said quietly, and he told Leach about Cass and the Winklers. Leach didn't even show interest. He sat there, his head sunk on his chest, staring at the table. Presently, he said, "Mickey, I can make this good with Fitz. I mean I got the money to do it, but"—and he raised harried eyes to regard Mickey—"what am I goin' to tell him? That they've got us on the run?"

"Who?"

"I wish I knew," Leach said savagely. "Fitz ain't pleasant to face. This time he's going to be wild."

Mickey thought a long moment. "Tell him you found Cass and the Winkler boys with the beef high up in the Calicoes. You took care of them, all right, and then you got to thinkin' and you decided to drive the stuff over to Warms—all of it, so long as you was close as you was. Then give him the money. What can he say?"

"He'll know I'm lyin'."

"He'd never know I was lyin'," Mickey said quietly.

Leach seemed not to hear this for several moments, and then he raised his head with a jerk. "That's it, Mickey! You tell him. Can you do it?"

"I never seen the lie I couldn't tell with a straight face," Mickey boasted quietly. "Sure I'll tell him."

"Right now. You ride over right now."

"Wait till tomorrow," Mickey drawled. "That'll give us time enough to have drove the beef over and come back."

Mickey started out at sunup for the Bar 33. At dark he was not back. He did not return that night, nor the next day. At midnight he was still not back. Leach, his eyes frantic, paced up and down the room, listening occasionally.

Sometime that night, as Leach lay on the rough and soiled sofa, staring at the ceiling, a thunderous knock on the door brought him to his feet with a leap, gun out.

He waited a moment, and then crossed to the door, listening, his hand on the knob. Then, gathering himself, he yanked the door open.

Something was standing there on the sill. Instinctively, protectively, wildly, Leach fired, but the body did not move. It simply toppled into the room at Leach's feet.

Leach looked down at it. It was Mickey. He was dead and stiff. On his chest was pinned a note, and, stooping slowly, Leach read it.

This was a mistake, Leach. Get that beef back or get out.

And Leach, trembling there in the guttering flame of the lamp, knew that war was declared, and he was afraid.

Chapter Seventeen: GUNFIRE BY NIGHT

WHEN TIP ROGERS WAKENED and struck a match to look at his watch, it was seven o'clock. He knew that if he was to get down to the dining-room and eat supper before it closed, he would have to hurry with his shave. Two days and one night in the saddle heading a posse had left him stiff and sore, but he was refreshed after fourteen hours of sleep.

Down in the lobby and heading for the dining-room, he thought of Nora inside, and his face settled into gravity. He knew that she must hate him now for the stand he had taken against Johnny, and he hated it, too, but the honesty in him would not let him do otherwise.

The dining-room was almost empty. Major Fitz and Bledsoe were seated at a side table in the corner, and Major Fitz's harsh and dogmatic voice could be heard the length of the dining-room.

Tip took a table, and Nora, who had been standing listening to Major Fitz, came over to take his order. Surprisingly, she smiled at him, and Tip smiled warmly in return. "Too late to get anying to eat, Nora?"

Nora shook her head. "No, I had the cook save something for you, Tip. Hungry?"

"Watch me."

When she returned with his food and sat down opposite him, he observed her carefully. She was a little pale, but her eyes looked bright, almost feverish, and her talk and even her actions were animated. Tip made a vow that he would not bring into the conversation any mention of things that might upset her, such as his activities of the last few days.

Nora, however, spoiled this resolution with her first question.

"Did you have any luck with the posse, Tip?" she asked.

Tip looked up at her, his face coloring. "Of course not. If I had, I'd have brought them in."

"Not shot them?"

Tip shook his head. "Why should I? I liked Johnny Hendry. Maybe he didn't do what he was accused of, but he'll never prove his innocence by running away."

There was a quizzically probing expression in her eyes. She said, "You'd have brought him back to stand trial, then—for his own good."

Tip grinned and shook his head. "No, I'll be honest. Not for his good, but for mine. I won't pass up a chance to find out who robbed the bank and got the gold."

Nora didn't answer for a moment, and then she said quietly, "Perhaps that's what he needs, Tip. Somebody ought to scare him, to make him prove his innocence, even if he didn't take the gold."

Tip laid down a fork and stared at her, as if he had not

heard rightly. Nora laughed a little self-consciously and said, "Why not? Johnny treats other people that way. Why should he expect more in return?"

Her voice shook a little with anger, but Tip was too much in love to see that Nora's displeasure with Johnny Hendry was dictated by her mind. It was something she felt—and tried to feel—because she thought she should.

"Treats them how?"

"Oh, he makes snap judgments, believes the worst of people. He's unfair and unjust."

"You think that's the kind of treatment I've given him?"

Nora nodded and said, "A little. But I can't blame you, Tip. You're only doing your job."

"And one I don't like," Tip said quietly. Nora did not answer. Tip ate in silence, frowning at his plate. Suddenly, he raised his eyes to Nora's face. "Believe me, Nora, I don't like this. I know how you feel about Johnny, and I could understand why you'd hate me for what I'm doing."

"How do I feel about Johnny?" Nora asked bluntly, looking him in the eye.

"Why—why—I've been seeing you for over a year, Nora, ever since I came here—when I ask you to marry me, you just laugh. And you've been just as nice, even nicer, to Johnny Hendry. But when he walks in the room, you're different. He's the one. My name could be Ted or Jim or Bob and you'd treat me the same. Don't you see? I may be one in a hundred but Johnny is one in a million—to you. Maybe he always will be."

All the while Tip was speaking, the flush on Nora's face was deepening. When he was finished, Nora said swiftly, "Tip, that's not true! You've been imagining it! I—I don't love Johnny Hendry. Maybe for a while I was infatuated with him, but I don't love him! And I've tried to treat you both the same—because I really do feel the same about you!"

Her eyes blazed.

Tip's mouth sagged open, and he could not speak for a moment.

"I know but—"

"And that's not because Johnny is in trouble!" Nora said defiantly. "I'm just as loyal to him as I ever was, Tip! I've talked to him since he was framed! If I wanted to, I could take you to his hide-out! But I won't! So you see, I'm not deserting him in his hard luck. Only, I don't want you or anybody else, Tip Rogers, to think I love him. I don't!"

Wisely, Tip held his silence, but he allowed himself a broad grin, and as Nora watched him, the fire died out in her eyes, and she began to smile. Suddenly they both laughed together.

"Finish your eating, Tip," Nora said. "I'm almost ashamed of myself."

Tip lifted his plate off to one side and leaned both hands on the table, and he began to speak in utter seriousness.

"Today, Nora, when I got in from the mountains, I went up to the Esmerella. Sammons, the manager, had some news for me." He paused, watching her. "He said the Esmerella will have to close. I'm out of a job. He offered me one with the same company down near the Mexican border. I'm not going."

"But Tip, why not?"

"Because I found out something tonight. If you like me as well as you do Johnny Hendry, then I'm going to stay here until you like me better. And the only time I'll take that job down there is when I can write the manager and tell him that he'll have to provide quarters for a new superintendent—and wife. Her name will be Nora."

Nora smiled shyly. "You're nice, Tip."

"Nora, will you marry me?"

"I—I don't know, Tip," Nora said. "Everything has happened so quickly. Tip, give me time. Please."

Tip reached out for her hand and spread her fingers out in his palm. On his own little finger was a ring, its band of silver, its stone of deep-blue turquoise. He took it off and slipped it quickly on her middle finger.

Tip said gently, "The Indian who gave that to me, Nora, told me that as soon as my greatest luck had come, to pass the ring on to somebody else I wished luck for. If you take it my luck has come. Will you wear it?"

His hand relinquished hers, as if he didn't want to put the slightest pressure on her.

Slowly, Nora raised her eyes to his. "Is this an engagement ring, Tip?"

"It's for you to name," Tip said gravely. "*I* want it to be that."

Nora looked down at the ring. It was beautiful, its stone cool and smooth and deep, but she was thinking of what this ring symbolized, what she could make it symbolize—a new life with a man she liked, a man who was steady and honest and patient, whom she could depend on, who would not change over the years, who, while he would not make her laugh and cry and be angry with him, would be as predictable as a calendar, as steady as the sun in its course. It would be refuge and security, something she sorely needed and wanted now. But did she love him? She looked up at his face, and saw Tip's quiet love for her shining out of eyes that were honest and very grave. For a moment, she remembered Johnny's eyes, careless, mocking, affectionate, lighthearted, quick as mercury—

"Let's call it an engagement, Tip," she said softly, stubbornly, and she hardly realized she had said it until she felt Tip's kiss on her lips. She laughed then, and pushed Tip back in his seat.

"Your supper is cold, and you've got to eat, Tip," she told him, but Tip was only looking at her, filling his eyes with the beauty of her. Nora rose and went out into the kitchen.

While she was gone, a man entered the dining-room and looked around him, waved to Tip, and went over to Fitz and Bledsoe's table. It was Les MacMahon, a tall, slim young man in careful black clothes who studied law at night and waited on customers at Bledsoe's store in the daytime. Tip was friendly with him and liked him. MacMahon talked quietly with Fitz and Bledsoe for some minutes, and Nora returned with hot food for Tip. She sat down by him again and made Tip eat.

Presently MacMahon left Bledsoe's table and came over

to speak to Tip and Nora. "It is true the Esmerella has closed down, Tip?" he asked. His sharp face was inquisitive, amiable. Tip nodded. "What are you going to do, leave town?"

Tip looked at Nora and smiled slightly. "No chance. I'll do something around here."

MacMahon leaned down and talked quietly. "I just had a funny experience, Tip. Six men—I don't know who they were—came in the store and started buying supplies— mining-tools, blankets, grub, black powder, and such. One of them, the man doing the buying, was drunk. He started talking to me about their claims, said they were the richest he'd ever seen. He told me quite a bit about them before the boss came over and shut him up."

Tip leaned forward, his eyes intent and excited.

"Did he say where they were?"

MacMahon flushed. "I know this sounds silly, Tip, but to begin with, they bought about a thousand dollars' worth of supplies. This drunk was bragging around that their assay showed higher than any mine that was being operated around here. I thought it was bluff, but when they'd gone out, I went over to the claim-recording office. Sure enough, six men had just filed claims together there. Furthermore, they just bought a dozen pack mules from McGrew down at the feed stable. Does that sound like it's a bluff? They paid cash for everything."

"It doesn't," Tip conceded. "Were they mining men?"

"Looked it."

"What do you want me to do?" Tip asked, interested now.

"You're free now. You know minerals. Get their locations at the recorder's office and go out and if it looks good, file on some claims. I just told Bledsoe and Fitz. They said if I could get a good man to look it over, to put their names down. I'll want one, too." He indicated Nora. "So will Nora, won't you?"

"Whatever Tip thinks," Nora answered.

Tip scowled. He had been around mining camps long enough to understand that fabulous mines had been discovered on just such thin rumors. A drunken boast, an incautious poker bet, a brag on a street corner had been the start of many a paying mine. He was free now with no job to hold him in town. Besides that, he hoped he would soon have a wife to support, and it had been Tip's dream that some day he would own a small paying mine. Perhaps this was the chance he had been waiting for.

"I'll do it," he said slowly, "only don't be disappointed when I come back and tell you it's phony."

MacMahon drew up a chair, and soon they were deep in mining talk. MacMahon had copied out the claim locations, and now he gave them to Tip. They discussed Tip's outfit, his expenses, and such, and while they talked, Nora listened, content only to watch Tip. She liked his quiet gravity, the slow and careful way that he arrived at decisions, the temperance of his speech, and the dry humor that crept into much he said. And she knew, too, that he would never change, that this was the way he was made, and the way he would always be. Moreover, she knew deep within her, that if her life with him would be dull at times it would be a generous life, with rewards and riches at the end.

Bledsoe and Fitz came over, and Nora rose and went about her business of clearing off the dishes. Later, when she returned to the dining-room, Tip was at the door, waiting for her. He drew her out into the dark lobby and said, "How does it sound, darling?"

"I don't know, Tip. What do you think?"

"I think I'd be willing to gamble anything to get money and presents and things to give you," Tip said quietly.

Nora squeezed his hand. "Not for that alone, Tip. You want to get ahead. You always would. Why don't you take a chance?"

"I am." He folded her in his arms and kissed her, and it was so strange that Nora almost protested, then smiled, and Tip vanished up the stairs. Back in the dining-room, MacMahon and Bledsoe were taking leave of Fitz. They were going to go down to the store to assemble Tip's outfit.

Major Fitz beckoned to Nora, and she came back to the table. "Sit down," he said. "I want to talk to you. Have I been drinking too much, or did I see that young scalawag kiss you, Nora?"

"You did," Nora admitted, blushing. "I like him, Major Fitz."

"Hmm. So do I. But I don't kiss him."

"I mean I like him awfully well."

"Better than Johnny?"

Nora looked him steadily in the eye. "Better than Johnny," she said quietly. "It's—it's just that Tip is steadier and more considerate than Johnny."

"Remember, Johnny was an orphan, raised in a rough town and with rough people, Nora," Fitz pointed out gently.

Nora patted his hand. She could not help but compare Major Fitz's tolerance and justice to Johnny's hotheadedness and his quick anger. Here while Johnny was hunting ways to prove Major Fitz a crook, Fitz was pleading Johnny's case with her, and a deep wave of bitterness passed through her. Whatever doubts she had had as to preferring Tip to Johnny—and they were few and dim, she thought—were vanished now. She felt anger toward Johnny, and pity and quiet affection for this loyal man across from her.

"I understand all that, Major Fitz, but it isn't as if I liked a man for his manners or for his polish."

"I know that. You like me," Fitz said, and smiled a little, "and I'm just a roughneck."

"And I was raised on a ranch," Nora said. "Maybe I wouldn't know good manners if I saw them."

"Nonsense. You're a lady because you can't help it."

Nora squeezed his hand, and there were almost tears in her eyes. "Don't be hard on me, old friend. I'm just trying to do what I think is best."

"I know you are. They are both fine boys." He shook his head slowly. "I wouldn't undertake to say which you'd be the happiest with Nora—if you can be happy with any of us men. Tip is steady, maybe a little bit dull. And Johnny is wild and a hellion, but more to my taste. But you're the one that's choosing. You stick to what you like and you—"

Fitz stopped speaking, and his eyes shuttled quickly to the lamp overhead. Its flame was guttering, as if a sudden draft had struck it.

And then, explosively, Major Fitz shoved hard on the table, so that it slammed against Nora and carried her over backward to the floor. He dodged aside, snaking out of the chair just as the blast of a shotgun filled the room with terrible noise.

Major Fitz, lying on the floor, whipped a hand to his shoulder holster, flicked out his gun, and in one snap shot at the lamp overhead plunged the room in darkness.

Then, on his knees, he swiveled his gun to one of the back windows and emptied it in thundering peroration, filling the room with the savage hammering of his gunfire.

When the gun was empty, he paused and waited. There was no movement, not a sound from that partially opened window.

Fitz pulled himself slowly to his feet. His knees were shaky, and he was angry at himself for the sickness deep in his belly that he recognized as fear.

"Nora!" Fitz whispered. "Are you hurt?"

"I'm all right," Nora said weakly. "What happened?"

Fitz walked over to her and lifted her to her feet in the darkness.

"If they'd hit you, Nora, I'd never have forgiven myself."

"But who was it?"

"I don't know," Fitz answered simply. "Evidently I have my enemies, like every other man."

The dining-room door opened, and the clerk came running in with a lamp. By its light, Fitz looked at the table. Its cloth was tattered, its top channeled with the blast of buckshot. And the lines it had drilled in the table top told their own story. By shoving the table against Nora and upsetting her, Fitz had saved her from taking the full charge of the buckshot in her body.

She looked at him, her eyes still wild with fright, and he folded her in his arms, trying to quiet her hysterical sobs while the clerk looked on in bewildered silence.

And looking at the scarred table top, Major Fitz knew that Leach Wigran had taken up the gauntlet.

Chapter Eighteen: FOOL'S GOLD

BACK AT HIS CAVE, Pick waited. He resolved to give Johnny another week before he rode over to the other side of the county and asked for news. If Johnny's self-made laws had stuck, then Pick's test was finished.

But while Pick was waiting, something happened. Days ago he had given up hope of ever finding the claim jumper again. Pick surmised that the man would take the ore down to Hugo and, when a less than mediocre report was handed him, he would forget the whole matter. Pick never expected to see the man again.

But one morning, several days back, at the very crack of dawn, when Pick pulled himself up to the rock rim and glanced down at the canyon bottom, he saw a campfire. Quickly Pick hid his rope, then made a wide circle up the canyon and took the trail to the bottom. By clean sun-up, he was hidden in the brush a hundred yards away from the campfire.

He counted six men, none of whom he recognized, but he did recognize what they set about doing just as soon as the light permitted. They were erecting claim monuments, piling rock, flattening poles, writing names and dates on these poles.

Pick observed it all with quiet amazement, noticing that the leader carefully consulted a paper. When they were finished, they had his test pits blanketed with their claims. Moreover, they had the canyon bottom well blanketed, too.

As soon as they were finished, they broke camp, gathered their horses, and moved out of the canyon down the mountain. Pick, after giving them ample time to be out of sight, came out of his hiding-place and examined the monuments. His leathery old face was grave, puzzled, and his bewilderment increased as he read all the names and found none of them familiar. Finished, he packed his pipe and squatted against a rock, sucking the rank fragrance of the smoke into his lungs.

This could mean just one thing. Whoever the man was

who took the ore samples had convinced these men that there was considerable gold here. He had sold them worthless claims.

"The fools," Pick said aloud, contemptuously. "The poor fools." Raised in the rough-and-ready school of the desert, Pick had no criticism for the man who sold the claims; it was for these poor misguided fools who had bitten on sucker bait that he felt contempt and scorn. Once, long ago, when he was starved and broke and sick, Pick himself had resorted to this very business of selling fools worthless claims. But in those days, Pick had taken the trouble to salt his ore with gold dust, so that the assay was good.

And remembering this, Pick had an idea. It made him smile, even laugh, so that his lean old body shook with silent mirth. Rising, he walked over to the test pits and looked down into them. He knew almost every rock and pebble down there. Outside of a tiny show of color which would not net a man a day's working wages, the stuff was worthless.

Again Pick laughed, his eyes musing. "Danged if I won't," he murmured. "An old man like me deserves some fun. Besides, this settin' is gettin' on my nerves."

He returned to his cave, packed a meager two days' food in his rucksack, and then struck off up the mountains toward the south.

Two days later he returned, his long and easy stride just as tireless and steady as it had been the hour he left. He went immediately to the cave, after first looking down at the canyon floor to see if the prospectors had returned. They hadn't.

Once in the cave, he slung off his flat rucksack and drew from it five soft doeskin bags. These were filled. Then he took up his shotgun derringer and his ten remaining shells, stuffed them all in his pockets and climbed up to the rock rim.

Twenty minutes later he stood beside the test pits again, that same smile still on his face.

Then he began his preparations. From the bottom of

one of the test pits, he brought up a quarter hatful of the loose volcanic breccia that made up this dike. With the butt of his derringer, he granulated a quantity of it on a flat rock. Finished, he emptied the contents of the five doeskin sacks into this heap of rubble and mixed it thoroughly. The doeskin sacks contained tiny nuggets of pure gold, which he had taken from his secret claims high up in the Calicoes.

Next, he turned his attention to the shotgun shells. From each, he pulled out the wadding and dumped the shot in his pocket. And each one, he filled with this mixture of gold and volcanic rock, and the smile on his face was broad and amused. Once the wadding was back in the gold-loaded shells, Pick cleaned up around him, so that not a sign of his activity was left.

Then he walked to the first test pit, loaded the derringer, aimed it at the pit and fired. He knew that the force of the shot would imbed the gold in the bottom and sides of the pit, and scatter it so that it would look as if it had been distributed by nature. At each of the other five pits, he did the same thing. With four shells left, he cast about, looking for a likely place to spend them. The dike continued on past the last test pit for about a hundred feet, and Pick, his gun held slanting toward the ground, covered it conscientiously with the rest of his shells.

His work done, he surveyed the job, an image in his mind of what would happen now. "They'll find color, have an assay, get a good report, and on the strength of it, they'll move a lot of equipment in. They'll tell their friends, and there'll be that many more suckers." And he laughed again, for Pick was a jealous old man. He had given a lifetime to gold seeking; he hated to see fools degrade a proud profession, and this was his revenge. The fact that it was costing him a thousand dollars did not matter.

Once that was done, Pick left that canyon for another one closer down to the foothills where his horse was staked out. That day and the following night, Pick rode straight for the north side of the county.

This time the first person he met was a woman driving

a buckboard, a child on the seat beside her. Pick hailed her, and they gossiped, and casually Pick learned what had happened to Johnny. "You mean they claim he blew the bank?" Pick asked incredulously after the woman finished her recital.

"They did, and it was a cryin' shame," the woman said grimly. "It means that sooner or later all decent folks will move out of the county. Why, just this mornin' my boy come in with news that some of our beef had been run off durin' the night. That's where I been, to tell Baily Blue about it."

Pick said nothing, his face hard and pensive. He was not listening to her.

"He didn't do nothin' about it except give promises," the woman continued.

"What?" Pick said, jerked out of his reverie.

"I say, he only promised me he'd tend to it."

"Who?"

"Baily Blue."

"Tend to what?"

"My cows that was stole."

Pick looked at her blankly, almost irritably. "Cows stole?"

The woman regarded him with mild exasperation and shook the reins of the team. "Pop, you been livin' alone too long," the woman told him, gently but firmly. "In another year, you won't be fit to run around loose. Go see folks. Get acquainted. Have company. Why, you know you—"

Pick gulped miserably, wheeled his horse, and headed off into the wayside brush, with the woman watching his departure in grim disapproval. "Cranky old devil," she muttered at his back and whipped up the team.

Pick's prank with the shotgun shells started something that he was to not fully understand for some time to come. The day after Pick left for the north end of the county, Big Westfall, Fitz's man from Warms, returned to the canyon and his claim with his five men and the pack train of supplies and lumber and tools.

The first thing Westfall spotted when he entered the canyon was a small tent at its head. The *rap, rap* of a pick came to him, and he reined up and threw a leg over the saddle horn and waited for his companions. Westfall had come by his nickname rightly; he was a giant of a man with a broad, aggressive jaw and fists that were massive and work-worn. Even motionless he had an air of command, and when he spoke, his voice was soft, low-pitched, as if men were used to listening to him and heeding what he said.

"Company," he said mildly, as one of his companions drew up beside him.

"Now how did that happen?" the other asked.

"Bud shot off his mouth considerable in Cosmos. Maybe somebody heard him."

"It don't matter, does it?"

"Not a hoot. I'll go talk to him."

While the others unpacked the mules, Westfall rode on up the canyon until he was by the tent.

Tip Rogers saw him and waved and left his work to come over.

"How'd you stumble on this?" Westfall asked, indicating the workings. He saw already that the monuments were up on Tip's claim. Tip grinned up. "Through your men. One was drunk, I believe."

"That's right."

"Well, I figured even a drunk can tell the truth. According to what I heard, you thought you had a good thing."

"We have. What have you got?"

"A blamed good thing!" Tip said excitedly. "I haven't put an awful lot of work on it, but it sure looks good." He went on to say that while eating his lunch today, he had idly picked up his shovel and found flecks of loose gold on it. This of course was the result of Pick's salting.

"I believe it," Westfall said. "I'm glad you've run into it, too. There ought to be enough to pass around."

They chatted a moment longer, and Westfall went back to his claims. Tip returned to work. He was sacking ore now, taking samples from a dozen different places along the dike. It was hard to work here, knowing that each hour he put in here in the canyon would postpone just that much longer telling Nora about his luck. For Tip, sober mining man that he was, felt deep within him that he had struck it at last, and that riches were in sight.

That night he fell into his blankets, exhausted, and early next morning he was on the trail, his five pack horses loaded with the sacks of ore for assaying. Next night, weary and footsore, he entered Cosmos, and the first place he stopped was at Hugo's assay office.

Hugo was working in the rear, but at Tip's knock, he came out and helped him unload the horses.

"So *you've* got the gold bug now?" Hugo observed mildly as he carefully marked each heavy sack at the table inside. He turned up the lamp wick, and Tip sat down.

"I've always had it," Tip said, and the excitement in his voice made Hugo look up to regard him.

"You sound excited," Hugo said.

"Man, I am. Open one of the sacks and take out a handful of that stuff."

"Come off it," Hugo scoffed. "What kind of a bonanza do you think you've discovered?"

"See for yourself. Open a sack."

Hugo, tolerantly grinning, did. And he drew out a handful of volcanic breccia, that ore which he had been looking for these many days now. This was the ore—unmistakably identified by the presence of volcanic breccia—that Hugo and Johnny Hendry had hoped would lead them to Picket-Stake's killer. And hoping to attract that killer, Miller had doctored up his assay report. But the plan hadn't worked out. The bushwhacker had disappeared, and Hugo's tricked-up assay started a false gold rush.

He stared at it for a long time, composing his face, and then he looked up at Tip. If there was any suspicion in his mind—and there was—it did not show in his face.

"It looks good, Tip," he said mildly. "Where'd it come from?" Tip told him, but that meant nothing. "How long have you been working on this?" Hugo asked.

"Four days."

"Find it yourself?"

Tip only grinned and shook his head. "That's what's

funny," he said, and he proceeded to tell Hugo about MacMahon's overhearing the drunk in Bledsoe's store. As he went on, Hugo breathed a quiet sigh of relief, for he had always liked Tip Rogers, and he did not want to believe that Tip was Pick's killer and claim jumper. But this man at Tip's diggings surely was the killer, the man Johnny Hendry would have given his soul to lay hands on. As Tip talked, Hugo began to wonder about this ore. When a sample of it had last been in his hands, it showed itself practically worthless, but now that it appeared again, it was obviously shot with gold. He frowned and scratched his head wearily.

Hugo heard Tip say, "But why am I wasting time telling you this, Hugo? I've got somebody else that'll be less cold-blooded than you. Good night, Hugo."

"So long, Tip." Hugo watched him leave, and for several minutes afterward, did not move. He felt his heart pounding steadily with the excitement in his blood. Right here he held the secret to Pick's death.

But where was Johnny? Where had he been for five days? Hugo didn't know, and behind the thought, there was a fear that he would not admit. Perhaps Johnny Hendry was dead. If not, why didn't he come?

Chapter Nineteen: TROUBLE FOR LEACH WIGRAN

ALWAYS A LIGHT SLEEPER, Hank was roused by the sound of crunching gravel. For a moment, he raised himself in his blankets and listened, then recognized the sound as that of two approaching horses. He knew this would be Johnny Hendry and Turk Hebron back from Warms, and he rolled out of the blankets and had a fire going by the time they pulled into the camp among the malpais.

Both were drawn and gaunt, but Turk was smiling. He met Hank with a shout. Johnny's greeting was more reserved, but Hank had become used to that these last few days. Johnny rarely smiled any more, not since that night he had last met Nora up above town, Hank remembered.

Hank helped them unsaddle and turn the horses into the tiny corral; then they all came back to the fire. Putting on the pot of coffee, Hank looked at Johnny, squatting over the fire warming his hands. His face was smeared with a quarter-inch stubble of black beard, and his cheekbones were wind-reddened and prominent. A week in the saddle had leaned him down until he was as fine-drawn and taut as a wire; his eyes were quick and feverish and, somehow, dangerous.

"Well, what happened, Hank?" Johnny asked curtly. "What did Leach Wigran do? Tell us about it."

Turk was standing behind Johnny, his hat cuffed off his untidy red hair. There was an arrogant, daredevil look to Turk, as if he were enjoying every moment of this, which he was.

Hank regarded Johnny soberly. "I've finally got all the proof you want, Johnny."

Johnny yanked his gaze up from the fire. "On Fitz?"

"He's not only a rustler but a killer."

Turk ceased rolling his smoke, his attention riveted on Hank, who was talking now. "I hung around the box canyon until a Runnin' W rider come along. That took two days. This rider didn't waste no time. He beat it back to the Runnin' W that night. Next mornin', him and two others and Leach rode up. They picked up the trail of the cattle, but I knew they wouldn't get far because of that last rain. Sure enough, they come back before dark and I trailed 'em back to the house. Later, Mickey Hogan rode in with five of the boys. Him and Leach talked a long while that night. I know that because I sneaked up to the window and—"

"Did you hear what they said?"

"No. I couldn't get clost enough, but I didn't need to. I saw Leach was mighty worried. Next mornin', Mickey rode over to Major Fitz's. But first he hung around Cosmos a few hours gettin' enough whisky to face the major, I reckon. Anyway, along toward afternoon, he lit out for the Bar 33, and I picked him up at the other side of town. It was dark when he got there." He paused, watching Johnny. "I did hear what he said to Fitz. I got right up to the window in Fitz's office."

"Well, what did he say?" Johnny asked impatiently.

"He told Fitz that he'd found the big bunch of Bar 33 cattle. Him and Leach tracked them up the mountain and found that Cass Briggs and the Winkler boys had stole them. They fought with Cass and the Winklers and cleaned them out. Then him and Leach got to worryin' about drivin' all them cattle back to Fitz, and they decided it would be safer to drive 'em—along with Fitz's first herd—over to Warms and sell 'em. That's what they did, Mickey said, and he come over and laid the money on Fitz's desk."

"Well?"

"Fitz never said anything for a spell, and then he said, real quietlike, 'Does Leach expect me to swallow that, Mickey?' And right then, Mickey made his mistake. He was a little drunk, I reckon. He said, 'He don't care much whether you believe it or not, Fitz. It's the truth.' I heard a chair scrape then and all of a sudden Mickey made a funny kind of noise in his throat and there was a shot. I pulled back in the bushes then, and Fitz come out. He went over and got Carmody, and Carmody brought Mickey's body over to the horse and staked it on and rode off. I followed him. He camped in the Calicoes, come day. Next night he started out. At midnight he rode up to the Runnin' W, stood Mickey against Leach's door, knocked, and rode off back toward Bar 33."

"And what did Leach do?"

"Ten minutes later, he rousted out all hands and put guards around the place. He never moved until the next afternoon, then he saddled up and rode into Cosmos."

Johnny sat down and pulled out his tobacco sack, but he forgot to roll the cigarette. Hank watched him, looking occasionally at Turk, who was also waiting for Johnny to speak. Now that his suspicions were confirmed, Johnny was almost astonished. Believing Fitz a rustler and knowing it were two different things, and Johnny thought bitterly of what Nora had said to him that last night. For days now, he had ridden with a stubborn feeling of guilt, thinking, almost hoping, that perhaps he had been wrong. But now that he was proved right he did not feel any better. He didn't feel anything except bitterness at Nora

—that, and the grave responsibility of seeing Major Fitz punished.

"I'm hungry," he said quietly at last and Hank quit looking at him. He knew they would talk of this later. Pan bread and bacon and coffee were set out, and the three of them ate ravenously. Finished, a smoke rolled, Johnny leaned back against his saddle.

"What's the best plan?" he said abruptly. "We're three. Fitz and his crew are thirty, Leach and his outfit about twenty. We can't fight 'em all, can we? Why not play 'em against each other, like we have done?"

Hank said, "That's my idea."

"What about you, Turk?"

"Let 'em whittle each other down till they're our size," Turk said.

"In about twenty minutes, then," Johnny drawled, "we ride. And this time, we'll know what we're shootin' for."

Hank looked up at Turk. Hank had ridden long enough to know when a man had been in the saddle countless hours and was dead for sleep. Turk had that look now. He was starved for a good sleep, but Hank saw no sign of protest on his face. Johnny Hendry, when he wanted to, could drive a man hard, and he was wanting to now, Hank saw; and he sighed a little. This was really the beginning of trouble now.

Since Johnny had no means of knowing about Leach's attempted bushwhack of Major Fitz the night before, he reasoned that the next move would be Leach's, and that Leach would strike at the Bar 33. So, once they were clear of the malpais, mounted on fresh horses, Johnny headed down through the foothills for the Bar 33. As false dawn was breaking, they cached themselves in the brush of the ridge from which Hank had beheld that first suspicious parley in the corral lot of the Bar 33.

Johnny had the glasses. Hank and Turk lay down to sleep, and when then the first faint light of clean day broke, Johnny focused his glasses on the Bar 33. Already, he had seen the lights in the bunkhouse and the main house, and he was anxious to see what these betokened. His glasses told him. The whole Bar 33 crew was out in the corral lot, a cluster of them around the corral cutting out mounts. They were getting ready to ride.

Relentlessly, Johnny wakened Hank and handed him the glasses, saying, "What do you make of it?"

Hank looked a full minute and said, "Trouble for Leach Wigran."

Johnny took the glasses back. He picked out Major Fitz's horse, which was being saddled. Slowly the group took shape. As they mounted, Johnny began to count them. He could see only two men who were not ready to ride, and one of them was the cook. Surprised, Johnny studied them carefully, but again he arrived at the same count.

"He's a trustin' soul," Johnny murmured. "How many men do you see afoot, Hank?"

Hank looked and he reported two.

"Uh-huh," Johnny said softly. "Maybe our chance has come."

"Chance?"

"Wake up Turk."

Hank did, and Turk joined them, his eyes half closed for want of sleep. But as Johnny unfolded his plan, Turk's eyes opened wide, and he listened carefully. "Suppose we're seen?" Turk asked at the end.

"We won't be," Hank put in. "That one jasper will likely hit for this ridge to act as lookout, and he'll be asleep in a couple of hours. The cook will go back to the kitchen. Fitz ain't the kind of man who'll give anybody credit for thinkin' faster'n he does."

"Then what's holdin' us?" Turk growled.

They waited until the cavalcade of horsemen rode out of the Bar 33, headed for the foothills. Fitz, Johnny guessed, would take to cover, so as to keep his movements as secret as possible.

Then they got their own horses, mounted, rode along the side of the ridge toward the west. Soon the ridge petered out, but its bulk still remained between them and the house. Hank cut off straight across the flats until he came to an arroyo. "This is the one," he said. "This'll take us close."

They put their horses down into this dry stream bed, and Hank led off, first warning them to lean down over their saddle horns, so that their heads would not be visible above the banks of the arroyo. They rode in silence for a good twenty minutes, and as they progressed, the banks kept getting steeper and higher. Presently, Hank reined and motioned to the bank. "This is the closest spot."

Johnny dismounted, took off his hat, climbed the bank, and, where a clump of sagebrush raised its icy-green branches over the very lip of the arroyo, he stuck up his head.

The main house was only three hundred feet away. Between it and arroyo, there was a tangle of wild currant bushes which the major had left to serve as a kind of landscaping. The house was broadside to them, hiding the cookshack and most of the corrals.

Johnny beckoned them up, and crawled up himself. Then they started the careful approach to the house, keeping in the thick shelter of the currant bushes. Once they had achieved the side of the house, Johnny said, "Raise every window you can, Hank. And you and me, Turk, we'll gather up this dry grass."

A hundred sweeping winds had stacked tumbleweed at the base of every bush. They put them against the side of the house in a tinder-dry pile. As Hank raised each window —and none of them were locked—Turk and Johnny followed him with great armfuls of tumbleweed and dry brush, which they shoved inside. They worked fast and hard, and in ten minutes had contrived to pile an enormous amount of tinder inside the house. The rest was simple, and yet none of them wanted to strike a match.

Johnny, watching Hank's uneasy gaze, said grimly, "All right, I never asked a man to do a thing I wouldn't do."

"It ain't that," Hank muttered. "It's just— Oh, shucks, Johnny. This ain't no way to fight a man."

Johnny's hard eyes did not soften, but his voice was reasonable as he looked from Hank to Turk. "Nobody said it was. But you ain't fightin' a man—you're fightin' a jasper that'd shoot you in the back, and that'd steal a widow to starvation and laugh."

He whipped the match across his Levi's leg, and while

it was still flaring, he tossed it in the window. Soon Hank and Turk were at work. When, by hoisting themselves up to window level, they had made sure that the tumbleweed had caught, they returned to the arroyo, leaving the windows open to create a draft that would help kindle the fire.

In the arroyo, they wasted no time, but mounted at once and rode back the way they had come, again seeking the ridge.

When Johnny had the glasses again, he trained them on the house. Only the faintest smoke streamers were rising into the still air. The cook, busy at his work on the back porch of the cookshack, hadn't noticed yet. Soon the smoke started to darken, a sign that the fire had taken hold of wood and curtains and carpets. It was the other ranch hand who discovered the fire. He came running around the end of the cookshack, pointing frantically at the house, and the cook dropped his work to run with him.

They disappeared into the house, and the smoke at once increased as soon as the cross draft from the open door caught it. Almost immediately the cook and the puncher ran out again, coughing and rubbing their eyes.

Their attempts to put out the crackling flames were as ludicrous as they were futile. As soon as the water buckets from the cookshack and bunkhouse had been thrown through a window, the two of them realized the hopelessness of their fight, and stood, arms akimbo, watching the fire's hungry progress.

"That'll raise enough smoke for Fitz to see," Johnny said grimly. "And after that, he'll wonder why he ever waited this long to ride out after Leach."

The walls themselves were slow to catch since they were of solid logs flattened on both sides. But slowly and surely the interior was gutted, and the smoke that poured out rose in a dust-colored pillar to the cloudless sky.

It wasn't long before Hank, who had been watching in the direction where Fitz had ridden, turned and said, "And now, gents, we'd better ride. Here comes Fitz."

They didn't linger to see his arrival. Mounted, they turned east along the ridge, raised their horses to a smart trot, and headed for the mountains. The first step in fanning the Fitz-Wigran feud to open violence had been accomplished. And when thieves fall out—

The second step was to come later, and it was the fruit of the first. All day long, they traveled tirelessly and swiftly toward the Running W, so that it was late afternoon when they rode across Running W range. They crossed the road that ran between the hills to the Running W, and it was here that Johnny drew up.

"You've got your orders," he told them. "Scatter out. Give me the first shot. Watch out for any guards Leach has got out, and meet me on the same ridge where we watched the place before."

Hank and Turk rode north up one ridge, and Johnny crossed the road and went on up the other. He rode carefully in the timber, reining up occasionally to listen. He calculated his course as a long circle, which would bring him out above the Running W. Once, approaching the lip of a ridge, he dismounted and cautiously regarded the valley below him where the road ran. He saw the form of a horse in the trees below, and after a moment's search, picked out its owner crouched in the brush watching the road. Leach Wigran, at least, did not hold with the major's idea that the best defense is a good offense.

Johnny withdrew and widened his circle. Now he was on the downslope, approaching the basin from the west. His pace slowed now, he sought out a clearing where the Running W was in plain view. Then he reined up, drew his rifle from the saddle boot, and squatted beside his horse, rolling a smoke. When he finished it, his time was up and he set to business. Lying down in the short grass, he raised the sights on his rifle, leveled it, and then sent shot after shot whipping down the slope. The first shot only boomed hollowly against the house, but the next one knocked out a windowpane. A ranch hand who had been out in the wagon shed streaked for the house.

Johnny paused, listening. Another rifle across the valley was sending its flat and reaching whanging over the late-afternoon air; and even as Johnny smiled, the third one joined in. Reloading, he started shooting again and now that he had the range, he picked out window light after window light. A flurry of shots answered him from the house, but these were blind and aimless, mere bravado. When Johnny had exhausted half his shells, he rose, mounted his horse, and traveled along the ridge until he came to the spot where they had waited before. The other shots had ceased.

Observing the house, he saw no movement there. It was as if they were waiting for an open attack. Minutes later, he saw a horseman approach the valley on the far side and sit motionless in his saddle for many moments. Then this man put spurs to his horse and rode madly for the house and the shelter of a wagon shed. This was the first of the guards. In five minutes Hank arrived, and together they watching the second, third, and fourth guards approach the house in the same manner.

When Turk arrived, dusk had fallen, and he reported that he had almost been run down by a fifth guard hurrying for the security of the house.

This was as Johnny wanted it. He had planned to warn Leach to expect an attack, so that a surprise move on Major Fitz's part would not result in wiping out Leach and all his men. For Johnny's blood was up, and he was playing this hand with a strategy that would have done credit to Major Fitz.

"Why let Fitz clean out Leach or Leach clean out Fitz all of a sudden? Keep 'em fightin' and let 'em cut each other down. That way, we'll step in for the cleanup," he told Hank and Turk as they waited there in the falling dark.

Even after dark, not a light showed in the Running W. Johnny understood the feeling of those tense men waiting inside that house. The hours of watching, their nerves pulling more and more taut until Fitz finally arrived, would be an exquisite torture.

A fingernail moon deep in the west washed its thin light over the basin and house below, and still all was silent, watchful. Johnny began to grow impatient, and he strained to see the house. Once, long after dark, he thought he saw figures moving at the outskirts of the valley and close to the house, but this could well have been Running W men leading their horses to the safety of the barn.

And then, when he ceased looking at the house, and felt the sure grip of sleep take hold of him, a shot broke the stillness of the night. It was the signal for a hundred others. In five seconds, the valley had wakened to an uproar of gunfire, and Johnny knew that Major Fitz had struck at last. Leach had remained quiet, and Fitz, lured by the look of desertion about the house, had ridden up to it.

Now, looking down, Johnny could pick out the places where Fitz's men were forted up. In every corner of the barn, in the angles of the outhouses and corrals, little telltale pencils of stabbing orange light marked out their hiding-places. And from every window in the house gun flames were licking out into the night.

For a full ten minutes, this fumbling in the dark continued, Johnny watching it with growing impatience. This was not like Major Fitz; it had none of his daring and boldness. It might have been a scrap between two bands of peeved rustlers.

Hank watched, saying nothing. Turk, his will finally succumbing to his body, lay stretched out in sleep in the grass.

And then, suddenly, there was a rumbling, bellowing, earth-shaking explosion, and a great spout of orange light flared up by the house. By its vast and sudden blink, Johnny saw that one corner of the Running W main house had been dynamited. Following the blast, the wood of the house slowly started to catch fire. The savage hammering of the gunfire swelled the crescendo. At the same time, flames began to show in the big barn, and it seemed only a matter of a few seconds until the shadows of the basin were pushed back by the growing fire of both the house and barn.

"That's more like it," Johnny murmured grimly. "That's the real Fitz."

But as they watched, it became apparent to Johnny that Leach Wigran and his men were trapped in a burning house. Systematically, too, Fitz's men were firing the outhouses, leaving only the spacious wagon shed, where the horses were. Soon Leach would have to make the choice of making a run for it or burning alive.

Johnny rose and said to Hank, "Come on." As they made their way down the slope, Johnny could see the huddled figures of at least six men in the yard of the house. These were the first casualties, but they were not to be the last.

When Johnny and Hank got down to the lower fringe of trees, the fire was well under way at the main house, but the rifle fire had not ceased. Fitz's men were forted up behind water tanks, the well house, anything that would give them shelter, and were pouring a merciless fire at the house.

Watching it breathlessly, Johnny saw the first Running W man break from the house and run for the shelter of the wagon shed. In that confusion, he made it, and it encouraged two more. They also made it, but now the Bar 33 was rearranging its men, scattering them. It was hard to do, because the three in the wagon shed were sending out an answering fire. After the change, the fifth and sixth runners were cut down before they had run fifty yards.

The most telling fire came from four men forted up beside an overturned wagon by the windmill. Their backs were to Johnny, and he could see their every movement.

Another hardy Running W hand tried running for it, and he, too, was cut down. Swearing, Johnny rose and leveled a shell into his rifle. "This'll end too quick," he told Hank savagely. "Smoke those jaspers out from behind that wagon."

With monotonous precision, Johnny started firing. His first shot kicked up dust from the wagon bed, and one of the riflemen rose and turned to look behind him. His carelessness cost him a slug full in the back, and blindly he tried to run, only to dive onto his face out in the open. Slugs plucked at his body stirring it a little, for the Running W hands were taking no chances.

Johnny kept on firing, Hank joining in, and now the three remaining riflemen knew from what direction they were being harried. One of them made a frantic run for the well house, and he made it, although he had to crawl the last ten feet.

The other two huddled in abject fear. Not seeing any more gunfire from the wagon, the men in the house assayed the trip to the wagon shed. About half of them made it. That path of danger was strewn with dead men. When Johnny reckoned that only Leach Wigran and a few more were left inside, he started to harry the Bar 33 men again, for he wanted Leach Wigran to live. And Leach was the next to attempt the run. Swiftly, Johnny and Hank poured lead into the waiting Bar 33 men, and this time, they were answered. Three riflemen out there had their range, and the slugs whipped through the grass and trees around them.

But doggedly, one eye on Leach, the other on the Bar 33 riflemen, Johnny poured out a hail of lead. When he saw that Leach had reached the safety of the wagon shed, only then did he realize that he and Hank were just missing a scorching blanket of gunfire directed up at them.

They moved to one side. The Bar 33 men could not come over to get them, or they would lay themselves open to the fire from the wagon shed. The fight settled down now into a gun duel—or so Johnny thought until he saw the first Running W man leave the wagon shed and break for the near timber close to where Johnny and Hank stood. Again Johnny moved, and he and Hank again threw their protective fire over the wagon shed.

Wigran, as if he understood that these men on the timber fringe were his allies, took advantage of their blistering curtain of fire to evacuate the shed. Johnny, shooting blindly now, counted them. Including Leach, who was the last man to leave the shed, there were nine Running W hands left. They were safe now in the protection of the timber.

The firing trickled off, and Johnny waited to count the remaining Bar 33 hands. The house was one blazing bonfire now, throwing so much light that it searched out every shadow of this basin.

Instinctively, the Bar 33 men knew that they were on the defensive now that their enemies were in the timber, and one by one they ran for the wooded terrain opposite.

Johnny counted only fifteen of them. That didn't include Fitz and Carmody, who were probably watching from a ridge up the slope.

Satisfied, Johnny and Hank faded back into the deep timber. There were men calling around them now, and Johnny hoped desperately that Turk would not sleep through this until someone stumbled on him. They made their clearing. Turk was still sleeping, the horses behind him snorting and stomping with excitement.

It was only the work of seconds for them to mount and ride up the slope. Turk, cursing his luck, heard the story from Hank as they rode.

"Nine to seventeen," Turk murmured. "That sounds better."

And to Johnny's tired ears it did, too.

Chapter Twenty: BOOM

SOMETHING HAD HAPPENED IN COSMOS. The streets were jammed with groups of men conversing excitedly, and the ore freighters roared themselves hoarse in an effort to clear a way through all the confusion. Slowly, two and three at a time, men were leaving town with pack horses and disappearing into the hills. For there was a rush on in Bonanza canyon. Gold had been found there!

And Bonanza canyon—for so it had been named by the hopeful Tip—was jammed with pack mules and horses, timber, tents, miners, and tons of freighted supplies. Where ten days ago a bleak and waterless canyon opened its sun-baked barrenness to the sky, a miners' shantytown was springing up. Since the original claims almost blanketed the sandy floor, the buildings were being erected on each side of the canyon. Two roadways had been laid out. In a small *rincon* on the northern side, Tim Prince already had a clapboard saloon thrown together, and his sign was out. All down the canyon, skeletons of buildings were rising among the tents. The ore-bearing land around the dike had long since been staked out, and now the speculators were selling claims on the rock rim and for a half mile beyond it. Sober townsmen who had never been known to spend a careless penny were paying fabulous prices for plots of worthless ground—and this on the sure rumor that both Westfall and Tip Rogers had struck it rich.

It was a sweating, brawling boom camp. Teamsters toiling to bring up the needed tons of construction material were cursing the up trail, their mules, the crowd, and their employers. Nobody seemed to know what to do, except to keep going. Half the mob was only curiosity seekers cluttering up the canyon and keeping the other half from getting anything done.

Westfall was working only his first claim, but he already had a wire fence up around his whole property. Inside the fence two big sheds had been erected, and for days now, he had had two shifts of men working night and day. Over the gate into the claim was a sign bearing the legend: *Glory Hole,* and the place had an air of hard efficiency already.

The smaller shed was the office, and it was in this that Big Westfall had his quarters. Two days before, he had sent off his first load of ore to the reduction mill in town. His freighters had had to fight their way down a tortuous trail through a continuous, close-packed line of men on their way to the boom camp. But today, as Westfall stood in the doorway of the office, his eyes bloodshot from lack of sleep, he felt more excited than he had since starting work.

"Sisson!" he bawled. From the shaft house, an overalled man came running to his side. "Put a man with a gun at that gate. I'm ridin' down to Cosmos now."

"For the reports?" Sisson asked.

"That's right."

Westfall went over to the lean-to beside the shaft house and brought out a horse, which he saddled. Then he set off on the road to town, his huge bulk a sort of wedge driven in this ceaseless stream of traffic making its way up to Bonanza canyon. Westfall regarded these pilgrims with some satisfaction. These were the people who always got left, the weaklings, the slow. They would get only the pickings from the camp, none of the real takings.

In the late afternoon Westfall passed through Cosmos and turned down the road to the reduction mill. Things were slack here, he saw, for he could only hear a few of the stamps going. With the closing of the Esmerella, the business of the mill had fallen off considerably. The mill hands were waiting impatiently until the ore from the Bonanza camp started to pour in to usher in a new era of wilder prosperity than Cosmos had ever seen before.

Westfall walked through the small office, nodding at the clerks, and knocked on Kinder's door. He was told to enter. Kinder sat behind his desk, a scowl on his thin face. He rose at sight of Westfall and shook hands.

"You're after your report." He turned to the safe. When he came out, he had a paper in one hand, a small package in the other, and he laid both on the desk.

"There you are."

Westfall seemed puzzled. He looked at Kinder and then came over and unfolded the package. It was a sheet of letter paper, and in the folds of it was a small heap of gold dust, its amount between one and two ounces.

"What's this?" Westfall asked.

"Your first ton of ore reduced netted that much gold. The second ton netted about a quarter ounce, which I put in with this other. Look at the report and you'll see," Kinder said dryly.

Westfall picked up the report and glanced through it, and laid it down again without saying anything.

"You've got a pretty sorry thing there," Kinder said gravely.

"But the assay showed it rich!"

"Does that look rich?"

Westfall scowled down at the paper. "What did Tip Rogers's claims show?"

"He hasn't brought in any ore yet."

For a long moment, Westfall stood there, regarding the tiny amount of gold. He could have told himself that later reports would show better, but he was a man little given to self-deception. The plain facts were that Major Fitz and Carmody had been roped in. The ore Westfall sent down was the best ore on the best claim, and *it* was no good.

Silently, he picked up the dust and tucked it in his shirt pocket along with the report.

"Will you send any more down?" Kinder asked.

"I doubt it. But I'll have to think it over, Kinder. Much obliged."

He rode back into town and ate a lone meal. When the clock showed seven he went out to his horse again, mounted, and rode out the south road. Once up on the ridge, he turned off to the left and rode until he came to a tall pinnacle rock, which was just visible in the moonlight.

Major Fitz and Carmody were waiting at the base of it, and they greeted him as he swung down off his horse.

"What's the report?" Fitz asked harshly. His voice was strained and impatient, almost angry. Carmody remained silent.

Westfall took out the two papers. "Two tons—an ounce and three quarters," he informed Fitz.

"What?" Fitz barked. "Let's see!"

Silently, Westfall handed him the paper, and Fitz struck a match. First he looked at the gold and cursed. Next he read the report, and threw it angrily to the ground. Then he came over and faced Westfall, his legs spread. He came nearly to Westfall's shoulder, but again he contrived to seem the master.

"Westfall, what happened?"

"You've got it right there. I built the shacks, put two shifts of men to work on what looked to be the best claim. Like I told Carmody, two days ago I sent two wagons of ore down, one in the morning, one in the afternoon. You can see for yourself on the report."

"Curse the report!" Fitz said angrily. "What's happened to the gold?"

"There ain't any."

"You're a liar!"

Westfall made an instinctive movement of protest when Carmody's voice cut through the night. "Slow down, fella. I got a gun on you." Westfall let his hands drop. Fitz hadn't moved, and now his voice settled into what was nearly a snarl.

"I don't know whether you're double-crossing me out

at the mine, or whether you and Kinder have it rigged between yourselves. But I know there's gold there and I haven't got it."

"How do you know?"

"Because my assay showed I ought to have fifty times what you've brought!"

"Who assayed it?"

"Hugo Miller, one of the few honest men I know."

Westfall knew Hugo, knew he was honest. There was nothing he could say in reply, but that did not help the smoldering anger within him. "Fitz, I'll take considerable off you, but I won't take that. You and your mine can go rot. I quit!"

"Oh, no, you don't," Fitz said with a terrible gentleness in his voice. "You won't do anything of the kind. You'll go back to that mine and you'll get some more ore down to Kinder. And when you bring this next report—say in four days—it had better be different. That is, if you value your health."

"I don't have to work for you, Fitz!" Westfall said hotly. "Who do you think you are that you can keep me there?"

"Tomorrow morning I'll have nine men in the crowd at that camp. If you make a break to get away, it'll be committing suicide. If you talk to anyone and tell them that I'm behind you, that'll be fatal, too. Do I make myself clear enough?"

Breathing hard with the anger that had taken hold of him, Westfall did not answer immediately. But he had excellent control of his temper, and he saw the uselessness of argument. "I reckon you do," he said, mildly. "I'll go back, Fitz. Only, I'm telling you right now, the next report you get on this ore will be worse than the first. There's no gold there."

"There'd better be," Fitz said.

Westfall mounted and headed up the canyon where he would pick up the trail back to the mine. He knew that within twenty minutes, nine of Fitz's men would be following him. If he wanted to make a break for it, now was the time. But Westfall was no puncher, no outlaw, and he had the great good sense to see that his skill in evading these trained men would never match their skill in catching him. And once they did catch him, there could only be one end for him. His forehead beaded with sweat. He was no coward; still, he was no fool. There was only one thing to do, go back to the mine, sort out every rock in the next shipment so that the next report would be better, and then, after Fitz had called off his men, dodge out of the country. That was his only chance.

Next morning, back at the mine, Westfall gave his instructions. Every shovel of ore that went in the wagons was to be hand-picked for the color shown in it. Both shifts of men were put to the work, but it still went with agonizing slowness. Twice that day, Westfall saw suspicious-looking hombres hanging around the gate of the Glory Hole, but the shed was shut, so that the secret of his scheme was kept.

That night, a ton of ore was ready for freighting. It was the best Westfall could do, and he directed the freighters to start out with it. Their instructions were to tell Kinder that he wanted a report on it by tomorrow night. At least this would give him time enough to think up an excuse in case the report was bad.

And it *was* bad. When he went down the next afternoon, Kinder greeted him with a shake of the head. "You've got a lemon, Westfall. Look at this."

He had a small box on the table almost filled with dust, and pointing to it, he said, "This assays out about forty dollars a ton. If you had a mile of claims, a million dollars in capital behind you, and a reduction mill on the property, you'd almost have a paying proposition. As it is, I don't think you have."

Westfall contrived a smile. "That's too bad," he said mildly. "What about Rogers?"

"His first load is in the mill now. I'll have a report in an hour."

Westfall picked up the box in his big fist, took the papers, and bid Kinder good night. In Cosmos, he dismounted at the Cosmos House, but he discovered he had no appetite. So for one solid hour, he paced the streets, oblivious to passers-by, cudgeling his brains for a way to break this news to Fitz. And he had the uneasy feeling that he was being watched all the while. At the end of the hour, he suddenly realized he was hungry, and he went over to the Cosmos House. Despair was riding him. There was no way out of this.

Chapter Twenty-One: CAPTURE

HUGO MILLER CAME BACK from supper at the Cosmos and let himself in the front door of his office. In the darkness he could see a pencil of light shining under the door of the back room, and instinctively he drew his gun. Tiptoeing back through the room, he reached the back door, noiselessly turned the knob, and slammed the door open—on Johnny Hendry.

Johnny was stripped to the waist and was standing in front of the mirror, his face lathered with soap, a straight-edge razor in his hand. He looked over his shoulder as the door crashed, and drawled, "You nearly made me cut my throat, Hugo. You're sure spooky."

Hugo holstered his gun and said, "Where've you been, Johnny?" Johnny started to tell him, but Hugo raised a hand. "I only asked because I've been wanting to see you for over a week now."

Johnny stared at him. "News?"

"Plenty. I've matched that ore of Pick's. I know who stole the location papers from Pick. I've been trying to get hold of you for a week." And swiftly Hugo told him the story of Tip's discovery, and of Westfall. He told him also about the rush which had started up in Bonanza canyon, and Johnny listened with a grim amazement.

Night before last was the night he and Turk and Hank had started the war between the Running W and the Bar 33. They had slept through the whole next day. Last night, the three of them had again raided Major Fitz's herds, and again successfully. They had planted them in a canyon behind the Running W, where Fitz's men had tracked them today. But Leach and his men had moved off up into the hills, and there was no one at the Running

W for Fitz to fight. It was this lull that had allowed Johnny a breathing-space, and time to visit Hugo. He knew nothing of the rush to Bonanza canyon. And now Hugo's story seemed almost like a fairy tale. But what was not a fairy tale was that Hugo knew the man who must have Pick's stolen location papers in his possession.

"You know this whippoorwill, Westfall?" Johnny asked slowly, his face still half covered with lather.

"He's down at the Cosmos House now."

Without a word, Johnny started to wipe his face.

"Finish your shave," Hugo told him. "He was just coming in when I left. When you're done, we'll go after him."

Johnny's hand was trembling so that he cut himself before he was finished, and all the while he listened to Hugo's description of the Bonanza camp, and of Westfall's tactics. And the more he listened, the more grim was the exultation that filled Johnny's heart.

"And there's another thing," Hugo said quietly. "I don't know whether I'm buttin' in on your business or not, Johnny, when I tell you this."

"What?"

"Nora is engaged to Tip Rogers. She's taken his ring, so folks say."

Johnny turned to the basin and doused his face. He could not trust himself to let Hugo see his expression. But when he stepped back from the basin and reached for a towel his face was cold, impassive. "That so? Well, Tip'll make her a pretty good husband, I reckon," he said carelessly. But, lest Hugo think this unfriendly, Johnny grinned a little. "Me, I wouldn't. She didn't think so, Hugo."

"I'm sorry, Johnny Hendry."

"So am I. But I know when I'm licked," Johnny said grimly, and reached for his shirt. As he tested his gun, making sure it was loaded, Hugo outlined his plan to trap Westfall. Hugo would wait on his horse in the alley beside the Cosmos House. When Westfall came out and mounted, Hugo was to see which way he went, then ride out into the street and overtake him. Once he was past him, Hugo would slow down. The man following Hugo out of town then would be Westfall. With the glasses which Hugo would lend Johnny, he could keep a careful watch on the street from the south of town. The chances were that Westfall would ride south, and in that case his capture would be an easy thing to effect.

Johnny disappeared into the night to join Hank and Turk on the outskirts of town. Once with them, he told them tersely about Hugo's discovery. He stationed himself on a little rise beyond the recorder's office and trained his glasses on the hotel. The waiting was intolerable, but when, after twenty minutes, Johnny saw a big man come out of the Cosmos House and mount his horse and turn south, he felt an excitement crawling through his blood. When Hugo, seconds later, wheeled out of the alley and trotted down the street, overtaking the man, then slowed down to a walk, Johnny was sure.

Up the road, where the trail started to lift out of the canyon, Johnny remembered a gnarled and twisted old piñon whose limbs reached out over the road. He and Turk and Hank made for this point. While Turk and Hank took the horses and hid them, Johnny pulled himself up into the thick branches of the piñon and snaked out on its thickest lower limb until he was directly over the road.

When Hugo rode under the tree, Johnny called softly, "Ride on ahead, Hugo."

A few moments later, the dark bulk of horse and rider loomed up in the road. The horse was walking, as if its rider were sunk in thought. As the rider approached, Johnny prepared himself for the leap. The horse walked under the limb.

Johnny slid off the limb and landed square on top of Westfall, and together they tumbled into the dust of the road. Even as they lit, Johnny's fists were flailing, but it was unnecessary. Westfall was cold. The fall had done that.

Turk and Hank and Hugo appeared, and they tied Westfall's hands behind him. It was minutes before Turk could catch up Westfall's horse, and in that time, Westfall regained consciousness and sat up.

"Are you Bar 33 men?" he asked quietly.

"Not much," Johnny said grimly, shortly, and turned to Hank. Already he could hear Turk returning with the horse.

"We'll have this session out in the malpais," Johnny said quietly. "You comin', Hugo?"

"Try and keep me away."

Soon Westfall was tied on his horse, whose reins were in Johnny's hands, and they rode silently single file through the dark on the way to the camp in the malpais.

Chapter Twenty-Two: CAMPFIRE CONCLAVE

HANK BUILT A BIG FIRE in the gravel while the rest of them untied Westfall and then unsaddled. By the time they were finished, there was a roaring fire going, and it pushed night far back behind the malpais walls. Neither Turk, Hugo, nor Hank talked, for this was Johnny's affair. They watched silently as Johnny led Westfall over to the fire and untied his bonds. They looked at the man, at his massive body, his openly puzzled face, and privately they wondered—all except Hugo. His ores had never betrayed him; this was the man who first started digging at Pick's ore, and it followed that he was Pick's killer.

Westfall looked at the four of them, his face—if not amiable—composed. But he was bewildered, too.

When the ropes were off, he chafed his wrists, and looked over at Johnny.

"You wouldn't know what this is all about, I suppose," Johnny said softly, scornfully.

Westfall shook his head. "No, I don't."

"You don't know me?"

"Never seen you before."

"Ever hear of Johnny Hendry?" Johnny asked, as he unbuckled his shell belt and let it slide to the ground.

Westfall nodded. "Sure. I've heard of you. You're outlawed now, ain't you?"

"Ever hear of Pick Hendry?" Johnny asked quietly, watching Westfall with unblinking, savage eyes.

Westfall shook his big head and glanced inquisitively at Hank. "Are you him?"

"You liar," Johnny said tightly, "you murderin' sneakin' liar!"

Westfall's grave eyes settled on Johnny again, and, seeing the agitation in his face, he wisely kept silent.

Johnny walked over to face him, and as he walked, he whipped off his hat. Facing Westfall, he said in a voice thick with anger, "You never heard of him! You killed him!"

"How do you figure that?" Westfall said calmly.

Johnny's lips were white. "Pick Hendry was murdered, his head half blown off with a shotgun. He'd been workin' there in Bonanza canyon and he'd struck gold. He was on his way to register his claim when you come up on him. You killed him and took his location papers and filed them, and now you're workin' the claim!"

"And how can you prove that?" Westfall asked, still curiously.

"Your ore matches the ore Pick had assayed!" Johnny said thickly, and then he did not wait for more. He lashed out with his fist, catching Westfall flush in the face so that he staggered back and fell. Johnny walked over to him.

"First, I'm goin' to give you the beatin' of your life, fella. Then, when I'm done, I'm goin' to give you a gun. If you've nerve enough to try and use it, I'll belly-shoot you! I'll stand by five days and nights and watch you die, you back-shootin' ranahan! Get up here and take it!"

Westfall was mad now. It didn't matter that he had been accused unfairly. This slim, furious cowpuncher before him had named him everything that he hated, and had knocked him down, to boot.

With a growl of rage, Westfall got to his feet and faced Johnny.

Johnny struck out again with the swiftness of a snake's tongue, and again Westfall went down. Johnny leaped on top of him and they were a tangle of flailing arms and legs. It was a bitter fight, with no cursing, no sound except the grunting and the smack of fists on flesh. Johnny fought like a maniac. Astraddle Westfall, he slugged blow after blow into Westfall's face, until that giant of man, goaded to desperation, heaved himself to his feet, shaking Johnny off. Erect, his face was already bloody, but there was a light of murder in his eyes.

He tried to clinch with Johnny, and in lofty and angry contempt, Johnny let him. They wrestled around locked in iron embrace, but Johnny pumped a dozen blows into Westfall's midriff before the bigger man was glad to break. But Johnny would not let him break; he followed him with implacable anger, his lean shoulder muscles corded with the overhand blows he was looping into Westfall's face. And with the blind anger of a bull, Westfall was fighting back. When one of his ponderous blows landed, it would lift Johnny off his feet and set him back a yard, but each time Johnny would charge in anew, fighting with the deadly silence of a man gone mad.

Round and round the fire they circled, and it was Westfall, in spite of superior weight, who was giving ground. With the dogged bewilderment of a cornered bear before hounds, he tried to protect himself, but he could not. His slowness left him prey to Johnny's lightning blows, and when each one landed on his raw face, he staggered a little.

In one last rally, he lowered his head, braced his feet in the gravel, and slugged wildly at the swarming figure before him. Johnny, blind with rage, drove blow after blow at those thick, protecting arms, and then in fury of frustration, he dived in and clinched with Westfall. The big man wrapped his arms around Johnny, trying to smother him, but Johnny, legs braced broadly, hunched his shoulders and heaved mightily. Westfall left the ground, and still heaving, Johnny toppled him over backward. Almost before Westfall sprawled on his back, Johnny was at him again, straddling him. And time after time, his fists raised as if he were pounding with a hammer, Johnny slugged down at that face. Abruptly, Westfall's arms ceased to move and sank down by his side, but still Johnny kept hitting him, his blows hard and savage, merciless, countless.

At last, struggling and cursing and crying, he had to be

dragged off by Hugo and Turk, who had a hard time hold-ing him until he came to his senses and calmed down.

"I'm all right," he panted finally. "Get him on his feet."

Johnny stood there, weaving on his feet, his shirt torn to ribbons, his face bloody, his body cut.

But Westfall was completely out. Hank slapped him, punched him, rolled his head, but the man remained as limp as a rag.

"Get him up!" Johnny commanded, his eyes blazing. "He's going to get the rest of it!"

Turk looked over at Hank. Neither of them liked this. It was as bloody and savage as two wolves fighting for the supremacy of the pack, and it sickened Hugo. But none of them objected, for they could understand Johnny's part of it.

Hank went over to the spring and filled his hat with water and brought it back and doused water in Westfall's face. Still he did not move.

After Hank had made ten trips with water, during which time Turk slapped Westfall's face until his hands were sore, Westfall moaned. Turk stood up and backed off, and slowly Westfall rose to a sitting position. For a long minute, while the rest of them watched him, he stared at the fire with the glassy eyes of a man who is only par-tially conscious. When he shook his head as if trying to clear his brain, Johnny strode over to him and hoisted him to his unsteady feet. What clothes were remaining on Westfall were covered with blood. His face was distorted with welts and bruises, and his lips were shapeless ribbons of flesh.

Sharply Johnny slapped him in the face until he flinched away and raised an arm, then Johnny let him go and backed off.

Westfall looked up now, and his eyes were clear.

"That's enough," he murmured wearily.

Johnny said nothing. He walked over to his shell belt, took out both guns, came over to Westfall and thrust one of them at Westfall.

"Enough!" he said savagely. "You haven't even begun to get it."

Westfall looked stupidly at the gun. "What's this for?"

Turk cut in gently, "Ease up, kid. He can't even count his toes now." But Turk had his six-gun out, trained on Westfall.

Johnny turned to Turk and said savagely, "Stay out of this!"

Wheeling back to Westfall, he said, "Get across that fire. I'll give any man a chance to defend himself, but when you turn around to face me, start shootin', fella, because I am!"

A gleam of intelligence returned to Westfall's face. He studied the gun a long moment, as if assembling his thoughts. Then he dropped the gun and looked up at Johnny. "Go ahead and shoot," he said wearily.

"Pick up that gun!"

"Huh-unh. Go ahead and cut down on me. I dunno what this is all about, but I reckon you got blood in your eye, mister."

"I'll shoot," Johnny said evenly. "But not before you pick up that gun! And if I have to tie it in your hand, I'll do that! Pick it up!"

Westfall heaved a deep sigh and looked steadily at Johnny with his one good eye. "That claim ain't mine, son. I might as well tell you. I never found it. I was paid to mine it."

"Crawlin'!" Johnny sneered.

Westfall shook his head. "You don't need to believe that, but it's so."

"Pick up that gun!" Johnny commanded.

"Wait a minute," Hugo cut in gently. "That could be, Johnny. It might have been sold to him by the man that really killed Pick."

"Who owns it, then?" Johnny cut in, his voice still scornful.

"Major Fitz."

At any other name in the world, Johnny would have laughed and sneered. But now he suddenly lowered his gun. "Major Fitz?" he murmured. "He sold you the claim?"

"No, I'm just minin' it for him. He didn't want his

name known, threatened to cut me to doll rags if I ever mentioned it to anybody."

Johnny shot one brief glance at Turk and Hank, and then walked over to Westfall.

"Go on."

"That's all there is to it," Westfall said wearily. "Hoke Carmody come over and made me the proposition. I couldn't see anything wrong with it. Carmody put money in the Warms bank for me, and I drew on it. I hired the men, bought the supplies, and started the work. Last night I brought the first report to Fitz and Carmody from the mill. Fitz accused me of holdin' out the gold on him. Said to go back and if the next report didn't show better, he'd turn them gunnies of his loose on me." He looked at Johnny and said simply, "That's all there is to it."

"You got the location papers, the original ones?"

"The ones Fitz gave me? Sure."

Westfall's hands were so cut and bloody that it took him some time to pull out the papers in his hip pocket. He stepped over to the fire so as to see better, and after he had fumbled through the mass of papers in his hand, he brought two out and handed them to Johnny. The others crowded around Johnny to read them. One was the original location paper, written in Pick's own handwriting. The others were the plats of the other six claims, just as Fitz had copied them down from Barney's description. These, of course, were in Fitz's handwriting.

When Johnny was finished, he folded them up and sank down by the fire, staring at it. He had forgotten all about Westfall. All he could think of was that Major Fitz, already proven a rustler and killer, the warm friend of Nora's, his own one-time friend and benefactor, was the man who had killed Pick Hendry.

"Tell me all of this again, from start to finish," he told Westfall. The story was almost the same. Westfall repeated conversations, and Johnny prodded him with questions. Westfall told of the happenings of last night, of his meeting with Fitz, of his conviction that he was being watched by hands of the Bar 33.

"Has Tip Rogers got his report yet?" Johnny asked.

"He got it tonight."

Johnny gazed pensively at his bloody fists, the germ of an idea formulating in his mind. He was wondering about Tip Rogers. Tip had every reason to hate him, if he believed that Johnny robbed the bank; but on the other hand, if all this evidence against Fitz was presented, wouldn't Tip be willing to help? Johnny remembered that grave, honest face. The thought that Tip had Nora now and would marry her was something that he put in the back of his mind. He was trying to be just. Would Tip help him, if all the facts were before him? Johnny thought so.

"Roll me a cigarette, Turk, will you?" Johnny asked. "Roll Westfall one, too."

Turk did, and they lighted up. All of them were waiting to hear what Johnny would propose, and when he was finished with his smoke, he told them. It was a bold plan, and risky.

"Hugo," he said, when they were finished discussing it. "Do you think you could get Tip Rogers and bring him here by morning?"

"I ought to be able to. He was at the hotel when I left. Likely he'll stay there the night."

"Then try and get him," Johnny murmured. "If he falls in with this, we'll not only kill Fitz, but we'll break him before we do, and that will hurt him worse than a slug in the back." He turned to Westfall. "Are you with us, Westfall? It strikes me that's the only way out for you."

"It is," Westfall said grimly. "I am. My life ain't worth nothin' as long as that coyote is loose."

By the time Hugo was ready to leave, Johnny and Westfall were sleeping in their blankets, side by side. Hank sided Hugo as far as the town, which was so dark and deserted at this hour that Hank decided to risk going in. At the tie rail of the Cosmos, he waited while Hugo went inside and inquired of the clerk, whom he had to waken, the number of Tip's room.

In ten minutes, Hugo returned with Tip. The Cosmos was utterly dark, and the store lamps across the street were long since dimmed, so that Tip could not see Hank very well. Hugo introduced him as Bill Petty, and Tip nodded.

"Why all the mystery, Hugo?" Tip asked, laughing a little. "Where are we going?"

"How did your report from the mill turn out?" Hugo countered.

Tip laughed ruefully. "Between you and me, it didn't turn out. There was nothing there—not a thing."

"Think you'd like your old job back at the Esmerella?"

"I would," Tip said shortly, "but there's not much chance."

"Maybe if you come along with me tonight, we'll fix that."

"Open the Esmerella?"

"I think so, and before very long."

Tip's curiosity was whetted down. As they rode out of town, he asked more questions, but Hugo was uncommunicative.

It was well after sunup when Hank guided them into the malpais field. Tip had spent the last hour since daylight trying to place Hank's face, and for the life of him, he could not. But he had the uneasy feeling that he had met the man before, and in a place where he could not see his face very well. Hugo, however, was whistling, and Tip trusted him, so that his faint suspicion did not make him balky.

Just at the mouth of the small canyon, Hank pulled his horse aside and motioned Hugo ahead. Hugo, in turn, motioned Tip ahead, and Tip went on.

Rounding the turn, he came square into the camp— and saw Johnny Hendry grinning at him from his place by the campfire.

Instinctively Tip's hand traveled to his gun, very suddenly, but he remembered that Hank was behind him. He wheeled his horse to confront Hugo.

"Since when did you turn crook, too, Hugo?"

"Take it easy," Hugo said, smiling faintly. "Don't talk until you've heard what there is to say. You're no prisoner, Tip, so cough the sand out of your craw."

Grimly Tip dismounted and walked over to Johnny.

"This your plan, Johnny?"

Johnny cheerfully admitted it was. He introduced Turk and Westfall, and Tip looked long at Westfall, trying to explain his presence here. Tip concluded in one short moment that there had been a fight here between Johnny and Westfall, but beyond that, he could not hazard a guess.

"How'd your report turn out, Rogers?" Westfall asked him.

"Sorry. How did yours?"

"The same, and for a good reason. There's no gold there," Westfall said, and laughed. Tip couldn't understand that, either. He took the breakfast offered him, and listened to the small talk between the others. Covertly, he eyed Johnny, and against his own wishes he had to concede that Johnny didn't look like a bank robber and never would.

When they were all smoking after the meal, Tip said to Hugo, "Well, Hugo, it's up to you. Do you think this crowd will get the Esmerella going again? Is that what you meant?"

"It is," Johnny cut in. "If we could nail the man who's been behind all this rustling and robbery, who's hired most of the hardcases in this town, don't you think we'd have a fair chance of cleaning it up?"

"With a good sheriff, maybe."

Johnny only grinned at that. His next question was asked in a calm voice, but it made Tip sit up in astonishment.

"What would you say, Tip, if I told you that Major Fitz is the brains behind all this trouble? What would you say if I told you that he killed Pick Hendry, that he started this gold rush where there's no gold, that he's behind Leach Wigran and all the rest of it?"

Before Tip could answer, Johnny started out on his story, and to begin it, he went back to the time Pick was killed. He told of the poll of the ranchers, which really first put him on the trail of Fitz. All the other things he and Hank and Turk and Hugo discovered came out, sometimes from Hank's lips, other times from Johnny's. Westfall told his part of it, too, and three good hours passed in the telling. At first Tip was skeptical, almost hostile, but he was answered reasonably. No one made any false claims, and everything they said Tip checked and found true. And slowly, as the talk passed around among these men, he saw what Johnny Hendry had done, and he felt a sympathy for him. Moreover, he saw that these men were telling the truth. And out of it, there came a picture of Major Fitz which was blacker than Tip had ever dreamed of. Part of the story—especially the burning of the Running W and the Bar 33—Tip could not verify, because he had been in Bonanza canyon, but Hugo vouched for the truth of it all. He had heard it. Almost everybody in town had, but its importance was lost in the excitement of the rush.

When that was out of the way and Tip was silent with all this knowledge, Johnny broached the subject of the scheme to trap Fitz.

When he was finished, Tip said, "But why all the scheming? Go up and get him."

"I'm an outlaw," Johnny said dryly. "A wanted man."

"Have Hugo tell the sheriff, Baily Blue."

"Hasn't it struck you as pretty queer, Tip, how Blue won that election? Think back. Who'd be the worst hit if an honest lawman got in office?"

"Fitz."

"Who did get in? Blue. Who was interested in puttin' Blue in—a man who wouldn't stir a finger to clean up the county? Fitz. Then, knowin' what we know now about Fitz, it could be that Fitz crooked the election. He had the men and the money to do it, didn't he?"

"Then you think Blue is in with Fitz?" Tip asked.

Johnny spread out his hands in a gesture of negation. "I'm not accusin' any man till I have the facts, Tip. Maybe Fitz robbed the bank to get me, an honest lawman away, but I don't know. But I don't think Blue would arrest Fitz. I don't think he'd get the evidence on him. And once he did, and Fitz was in jail, how long do you think Blue would keep him locked up? If it ever come to a peaceful trial, do you think there'd be a witness left to testify against Fitz? Do you, with all those gunnies he's got and the money he's got to buy more of them?"

"Maybe not," Tip said. "But how is your scheme any better? It'd just break Fitz, strap him."

"There you've said it!" Johnny said swiftly. "Take his money away from him so he can't buy gunmen, can't bribe people, can't pay them killer's wages, and then who's goin' to stick by him? Nobody. Rats leave a sinking ship, Tip, and Fitz will be sunk."

Johnny rested his case on this, and Tip smoked in silence a long time.

"That's all you want me to do, then? Just get a quarter of a bar of gold and give it to Westfall?"

"That's all we need. Fitz will do the rest." Johnny regarded Tip with serious, sober eyes. "We came to you, Tip, because you're the only man who can get us that gold. You can get it from Sammons. We can't go to Kinder, because this has got to be secret. Sammons will believe you. It'll be a risk, of course, but as long as I can stand on two feet and give my promise, I promise that you'll get that gold back. Can you do it?"

Tip nodded his head slightly. "I can. I'll do it, too. It's a plain business gamble. If it works, the Esmerella will open. If it doesn't—"

"It will," Johnny said grimly. "It will if I have to ride the owlhoot the rest of my life for the murder of Major Fitz."

Tip rose, and the meeting broke up. Johnny followed Tip over to his horse. Tip was just ready to mount when Johnny said, "I heard about you and Nora, Tip. I wish you both luck."

Tip turned, to see Johnny holding out his hand. He gripped it and said, "Thanks, Johnny, I'll tell her."

"If anyone can make her happy, I reckon you can," Johnny said gently. "But if you can't, Tip, promise me one thing."

"What?"

"That you'll clear out when you see it doesn't work."

"It will work."

"I think so, too."

"I'll clear out if it doesn't," Tip said. "She's too fine to have her life cluttered up by a man she doesn't love, John-ny—either you or me. Do you understand?"

Johnny nodded. Tip mounted. Hugo and Westfall were waiting. They rode out of the camp, and with them rode the success of the scheme. And somehow, remembering Tip, Johnny felt it was in good hands. The waiting on the results would be the hardest thing to bear.

Chapter Twenty-Three: RAT TRAP

WITH THE FORGED REPORT in his pocket and the two-pound bar of gold in a sack resting on his saddle horn, Westfall rode up on the ridge above town and turned to the left again. There was a cool wind tonight riding off the bench, and it felt healing to the scars and bruises on his face. He whistled softly between his teeth, relishing what was about to happen.

The moon was brighter tonight, and from quite a way off he could pick out the horses of Major Fitz and Carmody. As he approached, two figures moved out of the shadow to meet him.

Westfall reined up and dismounted stiffly, and again Major Fitz, like a brash little terrier, stood in front of him.

"Well, Westfall, you decided to reconsider, did you?"

"Not reconsider, Fitz," Westfall said, chuckling a little. "I just made a bad guess. I was lookin' on the gloomy side of it."

"What's the report this time?"

For answer, Westfall handed him the gold bar and then the paper.

"How much?" Fitz asked quickly.

"A little over eleven hundred dollars from a short ton of ore," Westfall said calmly.

Fitz's hand tightened on the bar, and Westfall could hear his breath coming quickly.

"Eleven hundred dollars!" Fitz exclaimed softly, and he opened the paper with trembling fingers. The moon was so strong that he did not need a match to read the figures and the signature at the bottom.

"Well, how'd you do it?" Fitz demanded brusquely.

"Like you told me to, I got another ton down," Westfall said quietly. "It assayed only forty dollars a ton. But I knew I was on the track of somethin'. I didn't want to come back and tell you. I figured you was just about red-headed enough to gun me if I gave out that report. So I worked the men both shifts through the night. I changed the course of the shaft, workin' in more toward the dike and even into it. Come mornin', I knew I had it. I could tell by the look of the ore. I hurried it down to the mill, and Kinder put a rush job through for me, and there it is."

Fitz laughed with pleasure. He could afford to be magnanimous now. "You mustn't take me too literally, Westfall. I was upset. I'd lost my place the night before and I didn't know what I was doing."

"No offense," Westfall said easily. "I knew it was up to me to either produce or get out. The gold was there, and you knew it."

"I did."

Carmody took the bar now and hefted it and whistled in exclamation.

"You reckon you're in a pretty good humor now?" Westfall asked.

"Best ever." Fitz laughed. "Come over and sit down and let's smoke. You want to ask me something, don't you?"

"That's it." They walked over to the base of the pinnacle rock and rolled smokes. Westfall took his time in starting, for this was the part that would need skill.

He began thus: "You're a kind of hard man, Fitz, but I like to work for a driver. And you've done well by me in the way of wages. With the men, too."

"I've tried to," Fitz said with some satisfaction.

"I just had an idea when I got that report from Kinder," Westfall continued, after a moment's pause. "It come to me so quick I acted on the spur of the moment."

Fitz said nothing.

"It come to me," Westfall said slowly, "that if I didn't do somethin' to keep his mouth shut, Kinder would spread this news about our strike to the four winds."

"Yes?"

"So I give him three hundred dollars—all I had in my pocket—to keep this a secret for three days." He paused, and glanced obliquely at Fitz, who was listening carefully.

"What for?" Carmody put in.

"Well, I figured it this way," Westfall drawled. "Tip Rogers got his report last night. It was nothin'—worse than mine. That news is out in camp. Also, the news of our first report is out in camp. The whole camp is discouraged. This mornin' when I left, there wasn't but five or six men workin' their claims. Already some of the saddle tramps have started to pick up and leave. See what I mean? They're licked up there already!"

"Yes, yes," Fitz said impatiently.

"Here's my scheme, then. What if I was to go up there with a report signed by Kinder—that report that says the ore only showed forty dollars a ton? I'd show it around. Well, that would discourage the rest of 'em. No man, unless he's got a company behind him and a whole ore field to work on, is goin' to make money out of forty-dollar-a-ton ore, is he?"

"Hardly."

"Then what if I was to go up there and call the camp together and say, 'Look here. This ore is worth forty dollars a ton. It's no good to you jaspers unless you can sell out to a big outfit. All right, I'm the big outfit. I represent a million dollars lookin' for a place to mine low-grade ore. Sell me your claims. I'll pay you a reasonable figure for them. And once I've got them, all of them, enough to assure me that I'll have lots of ore to work, why I'll put in a big mine and mill here and start operations.'" He looked at Fitz. "How do you think they'd take that? Don't you reckon they'd jump at the chance to sell? And once I had all the claims, I could scrape away that top rubble and we'd open a vein of gold that would be worth millions, yes, millions!"

For a moment, Fitz did not answer, and Westfall could almost see the greed in him at work.

"Good Lord!" Fitz said softly, almost to himself. "What a fortune!"

"You see, Kinder will keep his mouth shut about my

strike just as long as I pay him a hundred dollars a day. We'd have to act fast, before Rogers or any of the others strike the vein, too. But inside of three days, I judge, I can buy out every claim in that canyon, and for a song." He paused and regarded Fitz openly. "Only I ain't got the money to buy the claims. Have you?"

In his excitement, Fitz jumped to his feet and walked out to the horses. He wheeled and came back toward Westfall, and he was talking so loud he was almost shouting.

"Money! Of course I've got the money! How much will it take?"

"A hundred and fifty thousand, anyway," Westfall said. "Have you got that much?"

"Nearly. But the rest won't matter!" He paused, and said more slowly, "How long have I got to get it?"

"Three days, I'd judge. By that time Rogers or some of the others will be about down to the vein. The time we wait after that would be risky."

"My money is over in Warms," Fitz said swiftly. "I could make it back with the cash in two nights and a day."

"Well, I reckon you've got a gold mine, then," Westfall said calmly. "I don't see how it will fail."

"What's your cut on this, Westfall?" Fitz demanded, his excitement making his voice quaver. "Ask for anything reasonable, and it's yours."

"Five per cent," Westfall drawled. "That and a job as superintendent at the wages you're givin' me. It ain't much, but then I ain't puttin' up any of the money. All I want is a nice stake out of it."

"Done!" Fitz said. They spent another ten minutes talking over the details and arranging a meeting-place, and then Fitz fairly ran for his horse, Carmody behind him.

As he was ready to ride off, Westfall called, "Fitz, you're leavin' this brick!"

"Keep it," Fitz yelled. "I'll pick it up when I get back!" And he and Carmody thundered off into the night.

Westfall watched them, chuckling through his cracked lips. And then he spat loudly to take the taste of it from his mouth.

When Tip came down to breakfast the next morning, he laid a burlap-wrapped object on the window sill, and when Nora came to take his order, she saw it.

"What's that, Tip?"

"Bait," Tip said wisely.

"For what?"

Tip grinned up at her and touched the brick which Westfall had returned to him early that morning. "You'll know in a couple of days, honey."

Nora made a face at him and took his order. When she returned with it, she sat down opposite him and watched him eat.

"You've been awful quiet lately, Tip. Aren't things going well at the camp?"

For a moment, Tip did not answer, and Nora saw him scowling at his plate. He had not told her about the report he had got from Kinder, thinking to spare her a share in his own disillusionment. But now he looked up at her and watched her closely as he said, "That mine is a fake, honey. There isn't a hundred dollars in the whole acre of it."

"When did you find that out?"

"Day before yesterday."

"And you haven't told me?" Nora exclaimed. "Why, Tip? Don't you think I can accept disappointment, too?"

"I had my heart set on it," Tip murmured. "I was a fool, Nora. In my own mind I had a home built for us. You were traveling—China, South America, Europe, anywhere. I was with you. We took the finest boats, bought the most expensive things." He grinned shyly. "I'm pretty much of a fool."

"Then it's no good? No good at all?"

"Not worth a hoot. Does it matter to you?"

"You know it doesn't, Tip." She smiled warmly at him and patted his hand. With a sigh, he picked up his fork and started eating again.

Nora hesitated a long time before she asked the question that was uppermost in her mind, but she determined to get it over with.

"Are you sorry you didn't go to Mexico, Tip?" she

asked gently.

Honest bewilderment showed on Tip's face. "Nora! What made you ask that?"

Nora shrugged. "It's kind of tough to have big, wide dreams and then come down to earth. It's bad enough when you're single. It's worse, I imagine, when you think you haven't done right by someone you love. And you do feel that way, Tip?"

Tip nodded. "Sort of."

"Don't do it. I don't mind no money, Tip. Our luck will change."

"What would you think if I told you it had changed already?" Tip murmured.

Nora only stared at him, her blue eyes wide and inquisitive.

"Keep this under that lovely blond hair of yours," Tip said, "but I think the Esmerella will open soon."

"Tip! You don't mean it!"

"I do."

"How soon?"

"I don't know. Nobody else does. But things are going to break here in this county. They won't break, they'll explode. And when they do, we'll see things the way we want them."

"That's strange," Nora murmured, her steady gaze on Tip. "That sounded like Johnny Hendry for a minute. You aren't having his delusions, are you, Tip?"

Tip laughed uneasily, and Nora could see the color creep up into his face from his neck.

"You've seen him, Tip!" Nora accused.

Tip avoided her gaze, and Nora knew instantly that what she had said was true. For a moment she hated to believe it. "Tip, you've talked to him, and he's got those wild schemes in your head! Oh, Tip, and I thought you were so steady and sensible!"

"Maybe I am," Tip murmured.

"Not if you can let Johnny Hendry sway you!" She leaned over nearer to him. "What is it, Tip? What has he done to you?"

"It's not *to* me, Nora, it's *for* me."

"Then what is it?"

"I can't tell you now. You'll just have to wait and see." Tip raised pleading eyes to her. "Believe me, Nora, I was wrong about Johnny. If you only understood. You were wrong, too."

"Not about the important part," Nora said firmly. "He's generous, Johnny is, but he's undependable. He's prejudiced, as suspicious as an old woman." Her eyes darkened. "I'd hate to take anything from him, Tip—I'd hate for us to!"

"Wait until you see what happens."

"I don't want to!" She spoke vehemently now, passionately. "Tip, if you love me, don't be with him! He's everything that's wrong in my world! He's everything that breaks a woman's heart, and makes her hate him!"

Tip said soothingly, "All right, honey. All right. But wait and see. Don't judge him until you know." He looked down at the tablecloth. "I did once, and I was pretty much of a fool." He rose now, and went over to her and kissed her, and then went out.

Nora watched him go, and for a while she sat there, ashamed of herself. What had made her speak so violently against Johnny, as if he had done something to hurt her? Really, he had never been anything but kind to her. And the thought crossed Nora's mind that perhaps she did not understand her own feelings, that she spoke out of resentment—much as Johnny had been known to do, himself. But she would not think this thought. She rose and hurried about her business, but if anyone had looked at her, they would have noticed that she was blushing deeply and beautifully.

Chapter Twenty-Four: A MAJOR KILLING

OVER THE APATHETIC BOOM CAMP of Bonanza canyon, the clashing of a dishpan hammered with a wooden spoon went out in loud waves. Lanterns hung from the ridge-poles of tents and in the doorways of open shacks. There was very little sound of merriment in the place tonight, for this was a gloom camp now. The two streets were hourly losing their crowds.

Men who clustered in silent groups of two and three pricked up their ears at the sound of the homely gong. This was the call to a meeting, where all the news, good and bad, was announced to the camp—and lately it had been mostly bad.

Big Westfall stood on the high front porch of Tim Prince's saloon, two old-fashioned kerosene flares on either side of the saloon door behind him. He clanged the dishpan with a hearty gusto and shouted out into the night for the crowd to assemble. They did, slowly, and among them were the figures of Major Fitz and Bledsoe. Baily Blue was with them. These three had ridden up to-day ostensibly to see how their claims were being worked. And in that crowd also, which moiled and flowed around the foot of Prince's porch was Tip Rogers. Behind the saloon, up on the cliff side, hidden in a sparse thicket of scrub oak, Johnny Hendry and Hank and Turk were waiting.

When most of the camp was around him, in front of and behind him, Big Westfall raised his hands for silence.

"I dunno whether you'll think this was worth callin' you for or not," Westfall began in his slow and homely drawl. "I just rode back from the mill and got my report on the second and third shipment of ore I freighted down. It was a bare forty dollars a ton."

A murmur of disgust ran through the crowd.

Somebody up in the front ranks said quietly, "Lemme see it, Westfall," and Westfall handed the report to the man without a word. It was passed around, talked about, until, from the very discouragement it bred, was handed back to Westfall, who pocketed it.

Westfall saw now that the crowd was turning to gossip again, and he kicked the pan with his foot to draw attention to himself.

Leaning against a porch post, he began again in a conversational tone which sounded as if he, too, was disheartened.

"This really ain't what I called you together for," Westfall said. "That was to kind of prepare you for the proposition I'm makin'. First of all, let me ask, has anyone in the camp got a better report than forty dollars to a ton of their ore?"

In various ways, the crowd of rough miners and punchers and townsmen told him no. They even ridiculed such a high figure.

"Well, then, I might's well make my proposition," Westfall continued. "It don't look to me like any of us is goin' to make any money in this camp except us that can afford to put in a big outfit here and a stamp mill and mine forty-dollar-a-ton ore. Does it to you?"

Again they said no.

"Well, I was talkin' to my bosses from Warms this afternoon. They come halfway over the Calicoes to see me. They read my report. They got the capital to put up the buildings and machinery and take out low-grade ore and reduce it and still make a profit on it. But they can't do it on the six claims I staked out for 'em. They told me to make you folks a proposition."

Here the general attention picked up, and when Westfall had waited long enough for their curiosity to be aroused, he went on.

"Me, I don't think much of it from their standpoint, but orders is orders. They said if you folks would sell out for a reasonable low figure, they'd buy out your claims. They aim to pay two thousand dollars a claim for all them that butts the dike, a thousand for them within five hundred yards of it either way, and seven hundred and fifty for all them rimrock claims within a half mile east of the canyon end. That's the proposition." He paused and spat and said negligently, "If you ain't a bunch of suckers, you'll take it. Not that I care whether you do or don't, though. I'm followin' orders."

A wave of talk swept through the crowd. Westfall sat down on the steps and cuffed his hat on the back of his head and idly gazed about him, as if mildly bored by the whole thing. He was the picture of a man wholly indifferent to his business.

Inevitably, men began to crowd around him and ply him with questions. He answered them curtly, indifferently, but beyond them, he could tell that the idea had taken hold of the crowd. Men were crowding forward to listen to what he said.

Presently, a voice rose over the crowd. "Westfall! Westfall!"

Big Westfall lumbered to his feet and looked over the crowd. Back deep in it, a hand was raised, and people craned to see who it was. It was, inevitably, Tip Rogers. He was elbowing his way to the front. When he was almost to Westfall, he said, "I'll take you up on that. I got a dike claim, and I'll sell it to you, clean and clear."

Westfall, again leaning against the porch pillar, appeared unimpressed. "All right," he drawled. "But one claim ain't goin' to do me no good. You get five other rannies with dike claims, and we'll talk business."

"Young man," a harsh voice called out. "I'll make it number two—and gladly." This was the voice of Major Fitz, and it came from back in the crowd. It got a general laugh, for it was tinged with irony.

"I'll make it three," Bledsoe called.

And suddenly, given this impetus by the best financiers and the best mining heads in the camp, others joined in, until there was a veritable avalanche of offers.

Big Westfall's face never changed. When the crowd had quieted a little to hear him speak, he announced, "All right. Tim Prince said I could use his place. Get your papers. I got the claim recorder here. Form a line and come into Tim's place. I pay in cash. You get your money, have a drink on me—and if you're smart, you'll git home and leave this gold minin' to a bigger outfit."

His announcement was met with a roar of laughter. Many of these men had sunk their last money in claim fees and tools and supplies, and this chance to unload at a profit, however small, was a golden opportunity. For none of them, not even the most sanguine, believed that there was any amount of gold here. Furthermore, they did not relish the prospect of having to prove up on their claims.

Tip Rogers was the first in the long line. He turned over his papers, had them checked by the recorder, received his money, took his drink, and, with a grin of pleasure, waved his money high over his head and disappeared into the night.

The whole crowd was gathered around Tim Prince's. Those who held claims were being chaffed good-naturedly and a little enviously by those who did not. But losers or gainers, everyone in camp was gathered at Tim Prince's saloon.

Tip Rogers headed back to his tent, but when he was out of sight of the saloon, he cut across toward Westfall's mine. At the shed to one side of the office, he opened the door and stepped inside.

"Tip?" Johnny Hendry asked from the depths of that darkness, and Tip answered. Hank and Hugo and Turk were here, too.

Baily Blue and Bledsoe and Major Fitz hung around the saloon for a while, watching the claims changing hands. From a big metal box on a poker table, Westfall was taking out silver and paper money. His supply seemed inexhaustible.

The sight fascinated Major Fitz. This metal box by Westfall's right hand represented every dollar, honest and dishonest, that he had managed to accumulate since he left the army thirty years ago. But if that sight was a little unnerving, he had only to think that what he was getting in return was worth a hundred times the amount held by the box.

Baily Blue, puzzled as to what was behind all this and surprised at Major Fitz's interest, was watching the major covertly, a glass of whisky cuddled in his hand.

Presently Bledsoe turned to Fitz. "I think I'll go look up some of the boys while they still have money. Most of them in this camp owe me for supplies. Coming along?"

Fitz shook his head, as did Blue. "I'll watch this," Fitz said.

He observed it awhile longer, then turned to go out. Blue followed him. Outside, the crowd had dispersed, and the camp was almost normal once more. The last of the line was already inside the doors of the saloon.

Fitz turned down the road, Blue beside him.

"I'd like to know what's behind this," Blue murmured. "Seems to me there's a lot of places here in the Calicoes that hold more ore than this canyon, and it'll produce more than forty dollars a ton, too."

Fitz only chuckled, and Blue glanced obliquely at him. "You know somethin' about this, don't you, Fitz?"

Fitz stopped and regarded him. "What makes you think so?"

"Several things," Baily said amiably. "You were almighty interested in what was goin' on here tonight."

Fitz did not speak for a moment, and then he said quietly, pleased with himself, "I ought to be, I'm behind it."

"Behind what?"

"I'm the company Westfall spoke about. He's buying the claims for me."

Blue cleared his throat and started to speak and then seemed to change his mind, for the words did not come.

"Say it," Fitz invited.

"All right, I will. Why are you payin' a thousand dollars a claim for ore that is common as dirt?"

"Who said it was?"

"Why, everybody."

"Ask Westfall to show you the last report he got from Kinder. The report he didn't mention. It showed eleven hundred dollars for a scant ton."

Blue was silent a moment, and then he started to chuckle, and then to laugh quietly. "I might have known that," he said at last. "Yes, sir, I might have known that. When they can outthink you, Fitz, then I'll take to herdin' sheep."

Fitz smiled with pleasure at this. "Come over to Westfall's shack," he invited. "You'd probably like to see just how much of an investment this is."

They turned down another rough street, which was dark, and made their way down the canyon to the Glory Hole. The office was unlocked, as Westfall had promised it would be, and they went inside. After first making sure that the burlap curtains were drawn tightly over the win-

dows, Fitz lighted the lamp and looked around him.
There was a deal desk in one corner, some rough benches,
and a straw-stuffed bunk at the far end.

They had only to wait a few minutes when the tramp
of Westfall's heavy step came to them. The door was opened, and Big Westfall, stooping to clear the frame, stepped
inside and closed the door behind him. He nodded to Fitz,
smiling, and then looked at Blue and nodded courteously.
His glance at Fitz was questioning.

"It's all right, Westfall," Fitz said. "He knows about it."

Westfall took off his hat and laid the box on the desk.
"There you are, Fitz. I ran out of money toward the last.
There were six claims up on the rock rim that I couldn't
buy, but I reckon they won't be rich enough to bother
with."

Fitz rose and came over to the desk and opened the box.
Blue stood behind him, looking over his shoulder.

Suddenly, a voice drawled from the doorway, "Evenin',
gents."

Blue whirled—to confront the six-gun in Johnny Hendry's hand. Johnny stepped forward, and Hank, Turk,
Hugo, and Bledsoe, a bewildered expression on his face,
filed into the room. Tip Rogers brought up the rear and
closed the door.

Major Fitz was the first to find his wits. "Well, Johnny,
my boy!" he exclaimed, elbowing Blue aside and walking
up to Johnny, hand outstretched. "We thought you'd—"

Turk was the first to see it. He leaped at Johnny, grab-
bing his left arm. Johnny's hand was fisted, his arm tense
and ready to strike, his lips drawn tight over his teeth.

Over his shoulder, Turk snarled at Fitz, "Keep out the
way, you, or he'll kill you."

Sobered, Fitz backed off, and Turk freed Johnny, who
glared at Fitz for a long moment, then shifted his attention
to Westfall.

"Big, bring that lamp over here on the table away from
that coyote." Westfall did. "Now sit down, Fitz. You, too,
Blue."

Blue wisely did as he was told, keeping silent, but Fitz,
always pugnacious, did not sit down. He looked at Johnny

and Turk and Hank and said scornfully to Johnny, "Have these outlaws' ways got the best of you, Johnny? I always believed—"

Cursing, Turk took the two steps to Fitz, grabbed him by the coat front, and slapped him again and again in the face. "Sit down and stay down and shut up!"

He rammed Fitz down in his chair and stood glaring over him. Fitz was subdued now, his thin fox face flushed with an anger which he was afraid to vent. Turk walked back and leaned on the table.

Johnny took over now, and he spoke with a slow easiness that was studied self-control. His gun was holstered.

"How much money did you spend for these claims tonight, Fitz?" Johnny drawled.

Fitz shot a wicked glance at Westfall, who was grinning broadly, but he didn't answer. Westfall answered for him.

"A little over a hundred and twenty-three thousand, Johnny."

"They're mine, anyway!" Fitz snapped. "They're registered legally under a company of which I'm the sole stockholder!"

"Did it take all your capital?" Johnny asked dryly, and again Fitz would not answer. He was puzzled by all this.

Again, Westfall said, "It cleaned him out, Johnny."

"Good," Johnny murmured. "Maybe you'd be interested in knowin', Fitz, that we framed up this deal on you— Westfall, Tip Rogers, and the rest of us. This whole canyon here don't hold a thousand dollars' worth of gold. That good report you got from Westfall was forged. That gold bar he showed you was borrowed from the Esmerella. Kinder was never bribed, because the only thing he could tell was that your ore was worthless."

Johnny paused, watching the color drain out of Fitz's face. "So you gave your money away, Fitz. You've spread it all around the camp, like the generous man you are. But you're broke, you savvy that?"

Fitz half rose out of his chair but sat down again when Turk took a menacing step toward him.

"About this fight with Leach Wigran," Johnny drawled. "I started that. I stole your beef, Major, and planted that

Running W gelding. I burned your place. I rustled that other herd, too, and you killed Mickey Hogan for it. Remember? I even helped Leach Wigran when you tried to wipe him out. Remember those rifles on the hill?"

Johnny was talking softly now, his eyes narrowed, a fixed, unpleasant smile on his face. Fitz's face was turning a dirty gray, but his fighter's jaw was still outthrust, belligerent.

"I did something else, too, Major. I did this on my own hook, because I don't like to be framed. I went back to the Running W early that morning after Leach had hit for the mountains, and I pulled Leach Wigran's red-hot safe out of that fire and I hauled it away. Do you know what I found in it, Major? I found a melted bar of that Esmerella gold. Part of it still held the mill stamp. You hired Wigran, Fitz. He couldn't move without word from you. He's the one that robbed the bank—and on your orders."

Tip Rogers said excitedly, "You didn't tell me that, Johnny!"

"Why tell it?" Johnny said softly, not taking his attention from Fitz. "I was waiting until I could get it all for you, Tip—and with the proof."

Baily Blue's face remained immobile, but he was barely breathing. This was getting uncomfortably close to him.

"Remember the poll of the ranchers I aimed to take, Fitz?" Johnny went on. "Remember, the lists come to the post office, and you sent a hardcase to steal them, and I killed him? Well, that vote was for you, Fitz—you were the biggest rustler in the crowd. It took me a long time to tumble to what everybody, other ranchers, suspected, but I proved it, Fitz. Wigran was the chief rustler and you backed him. The stolen stuff was driven to Warms and sold and the money deposited to your account over there."

Fitz's face seemed a little shrunken now, but he sat utterly still.

Johnny's voice got a little harder now and he shifted his feet faintly.

"But all this is just by the way, Fitz," he drawled pleasantly. "What I'm goin' to kill you for is this. You had Pick

Hendry bushwhacked."

"That's a lie!" Fitz said swiftly.

"Is it?" Johnny drawled. "Can you claim you didn't hire Westfall to mine a claim? Didn't you give him papers describing that claim?"

Fitz was silent for a moment. "Carmody did, yes. He told me about some location papers one day. He said he'd bought them over in Warms. I told him to take a look at the claim and if it looked good to go ahead with it. It was his affair. I loaned him the money. When they began to look good, I took them over."

"Wasn't that location paper in Pick's handwriting?" Johnny asked gently.

"I never saw it, I tell you. Carmody pointed it out to me on a map. I was indulging the whim of my most loyal hand."

"You lie, Fitz," Johnny said idly. "You lie in your teeth. You saw that location paper. I can prove that because you wrote out the other five claims in your own handwriting."

He turned to Westfall and said, "Big, give me those papers."

There was a swift movement at Fitz's chair, and Johnny swiveled his head, his hand streaking to his gun. But he was too late. Fitz had yanked out a .45 from a shoulder holster, and now he covered the room with it. He had taken advantage of that one second, during which everybody automatically looked at Westfall, to make his play. And it had succeeded. There was a full minute of dead silence.

"Don't want to try it, eh?" Fitz taunted them. "All right, Baily, cover them."

Blue rose and drew both his guns, and there was that old amiable smile on his face. He had been loyal, and his loyalty was repaid now, for no one man on earth could get the best of Fitz, he knew.

With three guns trained on him, Johnny did not take his eyes from Fitz.

"You're a smart young whelp, Johnny," Fitz said. "Too smart to live. I can't make up my mind how many people you've told about us. I—"

"Us?" Johnny said swiftly. "Is Baily in on it, too?"

Fitz didn't say anything. Baily chuckled. "Go ahead, Fitz. Tell him. Yes, I'm in on it, Johnny. I was in on it while you were my deputy."

Johnny's face did not change. It was flushed and tense, and his eyes were blazing.

"How many have you told, Johnny?" Fitz asked.

"Just these here."

"Now I know you lie," Fitz said. He shook his head reprovingly. "Well, I reckon we'll have to ride out of Cosmos, Baily, don't you?"

"Not without tellin' him what he wants to know," Baily taunted. "That'd be a shame. Did you kill Pick, Fitz?"

Fitz was watching Johnny, an evil smile on his face, as he said, "I had him killed, to be correct," and it gave him pleasure to see how this tortured Johnny. "I was convinced he'd struck it rich."

"All right, Baily," he said then, when Johnny didn't answer. "You start off. You've got two guns to my one, but save me—"

There was a crash of glass from the window behind Major Fitz, and in that stillness it exploded almost like a shot. Johnny saw the burlap billow out, saw Baily Blue jump with surprise, and then he streaked for his guns. Westfall was almost as quick. He swept the lamp off the table, and ducked.

But Johnny didn't. Before the lamp went out, he whipped both guns hip-high, and the thunder of his shot was first, cutting in ahead of Baily Blue's. Feet planted a little wide, one gun pointed dead ahead, the other at an angle toward Fitz, Johnny fanned the hammers frantically, cursing savagely.

And then the light winked out and the thunder of Turk's guns joined the chorus and then the whole room exploded with the concert of gunfire.

When, finally, in that dark, Johnny saw no answering flashes, he pulled up his guns and waited. The fire from beside him slacked off. All that could be heard was a small gurgling groan from the floor. Behind him, someone moaned and then cursed.

"Strike a light!" Johnny ordered.

Westfall's match flared, and he picked up the lamp. The chimney was broken, but the lamp was whole. By its guttering flame, they looked over toward the desk. Fitz was sitting against the desk leg, his head on his chest, as if he were trying to see the four neat holes that were spreading red across his shirt front.

Blue lay on his back, guns still in his hands, his face a bloody mess.

And then Johnny was aware that there was someone standing in the open doorway and he yanked up his gaze.

For a moment he was speechless, and then yelled, "Pick!"

In another second, he was beating Pick on the back, hugging him, trying to stifle the sobs of joy in his throat. Pick couldn't talk. For twenty-five years of his life, ever since the day he had found that tiny orphan in the shack, he had been wanting to know this. And now he did—knew that John Hendry loved him as a son loves a father.

Pick's first spoken words were characteristic, and they made Johnny laugh with joy. "I was squattin' outside that window and heard every word, but I didn't have a shell for my gun. So I heaved a rock."

Things happened all at once now. A crowd gathered, attracted by the gunfire, and it was Bledsoe who, on the steps of the shack, told them the brief story of Major Fitz's crimes and of his and Blue's death. Inside, Pick told his story, of his faking his own death and planting of the false papers, of salting the test pits and starting the rush. And while he talked, he watched Johnny, his tired old eyes summing him up anew. And he saw that Johnny had been through the fire and had come out steel—a man.

It was only later, after all the stories had been compared, that Hugo Miller asked for a bandage on his leg. His wound was the only casualty of their group.

Chapter Twenty-Five: A CASE FOR THE CLERGY

IT WAS MIDMORNING by the time Tip had finished telling Nora. At the end of it, she rose from the chair in the lobby and walked over to the window. Tip watched her, his eyes reserved, watchful. He had been the first to leave Bonanza canyon last night. He had wanted to tell Nora about everything. And halfway through his story, they heard the clamor out on the streets that told them Johnny and Pick Hendry had returned to Cosmos. That had been an hour ago.

Nora watched the street absently. Then she turned and came back to Tip. "It's grand, Tip," she said simply. "Everything bad I've said about Johnny Hendry, I gladly take back."

"I knew you would."

"I wish him all the success in the world," Nora said quietly. "Will—will he come to see me before he leaves?" she asked slowly.

"Certainly. Besides, his outfit is here."

They talked on a few moments more, and then the lobby door opened, and Pick and Johnny came in. Nora ran to greet Pick and gave his leathery old cheek a smacking kiss. They talked a long time, and then she turned to Johnny.

"I was wrong, Johnny, about Major Fitz."

Johnny's tense, clean-shaven face broke into a slow smile, but his eyes were veiled, black as night pools. "So were a lot of people, Nora—me among 'em."

There was an awkward silence. Pick sidled over to Tip and started to talk, leaving Johnny to face Nora alone.

"Tip told me you were leaving, Johnny," Nora said.

"That's right."

"For where?"

"I dunno. To see the world, maybe."

"But you're the rightful sheriff, Tip says. He said the commissioners are sure to recall you."

Johnny grinned. "Turk and Hank can take care of that job better than I can. Bledsoe has promised to make one sheriff, the other marshal as a favor to me. And they'll post a five-thousand-dollar reward to keep Wigran over the mountains. So it'll be easy."

"I wish you luck, wherever you go," Nora said. Johnny looked at her face, which was paler than he had ever seen it. And more beautiful—so that it hurt him to see it. His glance traveled down her slim figure, approving of the deep-blue dress. But it rested on the ring—Tip's ring, which she was wearing.

"And I wish you luck," Johnny said gravely. "I haven't had much of a chance to till now. But I do, Nora. You and Tip—you're both fine people."

And with that, Johnny ducked upstairs.

Nora was not in the lobby when he came down. Out on the street with his war bag over his shoulder, Pick beside him, they strolled toward the feed stable.

"I think you're bein' stubborn, son," Pick said with unaccustomed gentleness. "You don't seem to realize I'm a rich man."

Johnny teased him. "I think you're kiddin' me, Pick. I won't believe it until we ride up and see it tonight."

"But where you goin' from there?" Pick growled.

"Travel."

"And leave a good job and a clean town to be a saddle bum?"

"That's it," Johnny said crisply. He added more gently, "Pick, a man never likes to stay around a place where he's got a kick in the teeth, does he?"

"I reckon not." Pick looked at him. "You mean Nora."

Johnny only nodded. They swung in under the arch of the feed stable, and Tip Rogers, who had been leaning against one of the stalls, walked over to Johnny.

"Johnny, I'm leavin' today," he said simply. "I've got a job in Mexico."

"Good," Johnny said. "I hope Nora will like it."

"She doesn't even know about it."

Johnny looked Tip steadily in the eye. He said quietly, "You runnin' out on her?"

Tip nodded a little. "You could call it that, Johnny. You see, I don't like the idea of playing second fiddle all my life. No man does."

"Second fiddle to who?"

"You," Tip said quietly. He stuck out his hand and smiled fondly at Johnny. "Go up there and tell her you love her, Johnny. You do. She loves you. And treat her well, Johnny. I know you will."

Johnny took Tip's hand, but a frown creased his fore-head. "You're a jump ahead of me, Tip. How do you know all this?"

"About her loving you?"

"Yes."

"You can tell that when you watch her," Tip said evenly. "She was mad at you, Johnny. I came just at the right time. But now you're back, it's the way it always was. She's too loyal to send me away. She'd die before she'd admit to me that she loves you better. But I think she'll admit it to you after I'm gone."

Johnny wrung Tip's hand in one violent wrench and then raced out of the livery stable and up to the Cosmos House. She wasn't in the lobby. He slammed open the door of the dining-room, and there she was in the act of putting the silver out on the tables for the noon meal.

Johnny walked over to her, took the silver out of her hand, and dropped it on the floor with a crash, then folded her to him and kissed her time and again. She struggled violently to free herself, and when she finally did, her eyes were bright with anger.

"Johnny Hendry!" she cried, stamping her foot. "I'm an engaged woman!"

"You bet you are," Johnny growled fondly. "Engaged to me." He reached down for her hand and pulled the ring off her finger and threw it across the room, then, taking both hands, he said to her, "To think what a hammerhead I am! Of course you love me. Of course I love you. And we'll be married."

"But Tip—"

"Tip's a right nice jasper. And smart. He had sense enough to see that both of us would die without each other, so he just rode off for Mexico."

"But—"

"No buts. When do we get married?"

Nora gave a little moan of delight and threw her arms around his neck. "The sooner the better," she said, and she was squeezing him so hard he didn't have the breath to answer.